PRAISE FOR *IT DEVOURS!*

"Different from other mystery novels . . . As captivating and light as any mystery novel can be but explores one of the most complex issues: the conflict between science and reason on the one hand and, on the other hand, religion and cult"

Washington Book Review

"Thought-provoking . . . The relationship between science and religion is satisfyingly explored with humor and insight. Readers need not be familiar with the podcast or the previous book to enjoy this work, but fans will appreciate the cameos from well-known Night Vale residents"

Publishers Weekly

"Compelling . . . A confident supernatural comedy from writers who can turn from laughter to tears on a dime"

Kirkus Reviews (starred review)

"[A] smart exploration of the divide—and overlap—of science and religion . . . A thrilling adventure and a fascinating argument that science and belief aren't necessarily mutually exclusive"

Tor.com

"Very clever . . . With a gripping mystery, a very smartly built world (a place similar to our own world but at the same time distinctly other), and a cast of offbeat characters, the novel is a welcome addition"

Booklist

BY JOSEPH FINK AND JEFFREY CRANOR

Welcome to Night Vale: A Novel

It Devours!:
A Welcome to Night Vale Novel

The Faceless Old Woman
Who Secretly Lives in Your Home:
A Welcome to Night Vale Novel

Mostly Void, Partially Stars:
Welcome to Night Vale Episodes, Volume 1

The Great Glowing Coils of the Universe:
Welcome to Night Vale Episodes, Volume 2

𝕿𝖍𝖊 FACELESS OLD WOMAN
WHO SECRETLY LIVES IN YOUR HOME

You've been standing in that shower for ten minutes. I know, because I'm in here with you. A faceless old woman inches from your neck. You would feel my breath if I still breathed. I think it would be upsetting for you if you turned around. Better to let the water run over you. Better not to see.

PRAISE FOR *WELCOME TO NIGHT VALE*

"This is a splendid, weird, moving novel . . . It manages beautifully that trick of embracing the surreal in order to underscore and emphasize the real—not as allegory, but as affirmation of emotional truths that don't conform to the neat and tidy boxes in which we're encouraged to house them"

NPR.org

"The book is charming and absurd—think *This American Life* meets *Alice in Wonderland*"

Washington Post

"*Welcome to Night Vale* lives up to the podcast hype in every way. It is a singularly inventive visit to an otherworldly town that's the stuff of nightmares and daydreams"

BookPage

"Fink and Cranor's prose hints there's an empathetic humanity underscoring their well of darkly fantastic situations . . . The book builds toward a satisfyingly strange exploration of the strange town's intersection with an unsuspecting real world"

Los Angeles Times

"The charms of *Welcome to Night Vale* are nearly impossible to quantify. That applies to the podcast, structured as community radio dispatches from a particularly surreal desert town, as well as this novel, written by the podcast's cocreators, Joseph Fink and Jeffrey Cranor"

Minneapolis Star Tribune

The FACELESS OLD WOMAN

WHO SECRETLY LIVES IN YOUR HOME

A WELCOME TO NIGHT VALE NOVEL

JOSEPH FINK & JEFFREY CRANOR

www.orbitbooks.net

ORBIT

First published in Great Britain in 2020 by Orbit
This paperback edition published in Great Britain in 2021 by Orbit

1 3 5 7 9 10 8 6 4 2

A CIP catalogue record for this book
is available from the British Library.

ISBN 978-0-356-51505-2

Printed and bound in Great Britain by Clays Ltd, Elcograf S.p.A.

Papers used by Orbit are from well-managed forests
and other responsible sources.

Orbit
An imprint of
Little, Brown Book Group
Carmelite House
50 Victoria Embankment
London EC4Y 0DZ

An Hachette UK Company
www.hachette.co.uk

www.orbitbooks.net

To Meg Bashwiner and to Jillian Sweeney

CONTENTS

CRAIG

2011

I set your shoes on fire.

All of them. They're in the trash can by the rental office. They're still smoldering. The side of the plastic bin has melted away, and Stuart in apartment 413 has already made four calls to the super. He didn't answer because I locked him in his bathroom, because I didn't want the fire put out just yet.

It's nice: the smell of burning. I used to not like it, as it reminded me of a particularly bad moment in my early life. But that was so many years ago, and now I enjoy the smell of burning. Burning anything: rubber, cloth, skin in small amounts, hair (definitely hair), even wood. A fireplace on a cool winter night. A campfire on a warm summer night. A house as a family of four flees, leaving behind everything they've ever owned to be consumed by flames. Plus, there's true beauty in black ash quivering around bright orange edges. It's art, Craig. I know you appreciate art.

Also, the birds are alarmed, and I find that funny.

You missed your date tonight because you couldn't find your shoes, which is why I'm telling you now that they're on fire in a quickly melting plastic bin. Then when you tried to rush to a shoe store, your car wouldn't start because someone broke in and jammed glass shards into the ignition. Or at least that's what the locksmith said when she came to investigate the problem.

"Who would do something like that?" You wanted her professional opinion. She only shrugged and said she'd have to replace the ignition switch, which would take a couple of days and cost four hundred dollars.

I suppose I could have used the glass shards to slash your tires to keep you from your date. It would have been cheaper for you, but it wouldn't have been as beautiful. I don't think you noticed the perfect arc of blood splatter across the floor mat when you cut your hand on the ignition. You screamed in pain, ignoring the beauty of your own nature. So, please take a moment to look out the window by the shower and appreciate the artwork I have created. I call it "Craig's Impertinence" (multimedia: plastic, gasoline, and shoes). Ah, but you're too busy moping.

You've been standing in that shower for ten minutes. I know, because I'm in here with you. A faceless old woman inches from your neck. You would feel my breath if I still breathed. I think it would be upsetting for you if you turned around. Better to let the water run over you. Better not to see. You haven't even touched the soap. You look pathetic. Why? Because you missed a date with a woman who was pretty and shared similar loves and seemed genuinely interested in you? Or because when you went to try to reschedule with her she accused you of texting her an inappropriate photo, when in fact you did no such thing?

You can't hear me. These are rhetorical questions, anyway. I don't need a response. You wouldn't even know to respond to me. After all, you don't know I'm here, even after that one day a year ago when you passed by the living room and half noticed the strange new chandelier hanging from the ceiling, the one made from the twisted limbs and neck of an old woman, contorted into a shape like a spider. And then you thought, *wait, what did I just see?* And you backed up to find that the hanging old woman was gone. Almost certain she never was there. Probably you imagined her.

I can see why you're upset. The woman you did not go on a date with is too. No one wants to have a first date cancel on them and then have that same date inexplicably text them a photo of a raccoon having its intestines gnawed out by a coyote.

I mean, I would want that. But I've never really been into dating (although it is true that once I was deeply in love), so I can only assume most women would not like that kind of behavior.

I forgot to mention, she received a text from you while you were trying to get your car fixed that included a photo of a coyote devouring a raccoon. The coyote's fur was a glistening red about the mouth, its eyes golden like a cornfield. The raccoon's neck is clearly broken, and its organs are pink and gray. I'm sure she was disgusted, but honestly, she's made of similar materials. So are you, Craig.

I'm not sorry I sent her that photo using your phone. And you shouldn't be either. It was a good photo—a discomforting reminder of Snowden's secret, that man is matter. Did you ever read *Catch-22*? It's a funny and sad book about moral hypocrisy and self-interest. My favorite part is how cold Snowden got when his small intestine unraveled from beneath his flak jacket.

That's not a spoiler because that book's been out for decades, and you should have read it by now. Plus you can't even hear me.

You would have enjoyed your date with Giselle, I'm sure, but that's not the point. The point is that Giselle wasn't right for you. I know this because I've spent the past three nights in her home while she slept. I've skittered along the hallway stair behind her as she climbed, and I've burrowed into her trash to nap among the rotting things. She keeps her possessions quite organized. I like this about her. It made it easier for me to go through her photo albums, medical records, and diaries. I won't go into specifics because that would be invasive. I'm not like that.

Giselle keeps a great deal of physical photos. She likes to look through them when she is feeling nostalgic or overwhelmed. I took a crafting knife and carved away the faces from the photos. I only did this to people who were not her parents or grandparents. I think family is important. Children are the most important. Have you thought about children, Craig?

Giselle does not seem interested in having children. She wants to go to law school and open her own firm. She wants to travel a lot too. And you don't want that. Believe me. I've traveled enough for both of us. The world is awful. There is only flesh and illness out there. You'll be fine right here in Night Vale.

Don't worry. Giselle will find another person to date. They will travel and be selfish and not raise a family. They will never know the joy of raising a handsome, gentle, smart boy like you. And they won't care. That's good for them. I'm only saying *you* don't want that. I know you, Craig. I know what is good for you, and this would not have been good.

Anyway, that bridge is burned now, I suppose. Along with your shoes. You'll never hear from her again.

Nope. I was wrong. She just texted back. You're missing this while you're brooding in the shower, Craig.

WTF is wrong with you? she writes.

You two are done. Before you ever even got started.

Another text. Please don't contact me again. Please.

Okay, what I read initially as anger is probably fear. You scared her, Craig. We scared her.

I'm going over to her place now to block your number on her phone, so she doesn't have to deal with the emotional devastation of getting some mumbly apology text from you.

Done. She looks in bad shape. All her lights are out and she's sitting on the edge of her couch staring at nothing. Then for a moment she saw a flicker of me beside her, a crooked figure with no face. And she screamed. She is so dramatic about everything. You are better off.

Maybe this is a bad time to bring this up, but you need to pay your credit card bill. It's maxed out, and you've missed the past two due dates. And the thing is—and this is going to sound selfish, because it is—but your Netflix account got suspended, and I was only halfway through season three of *Cheers*.

The laugh track is a bit off-putting, but it's still a good show. I really love the plot twist that Norm's nagging wife, Vera, turns out to have been dead for ten years, and Norm has kept her memory alive by continuing a fictional narrative about her. Sam and Diane knew that Vera wasn't really alive and that Norm was delusional, but in episode seven, when they go to check in on Norm, they find him cuddled up next to her decayed corpse and reading her Lord Byron's "The First Kiss of Love," and he's crying. The stench is unbearable, but less unbearable than the brutal truth of the moment.

My point is, I didn't get to finish watching *Cheers* because you're behind on your credit card payments. I need you to deal with that.

Also you're wasting water standing in the shower for so long. Stop brooding, or I will run one of my jagged yellow fingernails along the back of your neck.

Your father used to brood all the time. Drove your mother crazy. He had a lot of stress and would come home crying. He would sit in his car, parked along a curb a block away, just breathing and sobbing, and breathing some more, until his eyes and cheeks were clear of their red lines.

Your mother thought he had depression. He did not. It's dangerous to do that to people, you know? Diagnose them with a mental health condition if you're not a doctor? I secretly live in everyone's home, and I have seen people coping (and not coping) with depression. Your father, Donald, did not have depression.

He had a difficult time coming to terms with his cancer, and eventually his body gave out. Lots of men in your family died young, but your father, comparatively, lived a long life. He got to see his forty-fifth birthday. He got to raise a son: you. When you were little, he called you Big Man. And then when you grew up—and you certainly grew up: six-foot-three, a quarter-foot taller than your own dad, by the age of fifteen—he called you Little Guy.

He loved you and cared for you like the father he never had. Your paternal grandfather, Jacob, died when your dad was only seven years old. But Jacob had been in a coma for four years before that, after the hunting accident that ripped away nearly half of his skull. He was carrying his shotgun carelessly. He tripped and the gun went off, as did a good portion of his head. The spray of blood really was beautiful, but I suspect you wouldn't have appreciated it then either. People so rarely take the time to appreciate what is around them.

Donald wanted you to have a loving father. Someone to teach you to ride a bike, to read, to be respectful to others, to be creative.

You were terrible at guitar. To be fair, so was your father, but the important thing was that it was something you could be terrible at together. And you've always loved music, even if you can't play a single instrument. Donald was a good and giving father. He loved you.

Having a father who loves you is so important. I know this well.

You're watching your diet, and this is good. I want you to be healthy. And you are. I took some of your blood the other night while you were sleeping. (Sorry I couldn't find a syringe and ended up using a knife from Rome that I've carried with me for a very long time.) I took your blood to the Night Vale General Hospital and surreptitiously replaced Harrison Kip's sample. Your blood work came back perfect. Apparently this was good news for Harrison too. He and his doctor were so amazed that his extraordinarily high hemoglobin count came back normal for once.

Your father's early death haunts you, I'm sure. That's normal. And I'm glad you are health-conscious because of it. Your father's body was filled with so many artificial chemicals and carcinogens over the years, his cancers (and they were many) were a product of personal choices, not genetics.

I'm old. Older than you can imagine. Probably older than I can imagine, and I have met nearly everyone in your family tree, going back well over a century. There's very little cancer there, rest assured.

Of course, you can't hear or see me, and I'm fine with that, because I'd prefer you stay on your healthy path. But really, please work on your finances. Pay that credit card bill. I want you to take care of yourself because I think you're a nice man, Craig. I've known you your whole life, and you have a beautiful heart. You care so much for your friends, your family, and even the people less fortunate than you. You had only three hundred dollars in your account last Christmas, and yet you still donated two hundred to Doctors Without Borders.

It's hard not to like you, Craig. I want to help you live a good life, raise a good family, to teach your future son to love and respect his children. It's what your father would have wanted, what all fathers should want.

But please. The water in the shower is starting to run cold, and anyway the firetrucks just arrived about the pile of burning shoes. Hurry and dry off so you can see the art I made for you.

Craig, I'm not going anywhere. You are part of my story, a story that started more than two hundred years ago on an estate by the sea. It is a long story, but don't worry. We have so much time still left.

AN ESTATE BY THE SEA

1792-1805

1

I was born on the Mediterranean, on the water itself, in a small boat that my father was frantically rowing in order to take my mother to medical care she would never live to need. What chance did I have when my first act was to take another's life?

My father let the oars fall once I had arrived and my mother had left. He cradled me with one hand and his wife with the other, and then he made his way back to shore. I was his first and his last child. From then on, we would only have each other. Maybe lesser men would have responded to the trauma of losing a wife by resenting my existence, or by forever associating me with sorrow. But my father was not a lesser man.

He buried my mother on the edge of our estate, on a hill overlooking the water she had died upon. When I was very young, he would take me to visit the grave regularly, but as I grew older, he realized I had no memory of a mother, and he himself needed no reminder, and so gradually we visited less and then eventually not at all. Still, once a year, he would go out by himself to the grave and carefully tend to it, clearing off weeds, making sure the path to it was passable, that the view from her plot to the water was unhindered. He never married again, nor showed any interest in women. This wasn't an act of misguided nobility. He was so fully occupied by raising a daughter, and by his mysterious work, that there simply was never space for a second act to his romantic life. Maybe if this story had turned out differently, he would have eventually, as an older man, found room in his life for love. But this story can only turn out the way things happened. I cannot conjure a happy ending where none exists.

I never missed my mother. I don't mean this to sound strong or uncaring. I just never knew what a mother was enough to miss one, and my father was such a warm and loving parent that I did not feel a missing piece in my life. Any sorrow I felt was on my father's behalf, for I loved him completely, and I knew that her death had been a great blow to him. So at night, in bed, listening to the whispering of the same warm seawater upon which I had come to be and my mother had come to pass, I would lay awake and wish that the tragedy could be undone. But it was never for my own sake. I only ever wanted my father to be happy.

Here is what an orange tree smells like.

At the base of the tree it smells of soil, the churn of earth, and the sun that heats it. If it is warm enough to grow oranges, then it is warm enough to bake the soil, and the scent will rise up, a dense, gritty smell, pleasant without being beautiful. When rain comes, the smell changes, becoming sharper, a smell that is as squishy and thick as the mud that makes it.

The tree itself smells like a house that will never be finished building, the dust of wood and all that binds wood together. It is a smell that grows with the tree, gaining the smells of what lives on and around it. A squirrel runs up the bark, and now the squirrel's nest, a faint trace of pungent animal, mixes in with the stolid smell of wood.

Between the continuous vegetable hum of the leaves, there are the flowers that smell more like fruit than the fruit itself, a perfume that smells like a miracle but also a reminder that life does not end with the humanity. The smell of the flowers is extra-human and it does not need us. It is the smell of running under a hot sun, the smell of falling into cool water. The flowers are the dream of the fruit, and the dream of sweetness to come. And then the fruit themselves, echoes of the flower's perfume, but more tangible. There is a weight to their smell and, when punched open with a thumb, the fizzy aroma of pulp and juice.

That is what an orange tree smells like.

Our estate had many orange trees, and many other fruit trees besides. It was a large and lush place, on a hidden inlet protected from the damage of storms and the curiosity of passing ships. The Mediterranean was a dangerous and wild place at the time, full of warships on patrol, and merchant ships passing to and from the ports of the east, and pirate and bandit ships, and other ships with strange flags belonging to mysterious organizations whose membership and purpose were unclear but whose menace was evident to all. Our tiny inlet was a blessing, allowing us a modicum of peace despite the apparent richness of our estate.

And our estate was quite rich. The land had belonged to my mother's family, wealthy beneficiaries who luxuriated in fine arts and foods, the fawning attention that comes from kind donations to the poor, and a carefree life not beholden to any business or industry. Wealth is either a blight upon the soul or a balm. My mother's family saw money as a privilege, allowing them to read poetry and explore intellectual gentility, which is why they approved of her marriage to my father, a working man with an average education. Few rich families of that time would have allowed their daughter to marry into a family without wealth, for fear that a dowry would be taken and the young bride and her family ignored.

As the son of a merchant, my father spent much of his youth traveling to farms to purchase livestock and produce to then sell at larger markets in the city. He met my mother one summer while stocking figs in a market not far from the estate. A quick errand into town to buy food turned into a long afternoon of discussion about the sweetest figs in late June. "You can tell the ripest by the smell," he told her, gently holding the green bulb to her nose, as she inhaled the aromas of golden syrup and earth. The long afternoon turned to weeks of not-so-accidental meetings between the two, and that became a courtship. The family trusted him so thoroughly, and my mother loved him so fully, that no question of the integrity of their marriage ever arose. They were married on the grounds of this estate, which was then handed over to the new couple by my mother's parents. My father loved this home. Why would he not? He had developed a nose for the finest produce, and here he could savor every rich grape, every spring onion, every plump orange.

Beside the citrus groves, there was the main house, a vast thing, inhabited now by only my father and me. There were servants' wings and towers that we left sealed to gather dust. Eventually, we reduced our presence to one small wing of the house, sleeping in adjacent bedrooms, using what was once a small kitchenette for the stable workers as our place for both cooking and eating. My father carried the habits of the small merchant family he'd grown up in and didn't know what to do with luxury on the scale it was being offered. Still, the lands were maintained by a variety of servants who came regularly, and the area of our house that we lived in was also well kept, and I did eventually begin to wonder, as the years went on, how my father was able to pay for the upkeep of such a large and lush estate when he did not seem to have any job in particular, having given up his merchant travels after I was born.

This was all so long ago. To parse through my earliest years is difficult. I am an old woman, perhaps the oldest there has ever been. A mind was never meant to catalogue this much. A life was never meant to be this long. But I do retain some memories of my earliest and greatest period of joy, when I lived in ignorance of what the world could do to a person.

I am three years old. This is my earliest memory. I am running through the orange groves. I am chasing my father, or he is chasing me. It is a radiant and clear day. I decide to hide. I wiggle my way up into one of the trees. I wedge myself against the trunk a few feet up into the leaves. I see my father looking for me. "Where is my daughter?" he says, in exaggerated confusion. "Where is her beautiful face? I must see that face again. Where could it be?" Soon I allow myself to fall onto the soft dirt, where my father scoops me up and both of us are laughing. Was my face actually beautiful? My father would say so either way.

Another moment. I don't know how old I am. Probably five or so. We are in our little kitchen in our big house, and my father is cooking. I don't remember what he is cooking, I only remember the smell, which is meaty and green, the smell of vegetables cooking in fat. He asks me to cut the bread for our dinner, and he shows me how, supervising my use of the knife, but allowing me to do it myself. "There are only two of us, little one," he says. "Both of us need to be able to take care of the other." He shows me where I should cut, but it is I who carefully lowers the knife through the hard crust. The smells of onions and herbs and lamb fill this memory, and anchors it forever in my mind.

One more memory of my earliest years is not like the others. I am six years old. Again I am in the orange groves, but this time on my own. My father is away for the afternoon on business, as happened every week or so, and I am left to play around the estate. I knew every disused shed, every good swimming spot, and each climbable tree in the groves, where I could hide and secretly watch the groundskeepers, or the ships in the harbor, or even the deer. I am playing in one of these hidden places and I see a shape moving forward in an odd, stop and start way across a line of trees. I assume it was one of the gardeners and called for them. No one answers. I am scared but determined to be able to tell my father how brave I had been, and so I run after the figure. Soon I reach the end of the line of trees and break out into the broad grass leading down to the shore. And there by the shore is a man lurching in a strange, stiff manner. He does not turn to look back at me, only shambles to the edge of the rock and then tips forward into the water. I run down to look. Where he had fallen, the water is clear and shallow, but there is no sign of the man. I decide I must have been mistaken and do not tell anyone what I have seen.

2

My father did not wish me to know what he did for a living, and if he had had his way, I would likely still not know. But few of us ever get our way in this world. We accommodate what life gives us and do our best to retain some sense of ourselves.

Father had a business partner, a man named Edmond. Edmond and my father grew up together, my father nearly ten years older. My father had looked after the younger Edmond, teaching him to fish and row a boat, teaching the young boy to be in nature, to find work that used the whole of his body, to take in the world through all five senses. But Edmond took a liking to math. He was a thinking man, enjoying calculations and finance. Life was Edmond's puzzle to solve. He was much smarter than most children, and despite their differences, my father had hired a twelve-year-old Edmond to help with bookkeeping and inventory at my father's warehouse, and that began a partnership that would last throughout my father's life.

Edmond would frequently join us for dinner, where he would pull faces that made me laugh, and ask me questions about what new parts of the estate I had discovered that day. I enjoyed his visits immensely, and it always made me angry when my father would tell me I needed to go to bed so that he and Edmond could have conversations for adults. At six, of course, I thought I was as adult as anyone could be, and it seemed unfair that I would be left out of these discussions as though I were a child. I would stand at my bedroom door, listening through the crack and trying to make out even a single word. But my father was aware of such tricks, and always moved the conversation to the far side of the kitchen, where even the sharp hearing of the young would be unable to eavesdrop over the crackle of the fire. All I could hear was the occasional roar of laughter from Edmond, always an enthusiastic man.

Despite the annoyance of secrecy, I enjoyed Edmond's visits, and in many ways he became a second father to me. He traveled much for work and was always bringing me little gifts and souvenirs. A painted seashell from France. A tiny bag of cinnamon from Morocco. A figurine of a horse from Svitz. He seemed to always be going to a new country, and he always had some trinket of that country for me. They decorated a shelf in my bedroom, and since I never left the estate, they formed a tactile map of the world. This is what Spain sounds like. This is what Franchia feels like.

Once in my youngest years I did stumble upon my father in the midst of his work. I woke up one evening from a dream in which my mother was alive, only she wasn't my mother, but someone very much like my mother. She had no face and was hiding somewhere in my house and I couldn't find her, even as I saw her moving in the corner of my eye. I was crying as I woke, the terror of an unknowable entity, an unseeable face, still causing me to pant. I ran to my father's room, but he wasn't there. I called for him, and there was no answer. Then I looked out the window and saw lamps down at the water. Frightened, but determined to find my father, I pulled on a shawl and ran barefoot down through the grass to the water. There I saw my father, and Edmond, and a third man with a rough, scarred cheek and disheveled clothes. They were pulling a rowboat full of canvas bundles onto the shore. The sharp oil smell of the lamps hit me from several meters away. The man with the scarred cheek saw me, and shouted an alarm, but my father waved him quiet. "There's been a shipwreck, little one," he said to me. "Fortunately, we were able to help with the rescue. Go back to bed. I'll tell you all about it in the morning."

In the morning, he refused to provide any details. Later I remembered that Edmond had not visited us in months. What had he been doing at the estate so late at night, when this shipwreck happened?

There is one other person left to mention from my childhood. I don't remember when it was that I met Albert, only that from my earliest years he was there. He was four days older than me, and so we grew in unison. When I explored the grounds, often Albert was with me. We would play hide and seek in the orange groves. We would swim together in the cove, daring each other to hold our breath longer, to dive farther, to grab stones at the bottom of the deepest point of the cove. He was a better swimmer than me by far. Despite my years with the water, my mother's death caused me to associate the sea with danger, and so I was not as fearless as Albert when it came to these challenges. Once he jumped from a cliff at least ten meters high, missing the rocks by a few body lengths. It wasn't the water that frightened me. It was the fall. I tried to imagine falling that far, then hitting the water and continuing to fall, deep below, until I settled on the soft sand of the bottom.

When Albert dared me to follow him, I demurred, pretending that I had to get home for dinner. I could see in his eyes that he saw through my excuse, but even as young as we were, he did not take the opportunity to mock me, instead pretending to believe me.

Other children from other estates came and went, but Albert was always there. My father, noticing our friendship, would sometimes invite him for dinner, but Albert always had to return to his house. I would ask him about which estate he belonged in, and he would point vaguely, in a different direction each time. It became clear he did not want me to visit his home. I sensed he was ashamed of his family, perhaps because they were one of the brutal landlord families always terrorizing the peasants in the nearby valleys, or because he belonged to a strictly religious family that did not like to fraternize with outsiders. Like my timidity with the water, Albert's evasiveness about his home became a thing we did not speak about, because there were always so much delight to do and see instead.

3

Although our estate was difficult to spy from the sea, there were places on nearby cliffs, easily accessible from our home, from which you could watch the passing ship traffic. And this I did often, enjoying identifying which of the ships belonged to governments, and which were merchant ships, and which were the pleasure yachts of royalty and the rich, and which the schooners of pirates and bandits that flew no colors, moving stolen cargo and attacking pleasure yachts that had not shelled out sufficiently for mercenaries and bodyguards. Soon, through the boredom and patience of a child, I had a better grasp on the routes of the various factions than the most well-informed spies of kings and emperors.

By age seven, I knew most of the ships in the region by name. If they passed close enough to our cliffs, I might even know the crew members by prominent physical traits. Here is the *Bee Sting* from Portugal, and the navigator has bushy red hair and a limp. Here is the *Lucky Bell*, a ship of bandits from right up the coast, their leader missing his left hand. And so it was a great surprise to me when I saw a ship that I did not recognize. The idea of seeing a vessel for which I had no information was astonishing to me.

With the serene certainty of a child, I knew all there was to be known about the world.

This new ship was smaller, like the ships of the bandits, but it flew a flag. The flag was black and had an insignia of a labyrinth on it. There was no crew visible, but the deck was stacked high with crates. It passed slowly, and quite close to the cliffs, but I never saw any movement on it. Down the coast, one of the regular bandit ships that often passed our home swerved sharply to avoid passing close to the ship with the sign of a labyrinth.

Of course I asked my father about this ship, and he frowned and kneeled in front of me.

"The organization that carries the sign of the labyrinth is an ancient and secret one, and you must never be seen by them. If you spot a ship with the flag of a labyrinth, I want you to run back home and stay inside until it passes. Do you understand?"

I didn't, but I also understood that I shouldn't ask any more questions. And so I kept quiet when I saw more and more of these strange ships. Crew were rarely ever on deck, and if they were they wore hoods and worked with their heads bowed. Always the crates piled high on their decks and lashed down with thick rope. And always a flag with the sign of the labyrinth. But I also refused to run away. I would stay hidden, and watch them pass until they were lost to the horizon or to a turn in the shore.

When I reached the age of eight, my father started to depart on regular business trips. "It would have been good to do this sooner," he said, "but I didn't want to leave you alone when you were so young. Now that you are a little older, I will occasionally need to go attend to affairs. I will return soon, do not worry."

He hired a series of caretakers for me during his trips, none of whom lasted long. My father assured me that this wasn't due to any sort of difficulty with caring for me, only that the young workforce in our rural region tended to immigrate to the great capitals of Europe seeking better jobs, and so one was always looking for good help. It was only much later it would occur to me that my father did not want any one person to know what the schedule of his trips were, and so was having the caretakers regularly replaced.

But I never used my father's absences as an excuse to cause real trouble. I took the responsibility he put on me seriously, and I wanted to prove, more to myself than to him, that I deserved his trust. And so while I would sometimes sneak out of bed after being put there far too early by some exhausted caretaker or the other, I would only use those hours snatched from sleep as an opportunity to read, or to wander the estate in the nighttime, when all familiar landmarks turned to indistinct shadow, or often I would just sit precariously on my windowsill, feet dangling over the lengthy drop, smelling the nearby sea. I had never in my life been far enough from the sea that I couldn't smell it, at least as a faint undercurrent under the other smells that filled my life.

On one of my father's trips, I snuck out in the morning to meet with Albert. We played hide and seek, and then ate a simple lunch of fruit and cheese on a rock by the cove, our toes dangling into the water.

"There are rumors about your father," he said.

"No there aren't." I glared at him. "What kind?"

"I don't know," he shrugged, and stuffed a large piece of cheese into his mouth.

"Tell me."

"People say your father is some kind of spy for a king, or

even an agent of the devil, and his journeys are crime journeys."
Albert nodded solemnly. "For crimes."

I shoved him into the water. He came up sputtering and I
kicked water in his face.

"That's stupid. Don't say stupid things like that to me ever
again." I ate the rest of the cheese all in a few bites, just to
punish him, although later this would be more of a punishment on me.

Despite my dismissal, what Albert said stayed with me.
What did my father do? How did we afford this estate? And
why was he never specific about where he was going on these
business trips of his?

I started to pay more attention to his comings and goings. I
noticed that there was a great variability in how he packed. On
some trips, he brought a full trunk, which he would struggle to
load into a carriage before leaving. But on the other trips, he
packed lightly and haphazardly, throwing only a few necessities
into a sack and then taking off on a horse. The care with which
he packed did not correlate at all with the length of his business
trips.

The mystery was deepened by an even stranger discovery.
One night, against the repeated and increasingly desperate
commands of my current caretaker, I was sitting awake in my
windowsill. Despite my disobedience, my body did very much
want to comply with the command to sleep, and so I was gently
nodding off, leaning against the sturdy stone frame, when I
heard a voice out in the garden. Hidden as we were, we never
had to contend with thieves, but ours was a large estate and
so theft was always a possibility. Perhaps our time had finally
come, and my father was not here to help. As I sprang up,
quite awake now, I realized, to my absolute confusion, that I

recognized the voice. It was the voice of my father. He was in the garden, two days into a weeklong business trip.

My first impulse was to run out and joyously greet him, assuming that he had returned earlier than expected. But something about the situation made me cautious. Instead I slipped out of my room, past my caretaker who had fallen asleep while reading at the table in the kitchen, and out the front door. I moved as quietly as I could through the fields and gardens, ducking behind hedges and trees. And there my father was, walking with a group of men down to the water. A rowboat waited on shore, and in the deeper water of the cove one of the small ships that bore no flag, one I recognized as belonging to bandits. My father was chatting with the men from the ship, and he even affectionately slapped the back of one. I had no idea what to make of this, but in my horror started to realize that perhaps Albert had been right. Perhaps my father was going on crime trips. To do crime.

As I came to this realization, I saw movement in the hill above the group of men. A figure was walking along the crest. No one but me noticed this figure. I recognized him. It was the shambling man whom I had seen disappear into the water a few years before. He walked along the hill with his strange, stiff lurch, too far away to be anything but a silhouette in the faint moonlight, but his movements were unmistakable. Then he crossed the threshold of the hill and was gone. I hurried back to my bed, where I lay, frightened and unsleeping, until my caretaker called me to breakfast.

When my father "returned" from the trip, I greeted him as normal, and said nothing for a few days. Then one day, during lunch, I casually told him that I had dreamed a vivid and unusual dream while he was away. He grunted interest but did not immediately pay attention. I told him that I had dreamed his voice in the garden while he was gone, that I had crept out and followed the sound, that I had seen him talking with a group of bandits down by our cove.

My father set his food aside and glared at me. He bit his lip, debating with himself for a moment, then sighed. "It doesn't seem like you are telling me a dream," he said.

"Papa, why were you here when you were supposed to be away on a business trip? Why did you lie to me?"

"Not everyone gets to know everything about everybody."

"Tell me," I shouted, a young girl despising her inability to control the tone and volume of her voice, her face trembling with the effort of holding in tears. My father nodded slowly, then he leaned in and addressed me quite seriously.

"All right, my little one. I suppose you would need to learn this eventually. I was hoping to wait a while longer, but life so rarely gives us what we want. I will tell you what it is I do on these trips, and let you into the secret of my life. But this is a deadly serious thing. And you must be responsible enough to tell no one, as one careless word from you is likely to get one or both of us killed. Can you promise this?"

I nodded, terrified but also determined to live up to that responsibility. My lips trembled and tears poured from my eyes, which I was ashamed of, but I was young and the heaviness of this moment was overwhelming. My father took my hands into his large warm hands, and his face softened.

"Very well," he said. "This is my secret."

4

Here is what the sea smells like.

It is more texture than scent, because the sea is primarily made of two substances that have no smell of their own: water and salt. Salt has no smell, but makes the air sting, and so all of the other smells of the sea are layered upon the pang of salt. Water has no smell but instead a comfort. We feel moisture as life and so the smells of the ocean are layered upon the contentment of the water. Salt is treble and water is bass. I don't know how I know this is true, but I know it is true.

The sea smells like old wood and wet leaves. Like cold mud and warm stone. Like every creature who has ever lived in it, a churning graveyard and nursery. Like winds from the inland carrying the hot circulation of life and winds from the ocean carrying the distant froth of waves against ships and islands. Like gray, only more so. Like blue, only less so.

A deep note of rot mixes with the sterile cleanliness of saline, and the result, a mottle of clear and foam, smells so much like itself that an old woman who hasn't smelled it in years, living in a desert town with no water at all, an uncrossable distance from the sea, smelling it faint on the breeze will stop and be cast back to her life on an estate by the sea, and for her, it will smell like her childhood.

That is what the sea smells like.

My father was a smuggler. He and Edmond, his business partner, had been running a smuggling business since before I was born and my mother had died.

"It wasn't always this way," he said. "Your mother's family had money. But they did not work, and the fortunes dwindled with age. By the time they died, we had far more property than wealth. There weren't the funds to keep up the grounds or pay the staff. Before you were born, child, the orange groves were filled with weeds. The gardens were tangles of overgrowth. Your mother and I didn't know what to do. I had no money of my own, no prospects. And there was no good way, then or now, for a woman to make a fortune in this narrow-minded country."

He guided me to the window and gestured toward the sea.

"Then one day, looking out this very window, I realized our salvation. The sea would save us. Our little bit of the sea," he said.

"Our cove." I looked out past his pointing finger.

"Yes, our cove. Difficult to find without a guide but deep enough for a small ship. Sheltered against storms. In the old days your mother's family used it to house their yacht. Amid a literal sea of fishers and merchants, your mother's family lived a life of privilege and comfort. They owned no business, generated no new wealth. They simply enjoyed that which they had.

"The money outlived your grandparents, but not your mother and I. We sold the yacht before you were born, along with jewels and art, no longer befitting our common status. I was good at selling and delivering goods, and I realized that our beautiful, hidden cove could be perfect for smuggling. But I didn't know the first thing about smuggling. I needed help."

"Uncle Edmond," I said. "He was a smuggler?"

My father laughed. "No, my daughter. Edmond is an accountant." He shook his head affectionately. "But a crooked one. He helped us through tough times utilizing . . . creative mathematics. I came to him with an idea. I would provide the perfect landing spot for smugglers, and an expertise in the local conditions and currents. He would find people interested in having their goods brought in without passing through the heavy taxes and duties of the ports. Such people, it turns out, were not difficult to find. And so gradually our business grew. Edmond finds clients, helps with the movement of the goods beyond our estate, and finds ways to hide our income from government inspectors. And I safely bring the ships in and out of our cove. Often when I am away on business, I am actually away. We must ensure that the goods reach their owners safely and secretly, and the overland travel is sometimes quite far. But there are times, yes, that I pretend to be away so I can work secretly at the cove on the arrival of a large shipment of merchandise. I apologize for lying to you. It breaks my heart every time, but it is only for your protection. I couldn't tell you why I would need to be awake and out all night, and asleep during the day, and I didn't want you near any of the sailors."

"Are they dangerous?" I asked, worried for the only parent I had left, but also a little excited at the prospect.

"No," he said, "but acts of crime tend to make even harmless people nervous. And nervous people can be unpredictable."

He shook his head. "Enough for now. The truth has been told. This is all too much for a young child. Let's get back to our lunch." But I wasn't hungry anymore. I was excited and scared. I couldn't decide which.

Years passed, as they do. I was nine, then ten, and then eleven. These were the last few years of true happiness I had left, although I had no way of knowing that at the time.

My father continued to go on business trips, although he no longer pretended to leave when receiving a shipment. He would only forbid me to go outside after sunset, and ask me to be in charge of my own meals the next day. I would sit in my window all night, anxiously waiting for his return, and so was always as sleepy as he was the next morning.

I looked at Edmond in a new light. Before, he had always been a purely friendly, goofy presence, full of jokes and games. He still was, but now I had the context of his job, and my respect for him deepened. Here was a man who could go out into the kingdoms of Europe, offering smuggling services to all sorts of low characters, and return to play backgammon with me at our kitchen table, attempting to cheat in intentionally obvious ways so that I could catch him and berate him, which amused us both.

Over one of these games, when I was nine, I stopped, unsure of how to say what I wanted to say.

"It's your turn, little one," he said. "Or do you want me to take another?"

"Is my father safe?" I asked abruptly, having failed to find a way to ease into the subject. "Will my father be okay when he goes out to, you know, do his work?"

Edmond grew serious and he pushed the game board aside.

"I will never let any harm fall upon your father," he said in a solemn voice, "and I will never let any harm fall upon you." He smiled. "Anyway, your father does the easy stuff. He'll be fine. I'm the one always sticking my neck out. Now, are you going to take your move or what?"

Albert and I continued to meet and play regularly. He asked sometimes about my father, and about the rumors, but I never answered one way or the other, preferring to change the subject by poking him or daring him to do some foolish act of bravery off one of the old, crumbling buildings of the estate. Eventually he understood that I would not say more than I had, and he stopped asking, and our friendship again became one of childhood joy and games and silence about any subject that could distract us from that.

Of course I regularly tried to talk to my father for more information about what he did. I wanted so badly to be of use, but he grew uncharacteristically stern at the subject, and would only shake his head. I never gave up, for I loved and admired my father, and knew that any work he did was work that I one day wanted to do too.

A change in our routine came suddenly, late in my eleventh year. It was a night that my father was set to receive a shipment. He had let me stay up with him as he waited, but when it arrived, he had put me in my bedroom and forbidden me to leave. I, as ever, sat awake at my window, waiting for him to come back inside so that we both could rest. I could hear the mindless babble of the waves, and, perhaps, although it might have been my imagination, the creak of wood from the bandit's ship that I knew was anchored in our cove. Generally this was all I ever heard or saw on these nights, the transaction done so quietly and quickly that no trace of it was noticeable even from our own estate.

That night, however, was different. I heard alarmed shouting, loud enough to risk alerting the inhabitants of neighboring estates. I rushed out of my room and out of the house without thought or hesitation. I would figure out how to help when I got to the cove. My father was all I had, and I would give up everything, down to my own life, to preserve him.

I raced barefoot through the fields toward the water, but some instinct made me duck behind a small rise before I got close to the source of the shouting, and from this hidden place I observed my father surrounded by the crew of bandits from the ship. They were the same group I had seen before with my father. But the circumstances were different this time. The man with the scarred cheek was holding a knife to my father's throat.

My father stood tall, unshaking, maintaining eye contact with his assailant. "I have no money here," he said. The bandits jeered at him, and the man with the scarred cheek pressed the knife into my father's neck.

"An estate this rich," the man said. His voice gave me a lurch in the gut, because it was not the voice of a man who was acting on a whim, but a man serious and set on a goal, and intent on achieving it. "And you a smuggler for all of these years. Don't lie to me or I will cut out your tongue before I gut you. If there is no money in this home then there will also be no life."

Before my father could reply in a way that might cause him harm, I took a large rock from the ground and hurled it with great accuracy born of years of dares and games with Albert. The rock thumped dully against the man's head, and he collapsed, dropping the knife. The other bandits were confused, having clearly been rallied by their leader and unsure of what to do without his motivation. My father immediately set himself upon them, increasing the confusion. I sprang forward, dashing for the knife. The man with the scarred face was dazed but awake. Blood ran down his face. He pawed about in the grass, his fingers batting the hilt, trying to get a grip. I made it to the blade first and without thinking fumbled it into my hands and in the same motion drove it toward the man with the scarred face. I struck something and heard a scream. The other men fled, and my father, bruises and blood visible now upon his face, scooped me up in a tight embrace. I looked down at the man with the scarred face, who I had stabbed in the thigh. He was bleeding from two different places, and looking up at me with a fierce hatred.

Edmond had rushed to the estate as soon as a messenger from my father had delivered the news. Seeing my father's swollen, reddened face, Edmond said in a lighthearted voice full of mock exasperation, "I suppose we have to find a new crew." My father sighed, and Edmond gave him a large hug and a laugh. "I'm so glad you're both okay."

Even in his joking, Edmond was right. They had used this crew for years and had trusted them. My father and he would have to start over finding a new group of confederates, and also now had learned to temper their trust in those who come from the world of banditry.

My father was quiet. He watched me with deep consideration. He had made sure I was physically unharmed, and then he had warmed some chocolate over the fire for me, which I now drank with the simple joy of a child who is awake past her bedtime and drinking chocolate. I was remarkably unbothered by what had occurred and about my own attack on that man. It had felt natural to me. This may have been the first sign of my vocation, although I did not recognize it as such. My father perhaps did, as he looked me over with deep thought and care.

"I suppose," he said, "that it is time for you to learn more about the business."

"Really?" I said with happiness.

"Really?" Edmond said with surprise.

"You didn't see how she handled herself out there," my father said to Edmond. "She showed foresight, she was quick. This won't be the last situation like this. We can no longer ignore the dangers of our business. And if my daughter is to be around this kind of danger, then I would rather she be prepared."

"It would be less dangerous," Edmond said, with the tone of someone bringing up an argument that's course had run for years, "if we partnered with The Duke's Own. Let them take the risk."

"We are not pairing up with those assassins and thieves," my father said, in the same tone. "We may be criminals, but we are honest criminals. I won't let my family name mix with an organization involved in murder, banditry, slavery, and who knows what else."

On the many nights my father had left me alone, I had taken to reading books in his small library. I knew all about The Duke's Own. They were a notorious syndicate of pirates, racketeers, and swindlers. Their reach was vast, covering Europe, Russia, and northern Africa. The Duke of The Duke's Own was a myth, a sleight of hand played by whichever pirate was handy when they needed a figurehead or a phantom for authorities to fruitlessly pursue. In actuality, the membership made decisions through general election, and in this way the organization was far more democratically run than any government on the continent. Still, The Duke's Own was also a brutal organization that pillaged small farms, abusing and often killing innocent people who dared to defend all that they owned.

The Duke's Own had politicians, military leaders, bankers, and merchants as members. The deeper their roots, the more secure their operations. I could understand Edmond's strategy for joining such a powerful group. They could protect us not only from smaller criminals like the ones who attacked my father, but also even larger, more frightening groups like the mysterious Order of the Labyrinth. If we made the right political connections, The Duke's Own could even protect us from the possibility of prison.

But my father was adamant, and Edmond backed off. "Perhaps one of these days you will change your mind," sighed Edmond.

"I will not have my daughter connected to a corporation of murderers and plunderers. Enough!" My father turned to me. "We must learn to protect ourselves from such people, not become them. Tomorrow we begin your education."

I learned first the complete structure of my father and Edmond's smuggling operation. Their clients were the owners of the merchant ships and pleasure yachts, bringing in fruit and spices and gold and cloth from ports in the east, or from Morocco or from Egypt. A close eye was kept on these shipments, because the various squabbling kingdoms of Europe all wanted their share of any goods passing through their ports. On the other hand, the Mediterranean was thick with bandit ships, and no eyebrows were raised at the occasional shipment of goods lost to pirates. A cost of doing business. But of course the bandits were my father and Edmond's bandits, and they did not take by force. They tied on peacefully to ships who had prepared for their arrival, and whose crew helped the bandits with the transfer of cargo. Then the bandits took the cargo to our cove, where it was unloaded, and transported by land back to its owners, minus a cut for the smugglers. The bandits enjoyed the situation too, since there was much less risk of violence and injury boarding a ship that wanted you aboard, and much less risk of jail since the ships always waited a considerate amount of time before reporting the "attacks." Edmond and my father had underestimated the bandits' greed, but the old crew was soon replaced with a new one, more carefully vetted and with less of a violent reputation, who for the time being at least seemed content with their roles. My father hired mercenaries to guard the estate for a year or so, in case any of the old crew returned seeking revenge, but nothing happened and eventually he decided he couldn't justify the expense and we returned to our old way of living.

Along with the details of the business, I learned much of the trade from my father, and from Edmond, and from the crews, whom, as I became involved in the business, I was allowed to interact with more. They treated me as a novelty, and from them I learned, unbeknownst to my father, how to pickpocket, how to open locks, and several other such tricks. I would make Albert act as my test subject, keeping a cork in his pocket all day while I would try to steal it as we went about our games. Albert never again brought up the rumors about my father, and I would have denied them if he had, but I could see in his eyes he knew they weren't merely rumors. For the first year or so Albert caught me every time, but eventually I was able to regularly slip the cork out without his noticing. He tried to learn as well, through my secondhand lessons, but he never could find the aptitude. I discovered great satisfaction in these new skills. I would sit for hours in front of the old back door, practicing breaking into the lock, until my fingers ached and the keyhole was fogged with perspiration from my nostrils.

Edmond, who networked with the wealthy and criminal alike, taught me much about the art of persuasion and manipulation. "Nothing must ever be your idea," he explained. "If I want you to go to bed, and I tell you to, you'll rebel. But if I simply set up a situation in which you will have the idea to go to bed yourself, then you will go with satisfaction, thinking you have won even as you do exactly what I wanted you to. Remember that, because it will get you far in life. Short-lived pride at winning a disagreement is a fool's game. It is far better to let the other side think they have won as they coincidentally decide to do what you wanted all along." He winked at me, and then tried to switch two pieces on the backgammon board and laughed when I slapped his hands.

For my father's part, he wanted me to be able to protect myself, and so taught me how to use a knife. I soon became adept at all sorts of defensive and offensive uses of a small blade, and I would, with my father's consent, practice fighting with the crew using short lengths of wood, until I was soon besting even the most skilled of them. I think my father allowed this practice because he wanted them to think of me always as potentially very dangerous. But even my father did not understand the full potential of how dangerous I could become.

5

At age thirteen I started to talk more openly about my future. I wanted to join my father's business, to accept it as my legacy and, when he grew too old, to inherit his place in the business. My father was adamantly against it. He had given in on teaching me to protect myself, and to understand the intricacies of his business so there would be no secrets interrupting our family closeness, but he wanted me to use the wealth he gained to find my way in the world of the righteous and law abiding. "Your mother and I dreamed such dreams for you," he said. "And none of them involved you becoming a smuggler or a fighter."

"What could I do in the outside world?" I asked. "Use whatever wealth we have to pretend at nobility? Drift through the world in a cloud of servants and days of leisure until the family money runs out and it all starts over again? Marry some wealthy heir, combine our fortunes, and spend my days serving him? There is no job in the world of the righteous for a girl. But here, among these so-called criminals, I could lead."

He shook his head, unable to argue with me but also unyielding in his insistence that I not enter the business. Edmond, when he was around for these arguments, would tussle my hair in a patronizing manner that would make me furious if it came from anyone else, but from him carried only affection. "I think she'd make a great smuggler. Better than a couple of bumbling fools like us."

"Stay out of this, Edmond," my father said, uncharacteristically cold. "She is my daughter, not yours." Edmond shrugged, a big, clownlike shrug, but I think the words stung him. This was one of only two subjects that he and Edmond diverged on, the other being the perennial argument about joining forces with The Duke's Own.

"It will only get more dangerous for us," Edmond would say. "Royal forces are aware there is something fishy about this stretch of coast. We could be caught. And then there is the Order of the Labyrinth. Their ships are sighted more and more often these days. We need protection. The Duke's Own can give us that. And we could make so much more with their distribution."

"My legacy will not go hand in hand with any band of murderers and slavers," my father would say.

He would embrace Edmond, a sign that he wished to drop these disputes for the time being. "Edmond, please, let me think about my family's future."

But there was little future left.

The Order of the Labyrinth was becoming more and more a worry, not only for my father but for anyone who lived or sailed upon the Mediterranean. Their ships, stacked high with crates, and bearing a black flag with the white sigil of a labyrinth, seemed to be everywhere. No one knew their purpose, who ran their organization, or what they wanted. What was known for sure is that they accepted no approach of their ships, and would viciously attack any other vessels that came too close. The various kingdoms and empires sent military craft after them, but none could catch them. Their ships were fast, and their captains appeared to know the waters better than anyone. There had been no sign of any of their ships arriving at any port, and so the rumor was that there were islands throughout the sea, seemingly deserted, that actually held hidden anchorages for the Order. No one understood exactly what or who the Order of the Labyrinth were.

There were rumors as large as legends, but the stories were so exciting and terrifying that the general assumption was that they must be at least somewhat true. Some said the Order only attacked at sea, late at night. They would use arrows to silently kill the lookouts, and then sneak aboard the victims' ship, slitting each sailor's throat and throwing the bodies overboard. They would carefully clean up all of the blood, and then abandon the empty ship entirely, the pristine ghost ship left as a warning to others of their presence. Some said the Order employed mystics who held the power of flight and the ability to reach into a man's heart and stop it by simply concentrating from as much as ten miles away. Some said the Order had been in the Mediterranean as long as humans had. Some said the Order had been there even longer than that, and that the first humans to reach Europe had found tall stone buildings already there, each carved with the emblem of a labyrinth. Those same people said that the buildings had no doors and no windows, and yet the hooded members of the labyrinth still came and went, through means no one understood. Of course, others said that the Order were simply bandits like any other, and the hoods and emblems were only a show to keep their victims disoriented and easily controlled. In any case, the mysterious aura of the Order was enough to make any man scared. Any ship bearing the black flag and white labyrinth was given a wide swath upon the sea. It was universally agreed the Order could be anywhere, at any time, and if they wanted what you had—whether it be wealth or life—they could take it from you.

All of this made my father nervous. He understood bandits and smugglers, the flow of goods, the motive of wealth. These were known quantities. He didn't know what to do with secret societies, with ships that could not even be sailed past safely. And these ships were seen more often near our shore. Whatever the Order of the Labyrinth was, they were expanding into our region, and my father felt this could only mean trouble ahead.

It was around this time that I, one evening, went out in the field behind the house to practice throwing my knife into the trunk of the old olive tree that had long since given up bearing fruit. Its bark was a patchwork of scars from my many previous sessions, and the scars had tended to group together closer and closer as my throwing became more precise. I could now easily land the knife within inches of where I had thrown it last, but I would not stop my practice until the blade landed every time in the notch left by the first throw. If I was to run a smuggling trade, and I was determined to do so, then I must be the best at every imaginable criminal feat. For crews of men to respect a woman as their leader, she must not just be their equal, but many times better, and I would not rest until I had achieved that.

As I threw, I felt a presence behind me. I turned, and there, quite close, in the gathering darkness, was a man. He was hunched stiffly, and I recognized him as the figure I had seen twice before through my life, always indistinct and distant. Now he was quite close, less than twenty feet, although he had his back turned, and in the dim of the gloaming it was difficult to pick out any detail about him. I quickly retrieved my knife and held it at the ready, but he made no move nor any sound. He only stood with his strange posture and distorted mouth, as though the basic functioning of his body had failed. I grew afraid, and, betraying an imagined self full of bravery and strength, I took my knife and ran inside. When I checked again out of a window, the man was gone.

6

Here is what a wet dog smells like.

A wet dog smells like everywhere the dog has been. Grass and leaves and dirt and stones, mud and rainwater and smoke and garbage.

Like everything the dog has done. It smells like saliva and adrenaline, like the furious joy of hunting smaller animals and the cringing confusion of being threatened by larger animals, or loud sounds, or a passing storm.

A little like ripe fruit. A little like shit, of course, but a little like flowers. A lot of funk, but a little sweet. Like food on the final moments before going bad. Like a compost pile when it has moved past the initial rot and starts the real alchemy of soil. Like grapes, a little.

A wet dog smells exactly of our idea of what a wet dog smells like. The comfort in complete comprehension. There is no fear in understanding. It is the smell of something we love, a smell we put up with because we love them. All loves are negotiations. We tolerate so that we may rejoice. The smell of a wet dog is part of that bargain.

That is what a wet dog smells like.

When I was fourteen years old, Edmond arrived late one evening to our house. This was not unusual, obviously, but his was a careful, tended-to schedule, and we had not expected to see him for some months more. He had never arrived early before, and my father looked deeply concerned. Edmond for his part was pale and had difficulty finding the words to express his reason for coming.

I heated water for him, and my father fixed a simple meal of bread and cheese.

"What is it, Edmond?" asked my father. "What trouble befalls us?"

"Trouble, yes," he said. "Great trouble. Oh, my friend, I don't know if we will make it through this one."

My father and I hunched in close to him.

"The Order of the Labyrinth," Edmond whispered. "I am hearing from all over Europe, from every criminal connection I have, that the Order is looking to take over all smuggling in the civilized world. They have been gradually eradicating smaller operations, by brutal and inhuman means. *The Noble Steed*, a ship we conducted business with last summer, was discovered seemingly abandoned in waters frequented by the Order. When bandits boarded the ship, they found the bodies of the *Steed's* crew burned to ash. I have it on several of my sources' accounts that we are the next target. The Order of the Labyrinth is coming for us, and they will destroy us."

I reeled with the news. My father took it even worse than me, and clutched at my arm.

"Should we shut down our smuggling operations?" my father asked. "Perhaps restart them when the threat has passed?"

"They already know who we are," Edmond snapped. "Their attack on the *Steed* was a warning to us. It is too late to hide."

"What can we do?" my father said.

"You know what we can do," Edmond said. "We have bickered about it before, old friend, but now it is an existential necessity. We must join forces with The Duke's Own. By ourselves we are powerless, but a grand force like that can provide countless fierce men to protect."

"The Duke's Own," my father repeated, and spat on the floor.

"Please, Papa," I said. "They can help."

"They are cruel and soulless men. They make their wealth off slavery and blood, and I will not accept that coin, even to save myself. We cannot mix their unspeakable crimes with our family's legacy."

For the first time, Edmond looked angry. "Then we are lost."

My father shook his head.

"No, there is another way. I have a plan."

At some point in our lives, we eat an apple for the last time. We smell coffee for the last time. We use a toilet for the last time, wash ourselves for the last time, get our last haircut. On a grand scale, very few of us are aware—as we have an experience—if it will be the last time we have that experience.

That same week that Edmond arrived, Albert came around and we went swimming in the cove. I was slightly embarrassed to strip down even a few heavier items of my clothes in order to go swimming as we always had done. Albert had grown up and was now much taller than me. He had the first faint shadows of a beard, but had not yet understood this to mean that he might need to start shaving. And in the quiet times between our games, I had noticed a new tension between us. There was a crackling energy that existed in the silences between our joking words, and neither of us knew what to do with that energy. We were just old enough to feel the first inkling of passion, but far too young to recognize it, not even in ourselves, let alone the signs of it in others.

So the afternoon I spent with Albert was halting and awkward, both of us a little shy for reasons we did not understand. But eventually we found the old rhythm to our days. We no longer played hide and seek or other childish games. We wrestled and raced, we ate cherries on our backs in the grass, and we giggled over private jokes that I cannot recall, although I have spent countless years trying.

Then the sun was going down, and Albert had to return to the family that I still knew nothing about, and I went back to my house in which the tension was fierce. Edmond and my father were leaned over a table, mumbling through the details of the plan. As soon as I walked in the door, I felt the stress of our situation return, and I looked forward to the next time I got to spend a carefree afternoon with Albert. But there is a last time for everything we do in this life. And, like anyone unlucky enough to be born into this world, I had just been carefree and young for the last time without knowing it.

7

My father's plan was uncharacteristically violent, but he was willing to do what had to be done. Quitting smuggling would not save him, and my father refused to join The Duke's Own, because he did not want his family name tied to their ruthlessness and violence. More than death, my father feared his only daughter used as collateral against him, or worse, herself forced into a life of banditry and murder. So he had his plan.

"A fake shipment," he said. "Here, a few miles down the coast. A cove very similar to ours, and next to dense, wooded land. Almost as good a place to bring ashore goods as our own. We stage a smuggling operation there and allow The Order to see us set it up."

"Won't they be suspicious that we have moved our receiving port?" Edmond asked.

"Yes, but we will assuage that suspicion on two fronts. Firstly, we will pay off one of the smaller royal boats whose crew we are friendly with to loiter in the waters near our cove, providing a pretext for the move. And secondly, we will move all our operations there, starting now. Once they see that this has become a regular place for us, they will accept it as the new status quo.

"Then," he continued, "we will hide a full regiment of mercenaries in the shipment. When the Order of the Labyrinth comes, our hired men will spring out and strike back mercilessly."

"The Order of the Labyrinth has many ships," said Edmond. "Even if our attack succeeds, they will be back with more soon."

"Their interest is secrecy," said my father. "And that secrecy is served better by picking on weaker operations first, rather than waging all-out war with the powerful. Otherwise it would be common knowledge even to the armies of the kingdoms and empires that this Order has become a warring state and must be crushed. So it is in our interest to establish a tone of difficulty. We strike first, and we strike with overwhelming brutality. When they understand that to approach us is to invite fierce and visible violence, they will move on to easier, smaller targets."

Edmond did not speak for several moments. Then, "You believe this will work?"

"Yes."

"It's risky," Edmond said. "You are dead set against joining The Duke's Own?"

"It will never be an option."

"Okay," conceded Edmond after a contemplative silence. "I will go about arranging the decoy royal patrol, and the mercenaries right away."

"Good. We keep a lookout at all times above this new location, and we board the mercenaries nearby. When we see the ship coming, we set up the fake shipment and prepare for their arrival."

Edmond shook his head thoughtfully. "I hope you realize the stakes here. If we fail or falter at all, they will crush us."

"They will crush us if we do nothing as well," said my father. He looked at me, and the sight of his daughter seemed to harden his resolve. "I don't know if we'll succeed. But I know that we must try."

Shrugging, and finding only a small part of his usual laughter, Edmond raised his glass. "Here's to our attempt."

"But I must help," I said. Or, more likely, I whined it. I hated that tone in my voice, but I couldn't help the rising feelings of helplessness and fury. "This is my family too. This is what keeps both of us fed. You must let me help."

My father raised an eyebrow, sighed, and motioned me to sit next to him. It had been some days, and smuggling operations had been transferred for the moment to the new spot miles down the shore. From our cliffs, I could just see the ships come and go from that new cove, but it was all so frustratingly distant.

"I have been trying to teach you what it is to live a life of crime," he said. "And much of that is understanding and managing risk. Those who rush blindly in are the first to fall or get caught or otherwise come up against misfortune. You must choose wisely when you put yourself in danger. One miscalculation could be the end of it all."

"But inaction could also be the end," I said.

"True, but we *are* acting. Edmond is managing the operation. Our mercenaries are in place. All that can be done is being done. Nothing about either of us being there or not being there would change how this will turn out. The only thing it could change is the length of our lives."

Still I could not be convinced, and what I felt was shame. I felt that my father was a coward, and that he was forcing me

also to be a coward, while others did the brave work of pre-
serving our lives for us. My father, seeing this resentment in my
eyes, led me to the window, from which we could see where my
mother was buried, a view neither of us ever acknowledged or
talked about. But this time he gestured toward her.

"I have a responsibility," he said. "And my responsibility isn't
to be the most wealthy, or cunning, or brave. It isn't to conquer
the world. It's to see that you flourish, not as a criminal, nor
someone indebted for life to criminals, but as a good woman.
That is what I owe your mother, and what I owe you, and what I
owe myself. Maybe you don't understand this now. Maybe you
never will, and you will resent me forever for my caution. But
none of those things will change the truth of my debt."

He turned me away from the window.

"Now," he said, "what should I make for dinner?"

Of course, that night I went. Quietly out of my bedroom, and
quietly through the house, and quietly out the door and then,
abandoning quiet, tearing through the grass toward the shore
cliffs and the ambush point ahead. It would happen soon, perhaps that night, and I needed to be there. It's not that I didn't
understand my father's warning. It's that despite my understanding, my faith in what was right would not let me do otherwise.

The night was warm, summer peering over the horizon of
spring. Bright too, a full moon turning the nighttime into a
slightly faded day. I could see the coast for a mile ahead of me,
and the white caps of the waves breaking against it. If I had
thought about it, I would have realized what a strange night
that would have been for the Order of the Labyrinth to attack,
when the cover of darkness wasn't dark. But I was not thinking;
I was believing.

I believed in my father and his righteousness. I believed in Edmond and his ability. I believed that our plan was foolproof. I believed in myself and my cunning. And most of all I believed that my time had come. Too long I had been a child, hiding behind the work of my father. It was time for my name to be known. For my face to be remembered. I would be my own person in this world of smugglers and thieves, and they would know who I was.

All of this went through my head as I, a child still, ran barefoot through that night until I arrived, panting, at the shoreline where Edmond stood, hands on hips, waiting to see if tonight was the night he would face attack.

He turned at my approach, his face passing through confusion and shock and worry.

"What are you thinking?" he said. "You must get home at once."

I was already speaking, already pleading my case. ". . . my legacy too. And when I'm old and looking back, do I want to have been hiding in my bedroom? It's time for me to take responsibility. It's time for me to help. You think so too. You said so. And I'm just doing what you said. But also I'm doing what I choose to do, because that's what it means to be grown up. And I am grown up. And I can help. I have sharper eyes than all the rest of you. I'll be able to see them coming from farther away. Please let me stay, Uncle Edmond. Please."

It had all sounded so much more dignified and eloquent in my head. Within me was a great general, surveying her troops and speaking stirring words, and it made me cringe to open my mouth and hear a child whining for approval. But Edmond heard the noble foundation under my mewling words, and he nodded thoughtfully. Or more likely he looked back at the night-shrouded coast and thought through the calculus of sending a child back on her own versus keeping her somewhere safe nearby.

"Okay," he said. "You can stay." He pointed up at a cliff well out of the way. "But up there. You keep an eye out and shout the moment you see ships."

I did not understand, or chose not to understand, the rationale of keeping me out of harm's way, but I nodded sternly, a soldier on a mission, and I ran, grateful, and ashamed of my gratitude, up to the cliff.

The night would have been the kind of quiet, beautiful night that I liked to watch from the window of my bedroom, the hiss of the waves and the wind through the trees harmonizing, and the world turned by the bright moon into a softer, bluer version of itself, permeated with the smell of night-blooming flowers. But now there was a sense of threat and danger under all of the beauty and it felt like the ocean itself was pounding as hard as my own heart. I strained my eyes watching the seas, determined that if I was to be relegated to this cliff, then I would certainly be the first one to see the oncoming ships, and it would be those few minutes of extra advance notice my young eyes provided that would make all of the difference in setting up our ambush. The line between success and failure would be drawn by my decision to come out this night. If another lookout saw the ships before me, then it was true that I was only a nuisance, an extra concern for Edmond on a night when he already had more than enough.

But try as I might, I could see no ships at all on the calm sea. The men sat around a fire on the beach, laughing and chatting. Edmond stood apart from them, staring at nothing in particular, with his arms crossed, frowning. He occasionally looked up at the moon, tracking the progress of the night. He was more worried than I had expected him to be, and it occurred to me that perhaps I had underestimated just how dangerous this position was. Perhaps I should return to my bed. But no, I was not a coward. And if I wanted to be counted in this world, then I needed the courage to stand up and be counted.

Hours passed. I could feel myself start to waver into sleep. There were no ships coming that night. Perhaps the ships would never come. Perhaps they had found a more worthy target, and we could go back to our usual business, and years later think back and laugh about this week where we all became so worried about a great attack that never came. This thought made me happy and I smiled sleepily. Then I shook my head and stood to wake up my body. Now was not the time to fantasize about what could happen. Now was the time to focus on what was happening.

I concentrated harder on searching the sea, hoping that this would keep me awake. And it was in this sweep from my vantage that I happened to turn and look back in the direction of our estate. I cried out, not anything as useful as words, but the strangled, grunting shout of someone who has been unexpectedly struck in the gut. Where the estate was, a thick black column of smoke rose into the bright night sky.

8

Edmond and the rest must have heard my cry, but I did not wait to see their reaction or consult with them on what to do next. By the time I understood what I was doing, I was already flying across the edge of the cliffs, a headlong sprint toward my home. The closer I got, the more unmistakable it was that the smoke was from our estate. And where was my father? I wished I could run faster, that my spirit could fly from this too-slow body, and I could transform into a being untethered to the physical world.

But on that night I could only move on the length of my awkward teenage legs.

When I rounded the last turn of the coast and the trees fell away, and I saw my home burning, those legs almost gave out on me. I stumbled and fell, my nose slamming painfully into the ground. I pulled myself up, tried to keep running at the same speed but my ankle was twisted and I could only manage a limping jog. I cried out my father's name, over and over, and then I saw him. He was hunched over, perhaps hurt, but he was alive, and I began weeping out of sheer relief.

"It's you, it's you," was all I could manage, and I came up to him but by then I had already realized something was wrong.

This was not my father. This was a familiar lurching figure, the one I had seen three times before. The figure turned toward me.

The man's face was completely pale, his eyes and mouth twisted into a look of absolute shock and pain. The front of his shirt was wet with blood. He gasped but couldn't seem to form words. There was something wrong with his throat, or his lungs. He could only wheeze. I stumbled backward. He reached out one hand toward me and I ran around him, stifling a scream, toward my burning home. By the time I thought to look behind me, the man had disappeared.

The attack had been swift and total. Doors kicked in. Windows broken. The inside of the house was a pure inferno, and try as I might, I could not even get close to it, let alone inside. Drawn in ash over the hollow, flame-filled entrances was an emblem I recognized very well. The sign of the Order of the Labyrinth. I called and called for my father, stumbling around the fields and the orange trees and the cove, but there was no sign of him, only violence everywhere I turned. Even the orange trees had been hacked at and burned, although their wet leaves and living wood only smoldered and smoked rather than cradling the bright bursts of flames the attackers must have hoped for.

In despair at my inability to find my father, I stopped in a field and looked at the moon, the same bright, mute moon that had watched me run from this house just hours before. And I had a thought that drove me further into darkness. I started toward my mother's grave atop the small hill overlooking the cove. Soon I came across a blood trail in the grass and I started to run faster. And then, some twenty feet from her grave, I found the body of my father.

9

Here is what my father's death smelled like.

It smelled like blood, which smelled like metal and panic. We have evolved to find the scent of the inside of our bodies upsetting. We recognize the smell of shit and snot and piss and all of the other fluids do not belong to the natural healthy order of a civilized society, and so they repulse us. But a smell like blood goes further than that. In this much quantity, where it fills the air, the smell floods us with adrenaline, and so it is not so much a smell as an experience of the flesh. My father's death smelled like blood and so it smelled like tingling hands and a dry mouth and a scalp two sizes too small and skin that twitched.

My father's death smelled like smoke, which, combined with the blood, almost smelled like the preparation of a meal, but the disconnect between what I knew to be true and what the smell reminded me of caused an emotional motion sickness, and I staggered away from his body to throw up. Then his death smelled like my vomit, which smells like acid and disease.

My father's death smelled much like his life. It smelled like his clothes, and it smelled like his skin, which smelled exactly like his skin when he was alive. It smelled like his hair, and his hands, and the sharp peppery note of the grass he was laying on. The night breeze in from the sea still smelled like ice and salt and a deep organic undercurrent that was the combined smell of all things living in it. In other words, my father's death smelled most of all like any other night, like any other time that was not the end of everything I had ever known. There was nothing in the smell to indicate just how deep and terrifying was the reality, and that was the worst part of the smell of all.

That is what my father's death smelled like.

Edmond arrived soon after. He put one arm around me and one around my father's body. "What have we done?" he said. "What have we done?"

He cried. I had never seen him cry, and the surprise of this startled me out of my stupor for a moment. I reached up and wiped one cheek.

"I was foolish to think we could have set a trap for the Order of the Labyrinth," whispered Edmond through his weeping. "They instead set a trap for us. Drew me and my men away from the estate, and then attacked, following the same principle we had thought to follow. Strike first and strike so viciously and completely that no response is possible."

He shook his head and waved vaguely at the devastation behind us.

"I am a fool and a failure," he said.

His defeat roused action in me.

"We must go," I said. "We must go before they return. There is nothing for us here."

He nodded, seeming only an automatic gesture in response to my words. I helped him up, and together we went to fetch a wagon that hadn't been destroyed in the fire, and some horses that Edmond had tethered back at the planned ambush site. The smell of the still-burning building was a physical pain for me. It would take me many decades, longer than any human life, to come to appreciate the inhuman beauty of the smell of burning. Until then, it only brought me back again and again to that place and that night.

Edmond refused help from his men and carried my father into the wagon himself. As I was about to follow my father's body onto the wagon, I saw someone approaching from the woods. I turned, ready to fight, ready to defend, ready to die. But it was Albert. He looked about him with numb shock at the ruined estate, at me with my father's blood on my clothes.

"What has happened? Who has done this?" he croaked out. He saw the wagon. "You're not leaving. Where will you go?"

Where would I go? I would go with Edmond. I would travel the world and learn the ways of criminals, and live the life of a criminal, and use all of the skills my father taught me, with only one goal in mind: to utterly destroy the Order of the Labyrinth for what they had done to me.

"Go home, Albert," I said. Tears streamed down my face, and he began to weep too. I touched his cheek, only to comfort him, only to wipe away his tears, and then I found myself drawing his face toward mine and we kissed then, a long kiss, one that would have to stand in for the years of time together we would never get to have. His lips tasted salty, but his face smelled clean, like linen fresh from water. Finally, the kiss broke off, and I turned before I could begin to waver. "Good-bye," I said, with my back turned, and got onto the wagon.

"Good-bye," I heard Albert respond softly. I did not know if I would ever hear his voice again. I thought that probably I would not.

CRAIG

2013

You found the letters. I knew you would, Craig. You were supposed to. But I didn't account for your fretful nature.

It's good news though. After two stressful years of threatening letters and calls, Mastercard abruptly sent you a statement showing your account balance of $15,417.71 was paid in full. They also thanked you for your loyalty as they closed your account. I watched you stare at those statements for nearly an hour. I enjoyed how you reached for the phone, like you were going to call them to correct the error, but then you would retract your hand. I could see the moral machinations, and it was a delight.

Maybe they won't notice, I'm thinking you thought. *Maybe I benefited from a computer error?*

Then you stopped thinking about it for a while, and you looked genuinely happy. I want you to be happy. Genuinely. Craig, I will be with you from your birth to your death. It doesn't benefit me in any way to have you living a miserable life. Sure there will be misery. There always is. Trust me. But if I can keep you happy while you're trying to have a family, then I will.

I celebrated your new debt-free lifestyle by carefully placing tiny spiders along the back collar line of your shirt, where you wouldn't notice them for hours. Meanwhile your happiness waned, and you came to some internal ethical conclusion about what you should do. I hate that I can't see inside your mind. I hate that I can't put my fingers into your hairy little earholes and just poke your pink-gray lump of thoughts until it focuses on what's important. Ethics are not important. I'm trying to promise you this. Everything here is ethical in the way that anything is ethical, depending on whose decision it was in the first place. And this was my decision. You weren't doing anything about it, so I did.

You grabbed for the phone and you called Mastercard. I miss the old days of phones plugged into walls. I could just bite through the cord with my surprisingly sharp teeth, and voila, no more conversation. Or better yet, the old old days before phones, when it was easy to rewrite letters or throw them away before the postal carrier picked them up or, if absolutely necessary, cause a fatal accident for the postal carrier before they could be delivered.

But these wireless devices, I can't do anything about. I know I sound like an old woman, complaining about cell phones, but that's because I am.

Devin, your account representative at Mastercard, answered and heard you explain what you thought was a computer error, and that you never paid that amount. You then heard him say he'd have to check with his supervisor. Then you heard a crash in your bedroom. Devin heard the crash in your bedroom.

Then Devin heard you stifle a scream, which came out as a whimpered grunt.

Devin tried to ask, "Is now a good time?" but you had already tossed the phone onto the couch and run into the bedroom, where you found a gray fox on your bed. It had knocked your lamp off the nightstand (the crash you heard).

The fox had only one eye. Its left eye socket was swollen, but not entirely closed. The fur around it was brown from dried blood, which accentuated the two swaths of bright pink flesh hiding dark yellow fluid. The fox was cackling, like a baby laughing at a thought that exists outside of the bounds of language. It was not a sound you ever expected to come from an animal, and you looked frightened. You should have been. Foxes are not aggressive toward humans in the wild, but this little thing was not in the wild. It was cornered, scared, and wounded.

You stammered and backed up. The fox arched its back and growled. From the living room sofa, where you forgot to end your call, Devin was asking "Sir, is everything okay?" But Devin himself became distracted as the cursor on his computer screen began typing on its own. It wrote out the date and cause of Devin's eventual death (May 17, 2031. The latch holding up a second-floor fire escape ladder will fail just as Devin walks below it, crushing his skull and breaking his neck.). Then his web browser showed him photos of human corpses with crushed skulls—mostly from auto accidents and deliberate physical assaults, but a few from falling objects like window-unit air conditioners. Devin passed out and broke two of his teeth falling from his desk chair. Broken teeth are unfortunate, although not nearly as unfortunate as the broken skull will be.

Meanwhile, you were panicking over a tiny fox. Here's what I would have done. First I would have closed the bedroom door. Then I would have opened the front door. Then, I would have removed the four-day-old leftover beef tacos from the fridge and dropped them in a trail from the bedroom to the front door. It's not a large apartment, Craig. That animal is starving and would have gotten out in a hurry.

But you did not do that. You yelled at it, Craig. Why are you yelling "Get out!" at a feral animal? I don't need to explain the limitations of human language to you, do I? It is a fox, and it is disoriented and scared. Can you imagine how you would feel if a monster ten times your size stood above you and shouted incomprehensible noise? You'd feel terrorized, Craig.

I don't know if you'd turn that fright into a lunge, and a growl, and a gnashing of teeth on that monster's calf, but that's what the fox did to you.

There are certain ways I handle problems, and certain ways you handle problems. Either way, the fox got out of your home. It took a neighbor calling the Sheriff's Secret Police after hearing your screams, and animal control having to tase the fox and cart it off in a cage. (Don't worry. I snuck into their truck and released it later.) You were taken to the hospital and given sixty stitches and painful rabies shots.

While you were in the hospital, I called Mastercard back and asked to speak with Devin. I had to get through a fairly complicated phone tree, but I finally found him. I told him that the noise he heard was only a bad communal dream we both experienced, but now everything's fine. Devin was crying. He said he was afraid he was going to die. I said, as gently and honestly as I could, "It's better than the alternative."

Devin agreed to send you another letter double confirming that your balance is zero.

I hope when you're out of the hospital, Craig, you'll feel convinced and move on. The doctors say the infection in your calf is bad. It was made worse by you passing out when you saw your own fibula behind the flesh torn away by the fox. If you had gotten immediate attention, an early treatment of antibiotics would have really helped.

You're thoughtful and tender, Craig. It makes my task difficult sometimes.

Speaking of credit cards, today you received a low interest, low spending limit card (just $1,000) from American Express. This one doesn't come with any airline or hotel points. But it will help you rebuild your credit score, and I know you're not interested in traveling anyway. You have family on your mind, I'm sure, now that you've had a girlfriend for almost two years.

Two years! Amaranta is a lovely woman. Good sense of humor. Incredibly smart. Contagious smile and elegant style. Such lush black hair, like velvet drapes. She has a stable job at the bank, working directly under the vice president Steve Carlsberg, probably the nicest (if chattiest) person in town. He really treats his staff well, with good pay, benefits, and a positive work environment.

Amaranta's a good one, Craig. What a twist of fortunate fate, that fender bender. She hit her brakes for seemingly no reason, and you tried to swerve but clipped her bumper. Technically it was your fault because you rear-ended her, but she slammed on her brakes with no one in front of her. She said she thought she saw an old woman jump in front of her car, but no one else saw the woman there. Plus she couldn't remember what the woman's face looked like, so probably just a trick of the eye.

Blame didn't matter though. You two were both so apologetic. You're a gentle soul, Craig. I knew you would be forgiving about it. She's more emotional, and overly critical of herself. I'm sure this is because of her overbearing father, who constantly negated her achievements with his lack of enthusiasm for everything from Girl Scout badges to prophetic dreams to softball championships.

So a car accident, even a minor one at low speeds, was hard

on her. Had she been run into by a more selfish or aggressive driver, that person might have twisted the insurance reporting in their favor, or held out, or worse, sued. And she would have let it eat away at her like the infection eating away at your calf.

But it was you who ran into her. And your empathy is contagious. You put her at ease. And she brought out the best in you. She's practical and assertive. She helped make calls and fill out forms. She showed you the number to call for repairs. I hope her proclivity toward assertiveness rubs off on you.

The best part about that accident, though, was it happened at dinner time, right in front of that new Italian restaurant that recently opened: Maledizione. You both decided to step inside and talk through insurance paperwork over a cappuccino, but then that turned into a pasta dinner, tiramisu, and wine. You wanted to ask her for her number, but you already had it, and I'm pretty sure you backed down because you didn't want to ask if you could call for non-insurance reasons. But then, to your surprise, she called you a few nights later. Granted, she didn't mean to call you. Her phone just dialed your number somehow.

"It must have been a butt dial," she said.

"Ha ha," you said. Well, not *said*, but nervously choked out.

"I had a nice dinner the other night," she said.

"Me too," you said.

A pause. Say something, I hissed to you from the top of the bookshelves where I had wormed my way behind the potted plants.

"Maybe we can do it again," you said.

"That sounds fun," she said.

There was a longer pause. I was losing my mind that evening, Craig. If you had turned, you would have seen a strange, long hand absentmindedly tearing your potted plants to shreds.

Then she said, "Well, talk to you soon," and you both hung up.

After thirty minutes of pacing around your living room, you called her back. You did it on your own. I had unplugged your cable and internet so that you were unable to numb yourself with escapist entertainment. I certainly played my part, but you made the decision yourself. And almost two years later, you're still in love.

Lately, though, she's not been happy. I know you can't hear me over the commotion of the ICU: the other patients with their wounds and ailments, the din of the malfunctioning snack machine, the off-key cackle of a doctor down the hall, the furious buzz of the fluorescent lighting.

I thought you were losing interest in her, but it's your poor finances, isn't it? You were afraid you couldn't pay for dates with maxed out cards, that she would see your failures and not love you. So instead you pulled away from her.

I have taken care of your credit, Craig. You don't need to worry about how. I will not let you fail. I will never let you fail. I'm texting Amaranta right now to thank her for coming to see you in the hospital today. I'll leave some promotional cards for Maledizione lying around your apartment, so you'll get the idea that an anniversary dinner is in order soon. How romantic it would be to return to where you first met her. Such a good restaurant, traditional red sauce Italian, low lighting, good service, and waiters who mutter unhappy secrets to each other in the kitchen.

Take care of yourself, Craig, so you can take care of others. You'll never meet a woman as wonderful as she is. A mother as wonderful as she will be. I'm positive of it. Not in this small town. You two will be so happy together, I will make absolutely certain of it.

EXECUTION

1810-1813

1

Success is not in the idea, but the execution.

This was the first lesson of my life of crime. It was also my last, but I get ahead of myself.

Here I was, a woman of eighteen, seemingly alone on the streets of Hamburg. My eyes were closed, because what I needed to find was best found by hearing alone.

This is what Hamburg sounded like: cries of merchants trying to outcompete on prices for a clatter of ornate glassware from Venice, a shimmer of bells from the mountains of Franchia, and a thud of oranges from southern Spain, packed in straw and wrapped in canvas to try to mitigate their decay. The wet breath of horses and the clatter of their hooves. A swirl of German and French, a smattering of Dutch, shouts in the strange guttural language of Luftnarp. The muffled growl of the ocean, providing the reason for everything else I was hearing.

I let my mind drift over all of this, picking out the one sound I needed. There it was. A few words, in a dialect that was rare in this part of the world, a heavily coded slang used by certain sailors in the eastern Mediterranean. The chances of anyone but my targets speaking that were, well I had never had a formal education in mathematics but they didn't seem high. I opened my eyes and zeroed in on the rough-dressed men muttering and hurrying toward their ship.

Picking my way carefully through the crowd after the men, I inclined my head slightly in their direction. In response to my command, the most beautiful man in the city, quite possibly in Napoleon's entire flicker of an empire, stepped into their path. I say "beautiful" as an objective measure. His looks stopped activity in their tracks, and his smile caused symptoms that would give any doctor concerns. His name was André du Lièvre.

André broke into a smile that was both friendly and relieved, as though he had been looking all over the city for a filthy group of sailors and couldn't believe his luck that he finally had stumbled upon them. They frowned suspiciously as André lifted his arms in greeting.

"My friends and comrades," he said. God, he was nearly irresistible when he spoke in that friendly voice that was just this side of flirtation. "I'm told you are the best crew the North Sea has to offer."

It would be impolite and perhaps impossible to disagree with such a compliment delivered with such a smile, and so they could only murmur as he strode with them toward their ship, laying his arm across the shoulders of one of them causing him to jump nearly out of his rags. One would think that being so beautiful and charming, so impossible to forget, would be a detriment to a career as a thief, but André knew his tools and how to leverage them.

A large hand fell onto my own shoulder, and I patted it without turning around. In the cacophony of the port, I hadn't heard Lora approach. Despite her monumental size, at least two feet taller than me and with thick ropes of muscle, Lora could move

with utter grace and stealth. She was, through years of training and lived experience, extraordinarily aware of her body, the
limit and the length of it, and how to maneuver it through the
world.

"André is putting on too much of a show," she grumbled.

"Oh, let him have his fun."

The charming man in question had reached the ship which
was in the frantic process of unloading. Under new Napoleonic
law, ships were given free berth for the first half day. After that
a tax was exacted in the form of a length of wood from the
ship's structure. Neither the owner nor the captain had any say
on which part of the ship the wood was removed from, and it
could be as harmless as a panel from the Captain's wardrobe
or as vital as one of the ship's great ribs, leaving it floundering
in the harbor's shallow waters. This process was repeated every
half day until the ship either left port or was decidedly no longer able to, at which point it would be confiscated by the French
empire, and so the sailors hauled crates and bundles down the
planks at a furious pace. André left a wake of stillness in his
passage, as sailors and customs officials all stopped to gape.
Gathering those nearby around himself with a vague beckoning
of one hand, he began a long story, a story that had neither beginning nor end but a nearly inexhaustible quantity of middle,
leaving Lora and I ample time to get our work done.

We ducked around the piles of cargo, seeking a particular
chest of daggers. The chest was set to be delivered to a peas-
ant revolution growing in the frontiers of Svitz, a movement
called the Green and White. Our job was to divert that delivery into the hands of The Duke's Own, which would find a
more profitable and less righteous use for the weaponry. We
acted not out of any partisan fervor, but because the pay was

right. Motivation does not have to be complex. In our line of work, simple motives were generally better.

Lora, barely having to raise herself up, located the chest at the top of the tallest stack, and commenced heaving it out. I leaned nonchalantly against a crate, or as nonchalantly as I could. One sailor who was, for whatever reason, immune to André's charms, sauntered out from one of the rows and gaped at the young woman and the giant who were absconding with their goods.

"Thieves!" he squalled. I am unsure why it is the crew cared so much, since they owned nothing on the ship or the dock other than their own clothes and the promise of future pay, and, depending on their fortunes in the daily card games, sometimes not even that, but an element of pride made them fiercely protective of what they were unloading, and several abandoned André's morass of a story to charge us with fists and whatever weapons happened to be on their person. Unfortunately for them, they encountered Lora, who turned from her work just long enough to swat the first man to the ground with a tragic crack. I wouldn't have wished to be him in the coming weeks.

As more men barreled in, Lora turned fully to engage them and I tucked myself behind her. This position was somewhat safer, although I did find myself uncomfortably compressed every time she was jostled backward. From my position, I could not see the fight as it unfolded, but one only needs to hear so many bones break before one gets the gist.

The sounds of violence were halted by a voice habituated to immediate obedience. "Make way for her Ladyship."

I peeked around Lora to see the guard who had spoken. A lackey, but a well-dressed and apparently well-paid one. Behind him, a woman in the kind of dress that takes nearly as long for her to put on as it would take me to earn the money to afford.

She glanced at the mess of injured bodies with placid, polite eyes. A politician then. Some royals are temperamental, but some are survivors, with the skill of hiding what they feel. Those were the ones that truly had to be watched out for.

The sailors who were still able to stand all scattered as the woman and her retinue descended and crossed the port. None of us knew which royal family she belonged to or even if they happened to be in possession of any kind of throne at that moment. The details of power rarely matter. What matters is the impression of power. My crew, of course, had been well trained to be immune to niceties, so André took the opportunity to give a quick good-bye wink to the ship's cook and then performed a graceful dive off the dock into the filthy water of the harbor. Lora slung the heavy chest of daggers that now belonged to us onto her broad back, and the two of us began to hurry away.

One of the sailors, bug-eyed with rage but unable to give chase without crossing the path of the woman, spat at us, and the saliva landed a few feet from the noblewoman. A soft pop against hot wood. The sailor groaned. The woman stopped and turned her head ever so slightly toward the offending man. Her men tensed behind her. After a few seconds, long enough to communicate volumes of conceivable torture, she turned back to her dignified walk. Her guards kept their glaring eyes on the crew of sailors, helpfully keeping them too terrified to chase after Lora and me.

By the time the noblewoman was at a safe distance, we were long gone, and so the sailors went grumbling about their work, and later grumbling to their drink, a beer hall hanging over the water. Among them was the final member of my gang of thieves, one who was never noticed wherever she went.

2

Reunited in the attic that was our temporary haven in Hamburg, we opened the heavy wooden chest and inventoried the daggers inside. They were mostly undecorated, although each hilt had been carved with the sigil of a pineapple, an exotic and ridiculous fruit. As we worked, we dodged bats and listened to the twittering of birds. Below us we could hear every conversation, every potato dropped into every pot of water. It was an overload of sensory information.

We were finishing up when someone started pounding at the trapdoor, and André clutched his chest in what was only half a comedic exaggeration. Lora flung open the heavy trapdoor, a dagger decorated with the sigil of a pineapple hidden behind her back. A slight man in workman's clothes crawled up into the attic. He was spattered with blood.

"Rebekah!" I said in surprise. We had not expected her back for hours, if not days. Lora gently helped her up and Rebekah peeled off the layers of false hair and painted on features, revealing the small Jewish woman with a preternatural ability to look like anyone but herself.

"My god," said André, still holding his chest. "Rivkah, what happened to you?" During a boring ship ride she had once taught him her name in Hebrew, and he had found it delightful. Here it carried the tenderness he always especially showed her over all of us.

I checked her for wounds but she waved me away.

"Not mine," she said. "Not my blood." She managed, with a shaking, quiet voice, to tell us what had happened.

Rebekah, a master of disguises, had been the crux of my plan. She had joined the sailors on their last voyage disguised as a wharf rat named Henrik, willing to do backbreaking work in exchange for transportation to Hamburg. After the fight, and our successful theft, she had retired grumbling with her fellow sailors to the beer hall, where they had drunk and complained about thieves, and she had continued to gently try to guide them to the subject of where they had received the chest of daggers we had stolen. Our employers, as always, were The Duke's Own, who suspected that the daggers had been taken from one of their armories by someone sympathetic to the cause of the Green and White revolutionaries. The Duke's Own were not a group of people who liked being stolen from, and any information we could give them on the movement of that chest would help them string up whoever was ultimately responsible.

As the men grew drunker, and the relief of another successful voyage settled in, Rebekah felt them getting closer to revealing what she needed to know, but just as she was guiding them the last little way, she felt a surge of adrenaline. She had spent years infiltrating the lowest and the highest rungs of society, blending in seamlessly with every strata, and this had given her a pitch-perfect ear for when a scene was about to turn bad. And, as they chatted in that hall, she felt the scene shift suddenly and quite definitively bad. The door to the bar was kicked open and soldiers marched in, more and more of them, carefully taking positions in front of every possible exit. As soon as she saw this, Rebekah slid under the table.

"Henrik?" called out one of her fellow sailors, turning in confusion to find his friend gone. Rebekah crawled on her belly to the bar as the commander of the soldiers announced himself to the startled crowd.

"Let it be known," the commander boomed. Conversation died out instantly, and everyone fidgeted in the dangerous silence. "Let it be known," the soldier said again, "that her highness the Lady Nora of the royal house of Luftnarp was singularly disrespected while disembarking from her paid transportation to your filthy city. The penalty for insolence to royalty is death."

None of the soldiers were among the men that Lady Nora had been traveling with earlier that day. Those had been shouting scarecrows, suitable for pushing a crowd around. But these men were skilled and dangerous. Rebekah, having wriggled her way into a little nook in the bar, began searching her bag for any disguise that could save her. The barkeep glanced down at her, the only one in the room who could see her, and she looked back with pleading eyes. He said nothing about her presence, and she silently thanked him for his kindness.

Her bag contained a bewilderment of costume elements. It was too unwieldy to carry about entire disguises, and her skill was such that she didn't need them. Instead she carried bits of clothing, small props, wigs and false facial hair that could be assembled into some suggestion of a new person, a person then brought to irrefutable life by her performance. As quickly and neatly as she could, given the lack of mirrors and her awkward position, she altered herself to look like another barkeep.

"Fortunately for you lot," the soldier continued, "Lady Nora is the soul of mercy. And so she has granted her pardon."

The room, as one, began to breathe again. Rebekah didn't pause at her work, rolling out from her nook and popping up from behind the bar, trying to sell through her posture the idea that she had been there the entire time, even though many soldiers saw her appear. Her ability to inhabit a truth was more convincing than their own wavering memories, and their eyes slid past her.

"As a result of this pardon, we will only behead one in three men in this room. Soldiers, gather them."

There was an outcry and some desperate attempts to fight, but the soldiers were well armed and utterly ruthless, and even before the crowd was gathered, already several men lay dead. One of the soldiers eyed the two barkeeps, but the commander waved him away.

"Not them," he said. "The sailors."

And so Rebekah was saved, but still she had to stand and watch. The soldiers were true to their word, and they were very efficient.

Having finished her story, she slumped back onto the attic floor, futilely closing her eyes against the memory.

"Thanks to the Lord that you are safe," said Lora.

"Yes, I would have been heartbroken," said André.

I said nothing, only held her hand, felt relief with each pulse of her heart. Finally I spoke.

"Who in the hell," I said, "is this Lady Nora of Luftnarp?"

3

After the stern face of the North Sea it was a relief to return to the Mediterranean.

The way was dangerous because of the clashes between the Napoleonic army and the ragtag forces of the Green and White uprising. The war had started in a small region of Luftnarp where a group of peasants and craftsmen, outraged at the blatant thieving by the local lord from their guilds and fields, had formed a council to present their complaints formally to King Torrid IV. The King's advisor, Lord Fullbright, a kind man, had advised some swift show of justice, to demonstrate that the order of society was for the good of all, but the local lord in that region was a boyhood friend of Torrid, and so with some polite smiles and murmurs of appropriate action, the complaint was shunted aside.

Unfortunately for the King, the peasants could smell bullshit from all the way down in the fields, and so they just went and murdered the lord, who had been so confident in his safety that he had not bothered to use his ill-gotten gains on any real security. Even as the peasants pounded down his door, the regional lord sat smirking in an utter confidence that lasted the same few minutes the rest of him did. Their bloodlust and their sense of justice risen, the small army of peasants marched off to see if their neighbors had any problems with the nobility, which in fact they did. Soon the message and the methods of their army were spreading across the continent. It was said that their revolution spread as quickly as wildflowers and as hot as fire, and so they gradually became known by their colors: the Green, for the green of rapidly growing plants, and the White, for the pure heat of the flame.

The Green and the White from the east had met Napoleon's growing empire from the west, and soon the whole continent was roiling. A traveler such as I was sure to wear clothes that did not have any element of green or white, lest there be any excuse for my rapid execution. A war is only ever good for business, and so we of The Duke's Own slipped in and out of the cracks of this righteous uprising of the workers, making money where there was some to be made.

Soon I made it to the coast of Spain. It was brutally hot that summer in Barcelona, and so every window and door was left open, and that meant a constant cacophony was a trade-off for whatever breezes managed to make their way through the winding backstreets. An old woman stooped over the front step of Edmond's house, passing a frayed straw broom across it slowly.

"Good day, Señora Bover," I called. "You should be resting until the evening. It's so hot now."

She shrugged off my concern. "It'll be hot in the evening too. How is our girl, back from rolling up kings and emperors like a rug?"

"Tired," I said, honestly.

"We are all always tired," she said. "But we are all always working."

I laughed affectionately and passed her on my way up the stairs, three flights, to the door of the man who saved my life. Edmond called me in on my first knock. He had certainly heard me talking through the window, but made a show of fussy surprise from his desk.

"Oh, don't get up for me old man," I teased. "I'd hate to be what finally kills you."

He put a hand over his heart to indicate the depth of the wound I had dealt and then sprang up with an energy younger than his years and swept me into a hug.

"I worry so much when you're off doing a job," he said into my shoulder. "I don't know what I'd do if I lost you too."

"Maybe you should stop giving me these jobs," I said, as we disconnected and settled into chairs on either side of his desk, which was, as always, an eruption of papers and candles just this side of a disastrous fire.

"Ah, if you didn't get your crimes from me, you'd have to get them on the street. And my crimes are far more interesting."

After the Order of the Labyrinth had killed my father and burned his estate, Edmond and I had fled to a representative of The Duke's Own he had been in contact with, a gentleman of certain affiliations who kept an office on a narrow canal in Amsterdam. What I remember most are the sounds. The guttering cough of the candles caught in the draft. The soft splash of cold and clouded water outside, so different from the warm and clear water I had known my whole life. The heavy hiss from the largest man's nostrils every time he breathed out. The dark purr of the smallest man's voice as he put pause to Edmond's explanation and turned to me. "And who do we have here?" he had said. I trembled, but held his eyes. That moment of eye contact, where I looked back afraid but steady, was the start of my association with the organization. Everything that came after was a formality.

The more time I spent in the company of thieves and murderers, the more natural it became to me. This was where I belonged. I was good at this, and they grew to rely on me. I rarely thought of Albert, and our sunny days swimming in a secluded cove. I even more rarely thought about my father, because the hurt was so fresh that letting it in felt like poking at a bleeding wound. I trained myself to separate from the pain, in order to become more efficient at what was keeping us alive.

But back to a sunny day in Spain.

"About Hamburg," I said.

"I heard." Edmond frowned. "Dreadful."

"What do you know about this Lady Nora?"

"A cruel noble." He sighed. "My spies in her court say that she has a harsh reputation, even by the standard of nobility." Edmond, with his unintimidating presence but crafty mind, had quickly found his place organizing the spy rings of The Duke's Own. To make money off the troubles of royalty, one needs to know what was going on with the royalty, and so any noble of a certain stature had at least a few and probably several servants of The Duke's Own on their staff, and many of those reported in some way to Edmond or his underlings.

"There are limits even to a spymaster's knowledge," he said. "If I had known she was on that ship, I would never have sent your crew anywhere near her."

"I don't need protecting," I said with the absolute certainty of someone who probably does. "And now I'm interested in her."

"We don't need to be interested in anything," he said. "We're criminals. We steal. We smuggle. We collect gold. That is the goal."

"That is your goal," I said. "My goal is different."

He threw up his hands. "The Order of the Labyrinth. Haven't we learned enough to stay away from them?"

"They haven't learned enough to stay away from me." I saw the same terrible day repeat for me every time I closed my eyes. Memory lives inside the eyelids.

"I know. You have your plan," he groaned. "Impress the Order of the Labyrinth so much that they invite you to join, and then destroy them from the inside as an act of grand revenge. But have you considered what your father would want for you? And god forbid I mention so humble and meaningless a consideration as my own wishes for you? That you live a long and fantastic life? Can't the length and happiness of your life serve as revenge enough?"

I looked in the eyes of this man who had acted as my father since my father died. "It could," I said. But what I thought, and I hated myself for thinking it, was: What does it matter anymore what my father would have wanted?

4

From Barcelona, I made my way on horseback to Paris, the heart of Napoleon's empire. He had, through a combination of cruel imperial efficiency and the wealth expropriated from the lands he had conquered, managed to mostly restore the city from the liberated turmoil of the revolution, and now it was safely back to a thriving metropolis of suffocating order and brutal social stratification. A grand arch had been commissioned, a crown upon the head of that grand old lady the Champs-Élysées, but the construction had only just begun. In the meantime, a wooden and canvas version of the arch had been put on the site, a temporary and fragile approximation of grandeur, as good a monument to Napoleon's reign as any.

I went directly from the town gate to a towering structure on Rue de la Chaussée-d'Antin, the family home of one André du Lièvre.

André welcomed me at the door, beaming and tossing his hellos like they were flowers to adoring crowds. He had been raised in a merchant family that had done very well for itself during the early days of Napoleon's rise, and had established itself as a member of the post-revolution aristocracy, a less dangerous social status in Paris than it had been a few decades before.

The family must have been pleased to have a baby as beautiful as André, who became a child as beautiful as André, who became a man as beautiful as André. Early in his life, they introduced him to the work of negotiating and glad-handing with clients, and he took to it like beauty takes to a mirror, making others more charming as they reflected his charm back at him. When it came time for him to start courting, the consensus was that he had his pick of Paris, as long as he picked from the few correct families of course. After all, what woman would not want to be with a man of his panache and wealth? But André had no interest in women, which led to worried murmurs until it became clear that André did not have any interest in men either. André found people exciting, and wonderful to be friends with, and he had no interest in romance with anyone. This was not an absence from his life and it was nothing he regretted for a single breezy, smiling moment. His life was not better or worse for who he was, his life was the only version of himself he could be.

Unfortunately his family was less than understanding of his disinterest in marriage, which for them was a necessary social move and had nothing to do with their son's interest or lack of interest in romance. They pressured him constantly, until he decided that it would be easier if he got into business on his own. Seeking funding, and needing it quickly, he got himself predictably entangled with The Duke's Own. Being a low priority for their attention, they sent me, still only a few years past being a child. A test, perhaps. He tried to charm me, of course, but I had too much ambition to be charmed. Fortunately for him, I saw his usefulness, and instead of removing the digits of his hands one by one, the usual method for wringing coins out of a broke man, I offered him a job, which he eagerly accepted. While the start of our partnership might have been under duress, André took to a life of crime with absolute enthusiasm and glee. He found it thrilling, and I don't think I could have convinced him to quit even if I offered more gold than he could spend, or threatened him with every lowlife for hire in the City of Lights.

"Welcome! Welcome!" he boomed as I entered the home. His family, thinking he had in fact successfully started a merchant business, had grudgingly accepted him back in their lives, and their massive house in Paris was a convenient and secure place to meet. "We've all been waiting for you." He put his arm around my shoulder and swept me through the entrance hall.

Neither of us noticed the man in a well-worn soldier's uniform across the street, watching me enter, spitting on the ground, and slipping around the corner to let his superiors know I had arrived.

André led me up through the grand entranceway to the more modest bedrooms upstairs, the comforts of a family that had once held a lower station, and so preferred, in privacy, a simpler life. Still, each piece of furniture, each item on each shelf, was perfectly crafted and lovingly chosen. They valued what they had with the full sincerity and insecurity of a family pretending to have a place in life they didn't quite believe they deserved.

In his childhood bedroom, the other two members of our crew waited. Lora was stretched out on a divan at the base of the bed, her legs like two fallen trees, and her massive arms flung over her head. She was the picture of carefree relaxation.

Rebekah, on the other hand, stood in the corner, where there was the least light. She was never in her element when she had to be herself. She much preferred to be someone else.

André's father, a hard-faced but kind man named Gilbert, waved away the servants and served us a platter of expensive fruit carted in from Provence. Gilbert had always had a soft spot for André, even if the family's place in society always had to come first. He didn't approve of André's new life, just as he didn't approve of André's complete lack of interest in even the appearance of courtship, but he had come to a place of accepting André's happiness, and our group of friends made his son happy. Gilbert nodded his head at us silently, turned, stopped to fix a silver figurine on the shelf that was slightly askew, checked to make sure all other perfect objects were in perfect order, then left the room.

"Affairs certainly seem better here than the last time we visited," Lora boomed.

"Better, worse," André said. "They're family." He smiled and waved us to the food. "Oh Rebekah, come out of that corner," he said with a deep fondness. "If it helps you may put on a false mustache before eating."

She joined us without speaking. She never much liked to talk without her deep repertoire of put-on voices and accents. Whenever she had to, she spoke softly in an accent that sounded of the shtetl, of forest and snow.

We talked and ate, enjoying a restful moment in our hectic lives right up until the soldiers broke down the front door downstairs.

Shouting and screaming. The sound of many boots. Looking out the window I saw a small army gathered in the street. I recognized the coat of arms on their chests, two roses crossed over a growling dog. I had seen that same coat of arms on men in Hamburg only a few weeks before.

"It's Lady Nora's men," I said.

"Why in the world was she looking for us?" André asked, a more than reasonable question at a perhaps unreasonable time. He was preparing to fling himself out the door and take on all of the Lady's men in order to protect his family, but it was my job to recognize a hopeless cause when there was one.

We had to get out of this bedroom alive. Only then could we worry about protecting anyone else.

"Rebekah, meet us outside. Lora, André, to the window." Rebekah nodded. As always, she would remake herself into whatever identity was needed to slip out of the situation. She rummaged through her bag of disguises as she ran from the room. Meanwhile we went out the window, shuffling along the narrow stone of a decorative ledge, some stories above the neighbor's roof. The wind was fierce, and my shoes felt ludicrously slippery. Why had I worn such impractical shoes? I could almost hear Edmond in my head: *A good thief is always ready for a trip out the window or up the chimney.* Well, I wasn't ready, but here I was anyway.

Then my foot slipped.

I was upside down four stories above the streets of Paris, swinging like a clock's pendulum as Lora held onto my ankles with one hand and the frame of the window with the other.

"I have you," she said.

"Aaaaah," I replied.

I heard the boots of the men reaching our floor, and then bedroom door after bedroom door kicked down. They would find us soon. Lora and I made eye contact, her sweaty face upside down from my dangling view. The door to André's room crashed open.

"You have nowhere to go," I heard a man shout.

But he had never met Lora. "Oh, fuck this," she said.

She put one hand around André, pulled me up into her body with the other so that my nose was somewhere near her knees, and let herself topple from the ledge. "Lora, no!" I shouted but by then gravity had us. There was a horrible suspended moment and then we crashed into the neighbor's roof, Lora using her enormous body to cushion us. Even then the landing hurt. I couldn't imagine how it felt for her. She knew her own body though, and the limits of it, and hauled herself up, limping after the two of us as we fled across the roofs until we could find our way down to meet Rebekah at a café across town.

From Paris, the four of us went south to Éze, a village high in the hills above Nice. André's family kept a small home in the village under a different name. It was a family secret, a place that spoke to their humble beginnings, but it would hopefully be difficult for the Lady's soldiers to find. Reports we had gathered from fellow members of The Duke's Own had been fragmented but the general picture was clear. André's family was alive, but badly beaten. The house had been destroyed. Their fragile reputation was ruined. A lifetime of careful social climbing undone by their son and his friends. None of us talked much during the two-week journey south.

It was chilly in Éze, even as we looked down upon the sunny expanse of the Mediterranean below. When we were quiet, as we usually were, the faint fizzy slap of the waves below could be heard, one after another after another. Lora bought up half the village's market and made us a feast to distract us from the shame of what our actions had brought upon an innocent family, but the food mostly went to waste. André didn't eat a bite. He sat out on the cliff, staring down at the water. I realized it was the first time I had ever seen him without his easy, charming smile. Rebekah sat next to him, not talking to him, not touching him, only providing comfort by proximity. And for myself, I was too caught up in my own plans to think about food.

My life was for only one purpose, to get revenge against the Order of the Labyrinth. For that, I needed access to the Order. For that, I needed to get the attention of the watchers from the Order of the Labyrinth. These watchers were rumored to be everywhere in the criminal underworld, keeping an eye out for likely new recruits. To draw their attention, I needed to do a crime of truly grandiose proportions, which meant in turn that I needed a high-profile victim for this crime.

And here was the Lady Nora of Luftnarp, a walking monument to brutality and the misuse of power. She had hurt many people, but I believed she did not yet understand pain. I was eager to teach her.

So in front of an uneaten feast, in the cool sea air blowing up from the beaches below, I made the decision to destroy the Lady Nora of Luftnarp. To destroy her so thoroughly in such a visible way that the Order of the Labyrinth would have no choice but to take notice of my presence.

Having decided, I picked up a piece of bread, scooped it into a plate that Lora had given me, and began to ravenously eat.

5

First we came for Lady Nora's wealth.

Luftnarp, a tiny nation high in the Alps, is cold any time of the year, and even that summer night was chilly. But the fires that marked the road to the castle were blazing, and each individual carriage was festooned with lanterns. All of that flame served to dissipate the cold a bit. And then of course there were all the people. This was one of the social events of the season, and the rich and noble (one, contrary to popular belief, did not automatically mean the other) had traveled from all over the warring continent to arrive at the annual feast of Lady Nora of Luftnarp. Amongst them was our humble cart.

A canvas was pulled over the piled goods on the cart, and I sat cross legged atop the pile. Lora, impossible to hide, drove the horses.

Rebekah had gotten herself recruited as a guard in the castle some weeks ago, the commander of the guards being desperate for the extra help.

"Keep me safe, she says," the commander had muttered to himself. "Then invite every rich empty-head to come get drunk behind your open gates. Yes, keep the easiest target any thief has ever seen safe." Then realizing that Rebekah was still in the room, he had said tersely that she was hired, and marched abruptly out.

Meanwhile André had chatted up some prince or another in order to be invited as the prince's guest. "Tedious man," he said. "But not fundamentally bad. Let's hope he doesn't suffer any consequences from our actions." André had been in a gloom since his final break with his family, but I hoped he could muster some charm for tonight. We would need everything we had.

A line of guards stood along the road as our cart clattered along. One of them held up his hand and called "Ho!," drawing us to a stop. Behind him, I could see a second guard, a dangerous looking man with a scarred face, likely a veteran of a number of wars. Just the kind of person a member of The Duke's Own generally looked to avoid. I gave a nearly imperceptible nod to the scarred guard, and she winked back. Rebekah truly was a miracle worker.

"No sudden movements," called the gruff and dangerous guard. Even Rebekah's voice was unrecognizable.

Rebekah Barzani was born in the Pale of Settlement, a stretch of Eastern Europe which was one of the few places Jews were allowed to openly live. You could say that the attitude of the outside world to the culture she grew up in left her with a mindset well suited to making herself as invisible as possible. She was raised by a mother, a troublemaker and a saint, who believed that women should be educated just as much as the boys in the Yeshiva. Her mother strong-armed her husband into spending his evenings teaching their daughter the Torah, and also history and mathematics and the bits and bobs he knew from many other subjects.

Then, one night, as was frequent even in this scrap of land into which the Jewish people had been driven, a pogrom came. Their house was destroyed, and both of Rebekah's parents were killed. Running from the house, she had happened upon one of the perpetrators of the massacre, who was so drunk he had fallen face down in the street. She stripped him, and dressed as best she could to disguise herself as anything but what she was, a scared Jewish orphan, alone now in the Pale of Settlement.

Having survived that night, she fled to another community, and managed by cutting her hair short and adopting the right kind of posture and voice, to convince her adoptive town that she was a boy. She attended Yeshiva. As the years went on, her skill at disguise grew in order to allow her continued access to education. Out of this necessity she became an expert at hiding herself in plain sight. She was so good at it she began assisting the head rabbi at the town's synagogue. But eventually there was an incident at the mikvah and she was discovered. Her shocked community cast her out. This might seem cruel, and it was, but the constant harassment and persecution and pogroms had traumatized the Jews of that region, and they had responded by tightening the fist of tradition. Poor Rebekah sat squarely in the palm of that fist.

For the first time in her life, she left the Pale of Settlement, and began to wander Europe, seeking some kind of life worth living. It was easier to travel as a man, and so she kept up her disguise, improving and changing it as she moved from region to region. She learned new languages, new dialects and accents in order to survive. Of course, she also stole. How else was she to survive? As these stories often go, she eventually stole from the wrong folks, members of The Duke's Own. They were so impressed by how she had taken them, how completely she had seemed to be someone else, that they gave her a choice. Join The Duke's Own or die. She had joined, and like André, soon found her place in the organization. She was one of the first people I met when Edmond and I left that dark office years before in Amsterdam, both of us newly provisional members of The Duke's Own. She had been disguised as a harried clerk. I met her again as a stone-faced bodyguard, and then again as a graceful and cunning noblewoman. I hadn't known I was meeting her until the fourth time, at which point I noticed the drunk sailor I was meeting had the same freckle on his left hand as the noblewoman from the week before. It was the first time anyone had been able to see through one of her disguises, and our mutual admiration turned to friendship, two young women who had lost our families but found a new family, one that could be yours forever as long as you didn't mind stealing some gold and cutting some throats.

"You don't look like guests," the guard who had stopped us in front of Lady Nora's castle said.

"Good eye," growled Lora. The guard narrowed his eyes and put a hand to his sword. Behind him, I saw Rebekah tense slightly.

"We're a delivery," I said. "Take a look."

I lifted the canvas off our cargo to reveal cases full of wine. The guard pulled a few bottles out, inspecting them. The labels on them belonged to some of the more rare and excellent wines on the continent, although this particular guard likely couldn't even read them, let alone appreciate the estates they were grown on.

He looked through the cases and whistled.

"Has to be five hundred bottles in here."

"Six hundred, actually," I said. "A gift from a very generous guest."

"Well, certainly the Lady Nora will take well to this gesture. Go around the side to see the Warden of the Wine, and don't bother any of the guests. I expect to see you back within the hour or I'll come looking for you."

"Understood. Thank you," I said with my most winning and sincere smile.

Lora gave him a long look and then got the horses moving again.

"Please don't provoke anyone tonight," I said. "At least not until it's useful."

"I didn't like his face," she said. "I thought I could rearrange it into something better."

As we rode toward the castle, I heard footsteps off in the darkness. I looked, and in the moonlight I saw someone walking along a ridge, away from the party. It was impossible to see any details, but there was something familiar about the figure's strange lurching movements, stiff and clumsy. I shuddered, and turned away from that figure in the darkness, toward the music and the fires and the crowds of the feast.

6

Lady Nora of Luftnarp loved nothing more than wine. She was famous for one of the most extensive wine cellars in Europe, a fortress under a fortress, with a ventilation system hidden throughout the hills around the castle. The cellar had its own unit of guards, the captain of which was the Warden of the Wine. He had been a vintner until Lady Nora recruited him, having him trained in the basics of combat but primarily valuing him for his expertise in wine. He personally inspected every bottle before it left the cellar. Edmond's spies estimated that her collection was worth more than many kingdoms' fortunes, and no one was able to remove so much as a bottle without it being noticed. Fortunately, we weren't interested in taking any bottles out. Instead we had a few hundred bottles to bring in, which would be looked at far less closely.

The Warden of the Wine, an elderly but eminently sturdy man that I had no interest in annoying, stood in front of our cart, backed by a small army of guards.

"Gift for the Lady," I said, pulling the canvas off and showing him the cases.

He eyed the bottles and made a series of humming noises

that were meant to sound thoughtful but instead betrayed greed. The exquisite labels promising rare and expensive vintages were a trap set for this one specific man. As I expected, security wasn't much interested with what was going in, only what someone might try to pilfer out, and so he quickly waved us through and Lora had the cases unloaded down the steps in a few minutes.

As she worked, I looked over the party. Parties like these always orbited their most powerful guest, which tonight was the King of Luftnarp, Torrid IV, a direct descendent of the Luft royal line, and the man whose decision in favor of his rich friend had sparked the Green and White revolution. Most of these royals were a scrawny, gangly bunch, victims of genetic homogeneity, but King Torrid IV was a mountain of a man. He had been born with the look of a leader, and mostly had the bearing to back that up. His reputation had been good until the Green and White rose up against him. Now he was seen as a tyrant by some. For the kind of people who attended a party like this, he was a hero, standing up for the order of society against the rabble trying to tear it down. Next to Torrid IV was Lord Fullbright, closest advisor to the King, and perhaps the key to his successful leadership. It was said that Fullbright was not only extremely shrewd, but also truly caring and empathetic. He genuinely wanted the best for his country and his fellow people, and guided the King toward choices that would benefit even the lowest rungs of society. Still he had stood with the King through his harsh reaction to the Green and White uprising, and so his mercy only tempered justice so far.

But I could take no sides between the peasants and their rulers. I was seeking a different kind of justice against a different kind of adversary, and so I left the party behind and followed Lora down the steps.

We were met at the bottom by a pair of wine cellar guards, who were happy to show us where to put this new trove of wine. They were less happy when Lora knocked their heads together and placed them safely behind a sturdy stone column where they wouldn't get hurt. She had moved quickly enough that neither of them had made a sound that the Warden and his other guards up the long stairs to the surface might have heard. Without speaking, we first carefully placed half of our cases with the two unconscious guards, and then searched along the corridors, past countless priceless bottles, until we found a long stretch of wall that Rebekah had let us know was suspiciously free of wine. Here we made a pile of the other half of the bottles. I placed one last bottle on the top of our pile and lit the fuse. The two of us sprinted back to the entrance and threw ourselves on top of the guards in the safety of the thick column's shadow.

My plan centered on a simple fact. I didn't buy that the Lady needed that much security for a wine cellar, no matter how extensive. I believed she had hidden something else down here. It would be a smart place to stash the bulk of her fortune, because she had an excuse to put up a heavy guard without calling attention to what they were actually guarding. I wanted my hands on that fortune. So every bottle we brought contained not wine, but a powerful explosive created for us by a morally flexible chemist in Dubrovnik.

This was right around when André was supposed to be doing something quite loud and noticeable at the party. Setting off the feast's climactic fireworks several hours too early for instance. He hadn't entirely decided, and would scope it out when he got there, but I hoped, as I scrunched myself behind the pillar, that it was really loud and really noticeable. And just as I was thinking this, the explosive in the bottles went.

The explosion sounded like a mountain collapsing, like every animal alive crying out at once, like a thunderclap sounding the end of the world. The noise obliterated all of my other senses. It was literally too loud for me to see. Somewhere in that din I heard the once-in-a-lifetime sound of thousands of wine bottles all shattering at once. The best collection of wine the continent had ever known turned to vapor and, mixing with the acrid smoke, rose up the vent shafts, creating miniature smokestacks in the hills around the castle, giving away the secret location of their hidden outlets.

Two facts were immediately apparent: 1) We had used way too much explosive; and 2) Distraction or no distraction, every soldier for ten miles would be closing in on this cellar.

Before the rest of the castle could figure out where the explosion had come from, both Rebekah and André came stumbling down the stairs. André waved at the smoke as he coughed.

"I'm extremely eye catching, but there's only so much I can do," he said.

"What the hell happened here?" Rebekah said, still in the low, gruff voice of the guard.

"Our friend in Dubrovnik made his brew a little strong," I said, and ran past them toward the source of the smoke, keeping low to try to find any air to breathe.

Meanwhile Lora swung shut the heavy door and barred it. The guards above got over their initial shock and were pouring down, piling up against the door and pounding to be let in. Thanks to the massive ventilation shafts, the smoke was starting to clear, and so when I came to the demolished wall I could see enough to know that I had been right. There it was. Piles and piles of gold, bars mostly, but also sacks of coins from every empire that Europe had contact with. The source of the Lady's power. Her fortune.

"Holy shit," said André from behind me. Rebekah said nothing, only looked back nervously at Lora who was barely holding the door while as many guards as could fit on the narrow stairs attempted to ram it down. "How are we supposed to carry this much gold out of here?" said André. "Is there another exit I wasn't told about?"

I hadn't told them the rest of the plan, only letting them know that everything was in place and that they needed to trust me, which each one of them did, but Rebekah had spotted my intentions. I was smart, but she was smarter.

"We don't carry any of it out," she said, and I nodded.

"That's right, we're not here to steal from the Lady," I said. "We're here to destroy her. Help me with these." I ran back past the straining Lora, mentally giving myself only a couple minutes at most before the door gave way and started dragging the rest of the bottles we had brought. The shattered glass all around me was proof enough that the amount would be sufficient.

"Oh, this is a tragedy," said André. "I can't look."

Once the remaining cases of explosives were placed where they needed to be (I certainly didn't have time to figure out the mathematically most efficient way to do this, with Lora hollering at us for god's sake to move), I cut a length of fuse, making a hasty calculation of how much time it would take us to escape versus leaving any chance of some brave soldier stamping out the fuse at the last second. I hoped I had guessed right and supposed that I probably wouldn't be around to see it if I hadn't, and then lit the thing and ran like hell for Lora.

Once to Lora we all made eye contact, let a few breaths pass to sync ourselves, and then moved as one. Lora and I ran deeper into the cellar. The loss of her body weight from the door caused it to abruptly fling open, sending a group of red-faced and surprised soldiers tumbling in, where they ran head-long into Rebekah going the other way. She pulled André after her by the collar of his shirt. Her scarred face was twisted into a truly chilling snarl and she hollered at the soldiers: "I caught the bastards. But we need to run! A bomb!"

She didn't wait for a reaction. She pushed her and André through the jammed-up stairs, calling as she went, "It's all going to blow! Run for your lives!" Which the soldiers all did, reversing course and surging back up into the clear and chilly night air. Lady Nora, who had come to see who was trying to rob her, screamed at them to "Head back down. Where are the thieves?" By that point Rebekah and André had slipped out of the torchlight in the confusion of soldiers and were already gone into the night.

Meanwhile Lora and I made for one of those highly efficient ventilation shafts and began to furiously climb. I again considered the length of fuse I had cut and cursed myself for cutting it so short. What will it feel like, I wondered, to burn alive? The vents were well-protected by heavy grates at the top. Lora audibly strained, pushing upward with one hand while keeping herself stable with the other. I had no idea how much time we had left but knew we needed to be clear of the vents when the explosives ignited. The grate finally budged upward and popped open with a clang. We climbed up into the grassy hillside, landing on our backs and catching our breaths. The ground jumped, and the vent we had just come out of, and every other vent hidden about the hills, let out a great whoomf of fire.

It was a far more spectacular show than the fireworks that had been planned.

We scrambled to our meeting spot, a cliffside a quarter mile from the castle. André and Rebekah were already there. Rebekah appeared half the size she had been a few minutes before. I marveled at her ability to create the impression of weight merely through the way she shaped her body.

The four of us looked down at all the people far below, sprinting around the castle and shouting at each other, everyone trying to outdo each other in looking like they were helping, and the Lady herself on her knees outside her ruined wine cellar, bent double by what we had done to her. The anger and terror in her posture gave me as much satisfaction as I had felt in some time. And we were just getting started.

"All of her fortune," I said. "Blasted apart and buried under stone."

André coughed. "Well, not all of it." He pulled out a gold bar from his cloak and held it up. "I know you said, but it seemed tragic not to."

I laughed, and then we were all laughing. The cold air turned our laughter into a cloud between us.

7

We had taken Lady Nora's wealth, but I wasn't finished. To that end, over the next year, I visited three old friends.

The first was in Barcelona. I nodded hello to Señora Bover, who was painting the door to the building.

"Did it need repainting?" I asked her.

"I needed the repainting," she said. "We all need something to do."

Upstairs, Edmond was happy to see me safe. He had heard about the affair at the Lady's feast, and he was worried.

"My spies inform me that Lady Nora has reacted as one might expect her to," he said. "I'm told she collected thirty of Luftnarp's most well-known criminals and had them skinned alive. In front of her. I'm assured by trustworthy associates that she did some of the skinning herself."

I went a bit pale. I liked to think I was a hardened criminal, but I was also not yet twenty, and still approached the world with generally good intentions. For the first time I wondered if I was entering a world whose brutality exceeded my own limits. I smelled bile in the back of my sinuses.

Edmond continued. "They all cried that they had nothing

to do with the explosion at the feast, and she told them that she knew and she didn't care. She looked them in their eyes as they slowly died."

"Well," I managed through a dry throat, though it came out as an embarrassing squawk. "She is not yet done paying for what she does to people."

"Please listen to me," he said. "She is a charming woman and deserves all that's coming, I'm sure. But she is not to be fooled with. Be careful. My god," I heard the repressed pain in his voice, memory and love manifesting as a wheeze in the lungs, "if I lost you, too."

I knew little of Edmond's background. He often avoided talking about it. He was quite young when he began to work with my father, and while the subject of his family never came up, I knew that he had one and then had lost them. Through what painful circumstances he ended up an orphan on the street, he was never forthcoming, because he had no interest in being defined by pity. From the start, he wanted my father to see him as an equal, and my father had obliged. Still, the absence of a family, it seemed to me, would likely explain somewhat his fierce loyalty in keeping me safe, and in raising me to the adulthood that my father never lived to see. I resented it a little, as any daughter resents any father, but I was more glad than I was resentful.

I assured him I would be safe, although there was no way for me to be sure of that, and then left him for the docks.

I caught a boat from Spain around Britain to Edinburgh, an interminable matter of weeks watching gray water meet gray skies. Once in Scotland, I climbed Arthur's Seat in the company of a man wearing fine clothes but with a constitution manifestly ill-suited for the outdoors. Probably a wealthy scholar at the university, more accustomed to books than fresh breezes.

It was lovely seeing Rebekah again, in whatever guise she chose. There was no particular need for her to take on a costume in so remote a place. Our complete anonymity here was the reason we had, some months ago, arranged to meet there on that specific day. But I knew that she would be able to chat more easily this way. Rebekah was never comfortable unless she wasn't herself.

We sat near to the summit, and looked out over the city. It was a rainy, miserable day, as it often is in Edinburgh, but pillars of light pierced through the clouds onto the waters of the Firth of Forth. From our vantage, even with the dull slapping rain, we could hear the city, the steady clop of the horses, the bangs and shouts of men at work, the footsteps of students and of servants.

"And what news from the Lady?" I asked.

Rebekah had abandoned her soldier guise, the man who was now one of the prime suspects in the bombing of the wine cellar, and had re-entered Lady Nora's employ as a soft-spoken maid so loyal and so dull that hardly anyone noticed she was there.

"She's moved into the guest rooms of King Torrid IV. Some excuses were made about repairs needed at her castle, but the truth is that being around other royalty has allowed her to hide the loss of her fortune. Since everyone assumes she still commands immense wealth, it is easy for her to casually borrow whatever it is she needs, on vague promises to someday give it back."

I nodded. "A game that would someday catch up with her, but I'm not that patient."

Rebekah smiled, and through the wan face of the scholarly gentleman I saw the young girl I had met when I too was a young girl. "No one has ever accused you of patience," she said.

I smiled back. The truth was that all of my patience was occupied by my lifelong vengeance against the Order of the Labyrinth, and I had little left for anything else. If I hadn't developed a real instinct for the criminal life back on my childhood estate, picking those locks over and over and over, I would probably not be any good at all at this line of living, distracted as I always was.

"The King marries soon, yes?" I said.

"Yes. A princess from Svitz." Svitz, a thin crescent of a country, just west of the Germanic regions. "The hope is to crush the Green and White Rebellion by combining the strength of the two royal families."

"They are still worried about that rebellion?" I heard a violin from the city somewhere, a beautiful tune, played hesitantly, and occasionally restarting completely. Someone practicing what would someday be perfect.

"Terrified," said Rebekah. "King Torrid IV believes that there are even those in the court who are loyal to the Green and White. I would say that only Lord Fullbright is entirely above his suspicion, and that is only because without his closest advisor, the King is not much of a king."

"Lord Fullbright, the King's conscience."

"Kindest man in all empires."

"Mmm," I said. "Anything else?"

Rebekah lay back in the wet grass, and the rain played softly against the false parts of her face. "As you asked, I looked for elements of intimacy between the King and Lady Nora. The points where their friendship was strongest."

"And what did you find?"

"The King does not share much in the way of friendships, but he and the Lady spent their childhoods together, and so there is a history there. Specifically, there is a nickname."

"A nickname."

"A friendly one that she has for him. Strawhead. It seems his hair when he was a child . . ."

"Who knows about this name?" I asked.

"As far as I can tell, no one but the Lady and the King. She only uses it when no one else is around. Or at least when she thinks no one else is around."

"Rebekah, I couldn't do this without you."

"No. You absolutely couldn't."

I wanted to say something else. To express my gratitude for her friendship, and for her skills. But it was difficult to say these things out loud, and anyway she already knew. So I put my hand in her hand and we lay listening to the rain for a while longer. Then we parted, not to see each other again until the day of the job.

One final visit to one final friend, before the real work began. Dubrovnik, on the coast of the Adriatic, was all red roofs and blue water. It was a fortress of a town, huddled up against the mountains. It would seem to be in a fairly defensible position, but you wouldn't know it from how often it got conquered.

Lora and I walked along the town's wall, the top of which formed a fairly broad boulevard that allowed one to quickly circumnavigate the town. Below us, many of the buildings displayed, in defiance of the possibility of execution for treason, the banner of the Green and White. King Torrid IV would have been furious, and all of the gentle words of Lord Fullbright wouldn't have quelled his rage. In fact, all of the royal houses were terribly afraid of the precedent the rebellion set. I smiled thinking about their fear as I looked at the flags over the city. Let the powerful tremble.

"I don't think I could ever live anywhere too far from the sea," I said. "Once you grow up with it, it's hard to let go."

"I could live anywhere," Lora said. "I don't suffer under the delusion that I have to like where I live."

"A fair, if cruel, point," I conceded.

"Am I not fair?" she said. "Am I not cruel?"

I never learned Lora's birth name, I only knew her by the name she had given herself: Lora the Giant.

She reveled in her size, which God had bestowed upon her, and her knack for a fight, which she had bestowed upon herself. She was born a Spanish noblewoman in Madrid, big from birth. Her family had no idea what to do with a young noble girl built like so, and she showed neither interest nor aptitude in courtly manners or politics. A compromise was reached and she was quietly carted off to live in the family's country estate. There, more or less raised by the staff, she came to love the work of her hands. She would go out with the hunters, and tend to the garden, and haul feed with the farmers. None of them wanted to be caught leading a girl of noble birth into a menial position, but also none of them could refuse her, and she soon had befriended them all. When her family would come to check on her, she would unconvincingly pretend at the life of a girl of means, and they would unconvincingly pretend to believe her, and then they would leave again and she could go back to kicking every stable hand's ass in their weekly fights at which a good deal of wages were wagered on her reliable ability to win.

This period of happiness reached the conclusion life brings to all happiness eventually. There was a shift in the politics of the court, and her family came under attack. Quite literally, men with weapons arrived at their door in Madrid. Hearing the news, Lora demanded to be let back to the city to defend her family. Certainly she would have been a formidable opponent, and might have given them time to flee. But her family wouldn't hear of it. There was no part of any Spanish tradition that involved a teenager from a noble family getting in a brawl with soldiers. So her family surrendered, and were killed, each and all of them. The staff at the estate smuggled Lora off with one of the families working in the stables, so when the soldiers came she was already long gone.

Soon after, she left behind the family that had saved her, wishing them well, and sought out The Duke's Own. She knew that the Duke and his thieves and murderers wouldn't give a second thought to tradition and to what she was supposed to be. They would see her strength, and they would be willing to use it. And they were. Lora made an oath to her God, being still a devoted Catholic, that she would never let tradition get in the way of using her size and abilities ever again.

"You are fairly cruel," I agreed, and Lora laughed.

A small hut lay nestled in the rocks, just where the wall of Dubrovnik reached out from the harbor to the open sea. We entered blinking into its foul-smelling interior.

"I didn't expect to see you again so soon," said the chemist, who went by "the Seagull," because the only place in town he could do his work was right against the sea, where the foul vapors would drift out over the water. He was also only allowed, on pain of his neighbors showing up with torches, to work when the prevailing winds blew away from town.

"The substance worked well," I said.

"Too well," said Lora. "I lost half an eyebrow."

The Seagull cackled into the pot of a foul steaming sludge he was stirring. "I promise results. I never promise safety." He put the spoon down, and I couldn't help but notice that the spoon was starting to melt. I took a step back from the pot. "Don't trust anyone in this world who promises you safety," he said.

"I've come with another job."

"And here I thought this might be a social call." He sat in the one chair the hut could fit, and spread his hands. "What can I do for you?"

"A chemically reactive cloth," I said.

"All cloth is chemically reactive in some way," the Seagull said. "You'll need to be more specific."

And so I was specific. As Lora kept her head half out the door to try to catch a breath of fresh air, I laid out exactly what I needed.

"Is it possible?" I said.

"Possible?" he said. "Yes. But expensive. Very expensive."

I pulled out the bar of gold that André had liberated from Lady Nora's late vault. It seemed only fitting to use her ill-gotten gains to finance her own destruction. The Seagull's eyebrows fluttered up when he saw the gold. "Will this do?" I asked.

He wormed up from the chair, took the gold from me, cradling it like an infant and cooing slightly. Then he looked back at the two of us. "Give me two months."

We were happy to give him that and his fume-filled hut back. As we gratefully reentered the relaxed sunlight of a Dubrovnik afternoon, he called after us: "One more favor."

"What's that?" I said, trying to keep my nerves out of my voice.

"Never tell me what you'll use it for."

8

Five months later, the day of the King's wedding finally arrived.

The union between Luftnarp and Svitz was held on neutral ground, in the Sovereign Territory of Franchia. This was a strategic decision. No government claimed the land, so a ceremony in Franchia advantaged neither Luftnarp nor Svitz, while also not involving any other meddling royals. But it was an unsettling decision. Franchia was the only territory in the entire continent that had no population of any kind, and in fact, never had. Despite the lack of people, the land was filled with white stone arches, covering the plains and climbing the sides of the steepest mountains. From within the arches, sounds could be heard that the more rational promised was only the wind, but others knew was some sentience to the whole region, a jealous and xenophobic entity that wished no entrance into its realm. No one had ever successfully claimed Franchia for their own. Entire armies had been lost among the arches, the few survivors who found their way out swearing that the maze of arches went much farther than the small borders of the region would allow.

Given all this, the guests were nervous. No one liked to

spend the night in Franchia, and indeed the wedding feast had been set up just over the border, in the significantly less haunted region of Denmark.

The ceremony had been set in the closest counterpart Franchia had to a grand square, a large oval break in the arches, the ground cobbled with huge slabs of stone that had been there since long before humans had first arrived in Europe. I sat in between two of the arches up a hillside, so that I could get a sense of the whole scene. From behind me, I could hear that soft warbling of the wind, and I felt the distinct sensation of being hunted. I hoped we wouldn't have to be in Franchia for long.

All of the planning that could be done was done, and now it was up to my crew to execute it. Lora was atop the biggest arch, directly above the wedding platform, having disposed of the guards who had been sent precisely to make sure no one could lurk up there. André mixed with the crowds of well-dressed guests, sprinkling smiles and winks as he went, sending hearts and hands fluttering. And Rebekah, in her disguise of the meek maid, stood behind her master, Lady Nora, upon the wedding platform. Lady Nora was radiant in a dress that her most loyal maid had chosen for her, made by a young and upcoming tailor who was willing to work cheap in order to get his work seen. Rebekah had really outdone herself, having to play two different people in the same story, sometimes frantically switching from one disguise to the other while walking between rooms, or shouting from the hall as the tailor while still dressed as the maid. But as always, Rebekah had found a way to make it all convincing, and Lady Nora wore the dress made from a pale blue cloth that the Seagull had treated for us. Now Rebekah stood next to her master, and concealed in her palm a small vial of clear liquid, the other half of the Seagull's formula.

The ceremony began. It was a traditional Luftnarpian ceremony, which I found a little ostentatious even for a royal wedding. The bride played her part well, standing with a gaping mouth at the edge of the platform, making wide eyes over the crowd, oblivious to everything happening around her as her mouth fell wider and wider, more open than I had ever seen a human mouth extend. Meanwhile the King performed an off-balance and jerky jig around his bride, moaning and huffing and swinging his arms back and forth over his head. That part was actually pretty romantic. It was sweet how he hit his own stomach over and over, crying out in pain, but continuing to strike and strike and strike until he vomited a little on his own shoes. Lord Fullbright, standing at full attention next to the King, smiled at this understandable bit of mess and gestured for a servant to duck in and wipe it off. It was clear from the way Lord Fullbright gently patted the King's back the affection he felt. Their dynamic wasn't merely advisor and King, but old friends, and Lord Fullbright beamed beside his friend on his wedding day, even if the reason for the wedding was primarily political.

Lady Nora did not smile, and did not seem pleased to be there. Her lips were tight, as she looked past the ceremony, staring into the depths of some private abyss. I imagined or at least hoped that the loss of her wealth was eating away at her. I thought of André's family, their reputation ruined after generations of slowly working their way up. I thought of innocent men lying dead in a tavern in Hamburg. Of course, for me all injustices echoed the original injustice, and I thought of my father, lifeless in the grass. Let it eat at her. There would be more to come.

The drum solo signaled that there wasn't much left to the ceremony, and the moment in which a chicken was thrown into the air to land flightless and squawking back to earth was upon us. When the chicken's feet met earth, by Luftnarpian tradition, the marriage had formally begun. It was time. As though in celebration, I lifted up a bright yellow handkerchief and waved it lazily through the air. From that moment, Lady Nora's fate was sealed.

Two events happened at once, in perfect coordination, so that from the point of view of the crowd really only one action happened. The first event was that Rebekah misted Lady Nora with the contents of the vial, after which Rebekah immediately secreted the vial within her clothes and looked disinterestedly away over the crowd. We had asked the Seagull to make the substance as odorless as possible, but in the end it contained a strong scent of, strangely, bread, and so the platform must have smelled like a bakery. No one was paying attention to the out-of-place scent though, because the spray was reacting with a chemical embedded in the dye of the Lady's dress, and it immediately changed colors, from its pale blue into a bold dual-chromatic tone. Her left side bright green, her right side pure white. The second event was Lora, high on the second arch, releasing three banners declaring the justness and bravery of the Green and White Rebellion. The banners fell with a snap that caused the entire crowd to hush in their wedding jubilation instantly. The central banner contained a simple message that could only really have come from one person. "Surrender Strawhead."

The King turned in furious shock to Lady Nora, who, having not been looking down at her own dress, and with her back to the banners, had no idea of the horror that had just befallen her.

"You," the King said, in a quiet, pained voice.

"Me?" she repeated back to him, a question that sounded to everyone but herself like a confession.

9

I went to see Edmond. It had been over a year since our last meeting, and although I was sure he had heard through the organization at least some of what I had been doing, and likely had been able to guess the rest, I felt I owed it to him to tell him myself all that had transpired.

Barcelona in the winter is merely the Barcelona of the summer standing in the shade. It was with considerable happiness that I came across Señora Bover mending a shawl by the steps of Edmond's home. I greeted her warmly, and she stood.

"Ah, it has been so long," she said. "I was wondering if our city would ever see your face again."

"It has been a year, Señora, but I could never go too long without making sure all was well with you."

Bover gestured to the shawl. "I have work. What more could I ask of God?"

"Happiness? Wealth?"

"Happiness and wealth. They are matters mostly out of our control. But the work, *that* we can choose. Go on up. Your uncle must have heard your voice by now, and I'm sure he's pretending to be quite busy. Don't make him stare earnestly at the same boring piece of correspondence forever, waiting for you to catch him at it. Go on up and be duly impressed." Bover returned to her mending.

I climbed the stairway to Edmond's office, where, as the Señora had predicted, he was squinting at a letter with an ostentatiously serious expression. He looked up the moment I entered and let his face slide into a smile.

"I had thought you had forgotten me."

"Liar."

We embraced, and then sat across his desk from each other, and he leaned forward.

"You've been creating quite a situation," he said. "One would think you were trying to start a war."

"I am not interested in influencing Europe. Only the trajectory of Lady Nora's life."

"That you certainly have."

"She is finished," I said, with a bitter triumph I look back at now with shame.

"Finished," he tilted his head. "Ah, not quite. As good as, I suppose, but her friendship with the King was a deep cushion to fall upon. My spies tell me she is living in his palace, a prisoner, but a comfortable one. Still, you are right, that it has been a long fall from her former status in the world."

I felt a spike of pain in my stomach. "I would have thought treason would be reason enough for execution."

"Ordinarily yes, but the nobility is not ordinary by definition. This was my mistake. Oh, what am I saying? We should be toasting your triumph. You have set out to achieve the extraordinary, and you did so. Please forget I said anything."

"Of course. Yes. To my triumph," I said. I wanted badly to mean my words, but they tasted like nothing in my mouth. We ate dinner and took a slow walk through the city, and the entire time it felt like there was a ringing in my ears, a sound that I hated and that I needed to get rid of. Early the next morning, before Edmond had awoke, I was already gone.

From Barcelona I spent a slow winter making my way to Krakow, where the rest of the crew had stashed themselves. We met in a small river house, loomed over by the walls of Wawel Castle. I took stock of my people, and I wondered if I was still the leader they should be following. I thought the answer was probably no.

"What is my next role?" said Rebekah.

"It's time to get back to simple plunder and thievery," said Lora. Even André, for all the fury over his family, seemed to energize at the thought of stealing, rather than all the worry and fuss of ruining someone's life.

"There will always be a next job," I said vaguely, but I had no idea what it would be. I knew that I wasn't done with the job we had been working on, but also that I no longer needed them in order to do it. "But first, I'll need to leave for a while."

Rebekah studied me with concern. As it was the heart of her own skill, she had a sharp eye for the ways that people lie, and she read me carefully. "You're not done with Lady Nora," she concluded.

André groaned. "Enough with revenge, please let us do a dishonest day's work."

"I'm with them," said Lora. "Give me a target. Let me loose." Her broad body seemed caged in this little house in this little city.

"Soon," I said. "I have one more errand, and then I'll be back, and then we'll work." I was lying even to myself.

10

The giddiness and shock of the wedding feast had passed and now a businesslike solemnity lay heavy over the royal castle of Luftnarp. No one could believe the speed at which Lady Nora had fallen, the depth of her betrayal. The King had seethed, entirely putting off his new bride, who had moved her retinue back to Svitz to await a more welcoming situation perhaps in a year or two. This placed the King in a strange position of not living with his queen while simultaneously hosting the woman who, as far as he knew, had betrayed him. All in all, the partnership between Svitz and Luftnarp was going poorly, and the one person who no one knew was at blame for that was creeping secretly down the hallways of their home. I had come to finish what I had started. Perhaps Lora was right. Perhaps we had already done enough. But I didn't want to do enough. I wanted to do so much that I could not possibly be denied.

And so I crept down the halls, the sheathed dagger on my belt chafing against my legs. Above me, banners had the coat of arms for each of the sovereigns who had once held absolute power in this ancient kingdom. One coat of arms depicted a man holding an orange up to the sky, with a single ray of light striking the orange. A second was a human eye looking sharply to the right. Another took the form of a five-headed dragon, each head a different color. I studied this one with interest. No one had seen a dragon in hundreds of years, but it appeared that perhaps one had held the kingship of Luftnarp. A dragon would make a terrible leader, I decided, as it was well known that their many heads could never agree on anything.

I was alone in these halls. I did not want any of my friends to bear the responsibility of what I had to do next. They had come with me so far, and would likely have come even farther, but I could not ask that of them. As I had traveled to Luftnarp, I had kept an eye out for anyone following me. Our actions had created waves within the politics of Europe, and I knew that the attention of the Order of the Labyrinth must be on me. I was in every way a promising recruit. But try as I might, I could never catch any of their scouts. No matter. I knew they were listening, and I would give them something to hear.

I counted the doors. Rebekah had given me the information without knowing. I had asked her several disparate questions about the King's household, so that she would not be able to tell which item was pertinent. I didn't want her to guess my plans, partly because I didn't want her to try to help but mostly because I was ashamed. I could have asked Edmond to tap into his ring of spies, and he might have even helped me, but for the same reason I didn't want him to know I was in any way involved with this. What is the word for shame felt for an act that hasn't yet happened? What is the word for guilt felt for what has not yet occurred? The act could still be avoided. In the moment of putting my hand on the door handle, I thought about how easy it would be to just not pass through the doorway. And in thinking that, I entered.

The room was simple. A bed in one corner with a straw mattress. Windows with their shutters thrown wide open along one wall. A noble person's room, but a noble person in no position to show wealth. It would be unbefitting, given their situation. And now here I was, in that room. I drew the dagger and considered it. With this, I would end a life. It was not enough that Lady Nora be disgraced. She must die. And I had come to see that it would be done. It could be no other hand but my own. My hand was shaking. The weight of necessity lay heavy against it.

Even then there was a moment where I could have turned and left the room. I hadn't gone too far. Then I heard footsteps coming from the garden. I went to the window and peered down.

The sun was at its highest, and the garden was brilliantly lit. Despite the beauty of the spring weather, the garden was entirely empty except for a single figure. A man, hunched stiffly, and lurching his way down the garden path. I nearly dropped the dagger, seeing that figure that had haunted me throughout my entire life. I could hear the shuffle of the mysterious man's feet upon the pebbles, and for the first time I could hear the dry crack of his voice. "Why?" he was asking the empty afternoon. "Why?"

Behind me I heard a different sound. A door scraping open, and the shuffle of velvet shoes upon stone floor.

"Who are you, and what are you doing in my bed chambers?"

I turned and came eye to eye with the man who I had come to murder. Lord Fullbright, the conscience of the King. The wisest and kindest man in Luftnarp.

Lord Fullbright had survived in politics for a long time, and he eyed me appraisingly, trying to understand what I meant. He understood that while I looked like a person, I might be a political moment, and it was his task to determine what kind.

"Who sent you?" he asked.

The man was about to die, so I decided to tell him the truth.

"No one," I said. "I am here because I need something from you."

"Well," he said, smiling carefully, and taking a seat in a chair that, I noticed, was a few easy steps from the door. "Certainly my life's mission is to serve, but there are better methods of inquiry than sneaking into my bed chamber."

I found a chair that was close to his, but not so close that he would immediately flee, and I sat too, crossing my legs and matching his smile. The dagger was hidden against my thigh, but he would correctly assume I was armed. The joints of the chair grumbled as I shifted. "I wish there were a better way to make this particular request, but unfortunately I am not so wise as you," I said. "This is all I could come up with."

"I suppose shouting for guards would do no good."

"Your guards are alive," I said, answering two questions for the price of one. "But why shorten your life?"

He breathed out slowly through his nose, a soft hiss in a quiet room. "A man doesn't enter a palace like this without knowing how he may someday leave it," he said. "But I always thought if a moment like this came, I would know why. I've guided our king toward mercy and justice. Always I've consoled him that his is a position of service. We serve the people, not the other way around." He waved his hand. "And ah, perhaps he doesn't always hear me. Certainly the Green and White Rebellion and his wrongheaded decision that led to it is proof enough. But that can hardly be laid at my feet."

"You have done nothing wrong," I said. I knew he was a good advisor, but I hadn't counted on liking him as a person, and I tried not to.

"Circumstances would seem to speak differently." He dipped his eyes to my poorly-hidden blade.

I stood, and he stood. The act hadn't happened yet, but it was going to. There was no way down from here for either of us, and in that way we were bonded. We were standing atop something larger than ourselves, and both of us would have to jump. I thought of my childhood friend Albert, and wondered, as I often did, what he was doing. Living a good life, I hoped, free of pain. Free of vengeance. The kind of life that anyone should be able to live, if the world were a different place.

"You're a good man, Lord Fullbright," I said.

"As the hymn says 'Try, try your whole life to be righteous and be good,'" he said.

"I've tried," I said. "I've tried."

Even before I finished speaking, I pulled the dagger from my belt and without letting myself stop, afraid that if I paused for even a moment my hand would tremble away into inaction, I pushed the full length of the blade through his heart.

I let go of the handle, now sticking out from his chest, and he stepped back.

His mouth opened, maybe to curse me or maybe only to ask me a question, and either way I had no answer. And then he fell.

The sound of his body landing was softer than I thought it would be, like a falling of cloth. I stepped over him, leaving the dagger where it lay. It was a bejeweled ornamental dagger that Lady Nora was highly proud of. She had showed it around the palace for so many years that even the man scrubbing pans in the depths of the kitchens could have attested it was hers. As I went, I pressed a thin strip of fabric into the frame of the door, as though torn away in the hurry of flight. From one of the Lady's dresses, of course.

And once it was clear that Lady Nora, in revenge for her imprisonment, had murdered the King's favorite advisor, best friend, and the most popular man in the kingdom, I slipped away, hoping no one in the palace would remember my face.

11

In the end, after all her years of lording her power over those below her, Lady Nora wept as they carted her to the gallows. We all do, I suppose, in the end. Everything we build in our clumsy, teetering lives is a bulwark against this moment, and when that bulwark finally fails, what is there left but tears?

I didn't cry, even though I felt I could have. What point was there at that juncture? I had already come so far. Even as I could hear Lord Fullbright's final words repeating in my head, everything that I did was already done, and no weeping from me would change it. So I watched dry-eyed as Lady Nora was carried yowling from the cart to the platform. This is the sound we all make when we see that edge coming.

André stood next to me, as solemn and placid as I was. Here was the woman who had torn apart his family, and so he would face her fate with open eyes. He would see it through to the end. Rebekah was also calm. Here was the woman whose guards beheaded one in three sailors before her eyes. Lora, for all of her immense physical strength, did not take it as well.

"Do we have to stay and watch?"

"You don't," I said. "But when I start something, I see it through."

"You've seen it through."

"But we haven't *seen* it," said André. "I want to see it."

"Me too," I said. Once, I had the idea of destroying a vicious noblewoman. Success is not in the idea, but the execution, and here, finally, was that execution. Next I would bring down the Order of the Labyrinth and those who killed my father. If I could take down Lady Nora, the Order was within my reach.

Lora shook her head. "I hope you know what you're doing." She left the crowd. Rebekah didn't say anything, but she followed Lora away. And so André and I stayed alone to watch.

I wish I could say I felt something other than complete satisfaction. I won't lie to you.

"She deserved this," André said, and I don't know if it was a question. But either way, I didn't answer him. The moment came. The moment went. The body that had once been a person was taken away, and the crowd separated and turned back into individual people, a little ashamed of themselves for having watched. I left André behind and walked through the city. I heard footsteps behind me, and I turned to tell him that I needed a few hours on my own, but the person following me was not André.

"So accomplished for such a young age," said Señora Bover, no longer speaking Catalan but a smooth and fluent Luftnarpian. In that moment I knew that neither was her native tongue.

It was only by her face that I could recognize her. She was not stooped over some odd job as she had been every time I had seen her outside of my Edmond's home. At her full height, I appreciated how tall she actually was, and saw for the first time that she was also quite muscular. How had I missed all this for so many years? But of course, that was what she had intended. She had turned herself into a person I would overlook, and so I had obliged, as easy a mark as any.

"Come, this way," she said, and we started on the gentle sloping boulevard down toward the docks.

I must have looked stunned. She smiled. "Yes, I am not merely an old woman sweeping steps and darning cloth. There is a power in being unremembered, in being overlooked. You should remember that power. People who aren't seen can see and hear all."

"You've been watching me, all of these years." It wasn't a question, just a fact I now knew.

"Yes. Who would have suspected and so on. Come, I have something I must show you."

The woman I once knew as Señora Bover and I approached the docks, and, as we did, the deaths of Lord Fullbright and Lady Nora played again and again every time I blinked. Memory lives inside the eyelids. To distract myself, I tried to concentrate on the simple sounds of the city. The shouts of merchants, the conversation of simple citizens living simple civilian lives, the click of heel upon stone, the trod of hoof upon straw. I tried to listen carefully, because I felt that my life as I had known it was over, and some other life was starting, a life so completely different that the person I was now was, in some ways, about to die. My body would still be alive, but it wouldn't be the me within it. Or maybe not a death. Maybe it was a birth.

Señora Bover led me past where the boulevard ended onto the planks of the docks themselves, where cargo was carried by men with hard voices and hard lives, to a small ship tied at the quietest end of the busy waterfront.

"There," said Bover.

"What is it?" I said, trying to understand. As I asked, from some signal of Bover's I had missed, as I had missed so many things, the ship ran its colors. A black flag with the white symbol of a labyrinth rose up the mast. Seeing the sign of the Order of the Labyrinth, I heard a bell toll deep within my body, a vibration in my bones and blood. Acid washed through my mouth and I hoped it was what victory tasted like.

"That," said Señora Bover, "is your ship."

CRAIG

2015

I take care of you, but you refuse to take care of yourself, Craig.

I can whisper ideas in your ear while you sleep. I can pay off your debts. I can cause a perfectly responsible and considerate woman to wreck her car to bring you into her life. I can create scenes, leave cryptic notes, punish your enemies, reward your friends. I'm in your house. I'm in their houses. I am everywhere. All the time. Right now.

But those thoughts of yours. Or lack thereof. I can't do anything about that. You have to make your own choices. I can certainly urge you toward better options, but you have to make the decisions, Craig.

You've been seeing Amaranta for three and a half years. You're twenty-eight years old. She's thirty-two. All your hopes of raising a family are quickly passing you by. If you could hear me, you would say I sound like a controlling mother, wouldn't you? I'm aware of this, and while I don't disagree, I would argue that there's no reason to gender that statement. Men are far more controlling than women.

Mothers might put pressure on children to do well in school. To get married. To call their families. To be respectful to others. Men, on the other hand, hide the money, carry the weapons, direct the narrative, argue like they're in a Most Correct competition. Men rely on women to assist them, but they don't like it when we want to be collaborators.

Do you know the expression, "fish or cut bait"? Most people think it means you either need to commit to something (cast your fishing line), or you should just let it go (cut your bait loose). But there's another meaning. When fishers are preparing to cast their lines, they cut bait. They literally cut large chunks of fish meat into smaller bits to use as bait.

So to fish or cut bait means you can do what you came to do (fish) or you can put in preparation to do what you came to do (cut bait). It's not an either/or situation. You do one to be ready for the other.

You're doing neither. You're not preparing anything. You go to work. You eat lunch. You buy books or music or games. You go out on dates with your girlfriend.

Amaranta asked you what you want to do with your career. You've held the same assistant-level job editing press releases and marketing copy for the Ford dealership on Route 800. "Ford. Our cars are built strong. Our cars are built out of bones. Weird metal bones that we found buried in a meteor. Ford: Drive Weird Bones." That was your copy! That was good. A catchy and relatable marketing campaign that drew huge sales, but it was your boss who earned the raise. You're creative and indispensable to your company, but where are you going in your own career? That's what she wants to know. She cares about your life, sure, but she also cares about her own. If you have no direction within yourself, you'll have no direction with your relationship.

I want to take this time to point out—once again—that Amaranta wants a family. She wants to be happy, and to achieve that she wants you to be happy for longer than the present moment.

She loves you, and you're behaving like that love is a piece of art to be hung on a wall. A thing of beauty to behold each day, to revel in its colors and strokes of oil. But love is not a piece of art. Love is a tree that grows roots and needs sunlight and water all the time. Love experiences seasons. Seasons of lush leaves, of scorched branches, of starving insects, of brutal cold, and of sugar sweet fruit, which, when eaten, streams stickily down your chin. You're unable to take it all in.

A tree needs everything around it to contribute to its well being. And its environment is constantly changing. If you don't understand that, then the tree will die. Beetles will eat it. Or the blight will. Or larger trees will block its sun, overpower its roots.

Which brings me to Jennifer. You talk to Jennifer a lot. You work together, and your relationship is completely platonic, I know. I've read all of your emails and texts to her and listened in on your conversations at the dealership, as I crouched under the counter that holds the Keurig.

I'm not accusing you of infidelity, but why have you never mentioned Jennifer to Amaranta? She's met Julius and Brian and Orlando, all of your male friends. Is this a relationship you're hiding, not out of guilt, but out of protection? You're storing Jennifer away like a rainy day fund? Jennifer is a human, not a wad of cash, or a buried treasure. The problem is not that you're friends with a woman. The problem is how you treat that friendship. Either she's an open part of your life, which includes Amaranta, or she's not.

I've done what I can to help with this. Jennifer quit her job last night. You won't see her at work anymore. She stayed late to finish up paperwork, after everyone had left. In the middle of her task, all of the lights went out. In the first moments of a light turning out, before the eye adjusts, the darkness is absolute. She couldn't even see the desk in front of her. She tried shaking her arms in the air, but the office doesn't have motion-sensing lights. Her breathing sounded unusually loud to her, like it wasn't only her that was breathing.

"Who's there? Craig? Is that you?" she called. She thought of you, Craig. How nice. Footsteps circled her, a spiraling path in the dark closing in. She realized she had been holding her breath that whole time. Then who had she heard breathing? She scrambled back from her desk and ran for the break room, bumping painfully against furniture and walls as she went. There she fumbled for a knife from the kitchen. It is a miracle her hand found the handle and not the blade. Or maybe a friendly interloper turned it at the last second because that interloper wanted Jennifer terrified, not maimed. Jennifer poked the blade tentatively in front of her, announcing, "I'm calling the police."

But we both knew she had left her phone at her desk. She knew this because she saw her touch screen light up from across the office. I knew this because I had taken her phone from her pocket. She heard the sound of a bird, specifically a dove. "Coo Cooooo," the sound came lightly from the tiny phone speakers. "Coo Coooo," it sounded almost like an owl. Her ring tone had been "Party in the USA," but this was so much nicer. More elegant.

Now that the phone had drawn her attention, she saw, against the window behind her desk, a shadow of a person, hunched and elderly, crawling across the wall like a roach. Jennifer screamed. The woman on the wall screamed too, a perfect mirror of Jennifer's scream. As we screamed, the lights clunked back on, and Jennifer was alone. Or at least she couldn't see anyone else.

Jennifer walked to her desk and to her phone still ringing with a dove's repeating coo. Next to it, an actual dove, one of its wings missing and its head removed. (Likely by a feral cat. A coyote would have eaten the bird rather than mutilating it and moving on.) She picked up the phone. It was showing her mother's number. She answered the call. "Mom?" she said. A dry throated voice responded, a voice that was hundreds of years older than her mother: "YOU ARE NOT SAFE HERE."

Jennifer called her manager on her drive home and quit her job, effective immediately. Anything that she wasn't able to take on her first trip out of the building, she left behind. So, I suppose you won't be able to visit with her at work anymore. These things happen.

Although there is something even I don't understand about this story. As I've said, I don't breathe anymore. So who *was* that breathing? Ah well, Night Vale keeps its mysteries, sometimes even from me.

I'm sure you'll be saddened to lose Jennifer as a friend, but perhaps your mind is elsewhere these days. You've been seeing things lately. Things you are certain you have never encountered before, yet things that felt undeniably familiar. Last Monday morning, before leaving for work, you leaned in toward the mirror to examine a pimple on the side of your nose, and you saw something else. You saw someone behind you.

There's a thin line separating humor and horror, and this was that line. You were on the horror side. I was on the humor side. Your eyes got so large; your mouth dangled open. It felt like minutes, but was probably only five seconds. At first you thought it was a towel hanging from the door, or a trick of the light, or the sleepy remnant of a dream, but you knew. Your subconscious always knows, well before the rest of you. There was someone behind you. You attempted to find her face, but you couldn't quite make it out. Yet you felt her stare.

You jerked back and grunted. And no one was there. You ran out into the living room. No one there either. You shouted but I think you heard me giggle, because you stopped making any noise. You searched your apartment, checking closets and cabinets. You even looked in dresser drawers. Think, Craig. Who would be able to fit into a dresser drawer? (I can. I can fold myself wonderfully.)

When you returned to the bathroom, you sat down on the closed toilet, your towel still around your waist, and you breathed with your face in your palms. They were beautiful, cool mint toothpaste breaths. They felt wonderful on my own hands, hovering half an inch from yours.

I don't know if I've told you this before, you have pleasant breath. Even when you're sleeping. You're lucky. Or Amaranta is lucky, I suppose.

Craig, you're starting to hear a voice when you're alone, and it is the same voice that sometimes comes into your dreams. You think you are stressed and overwhelmed, yet Amaranta is so understanding, so patient. Maybe it's your job. Maybe Amaranta is right. You should find a better career with better pay, more scalable, a career you can support a family with. I know you're out of debt, but what if you started investing? I left a brochure detailing some nice investment opportunities, locally based companies, environmentally friendly and fair to their workers, in your mailbox. I think you could find real stability and real happiness if you weren't so stressed about money.

Just think of poor Stuart in apartment 413, whose unit caught fire last month. He lost everything. You went over to help him out even though you'd never met him before. You are a good person because you do good things. A person is only what they do. Having someone to cry with definitely relieved Stuart for a bit. It relieved you too.

In the process of consoling a neighbor, you also learned about Stuart's difficult life. His wife left him five years ago. Then he was laid off from his community relations job with the CIA. Then someone hacked his bank account a year and a half ago and stole $15,417.71. And now this fire.

He still remembered that exact amount too. $15,417.71. He just couldn't get over the seventy-one cents part. So specific, that amount. Maybe someone bought a used car with it, or got an all-inclusive vacation package, or paid off a debt.

"Paid off a debt?" you asked him.

"Such a specific amount," he said. "Could be."

And you said . . . well, you said nothing for a long time. Stuart actually had to ask if *you* were okay.

And you said, "The bank covered the theft though, right?"

"According to their records, I withdrew the amount myself. They have a withdrawal slip with that amount and my signature on it."

"And you don't remember . . ."

"I don't want to talk about it." Stuart looked annoyed. That was his old tragedy. He faced a new tragedy now.

If you could have seen my face, I would have looked annoyed too.

Focus, Craig. See how focused Stuart is? You are free from tragedy, and yet you don't savor the good fortune you have. You're free of debt. Now take charge of your future, of your family's future. Assert yourself. Don't look back. The only thing back there is regret. Also resentment. Also anger. Vengeance too.

You can't change what has already happened. You can only make things better moving forward. Amaranta loves you.

Cut bait. Then fish.

THE CAPTAIN

1814-1829

André cut open the pomegranate with his dagger. The red juice pooled along the heavily stained wood counter in the galley. He quartered the fruit and, with his thin fingers, pried out seeds in quick bursts from the pith.

He dropped them into a bowl in front of me and I ate them. I savored each small pop of the soft skin, the burst of tart juice. André found pomegranates too sour. They made his tongue hard and the insides of his cheeks feel fuzzy, but these seeds quenched my dry mouth, a splash of juice on each gentle crunch of their core. Squish, squirt, scrunch.

In the hold were five hundred pounds of pomegranates. We had stolen them from an orchard in Malta. We were not ordered to steal the pomegranates. We stole them out of the goodness of our hearts.

Nine years earlier, Señora Bover, on behalf of the Order of the Labyrinth, had granted me this small cutter called *The Wasp*, along with a crew of about twenty men. I didn't love the name of the ship, because of my distaste for that particular insect, but it was fitting for a quick little vessel that could make life miserable for others. Bover told us we were to report to a man named Holger in Ca'Savio, near Venice, for all details of operations.

I had collected my little band of thieves, and told them the good news, that we could go back to a life of banditry and profits, and they had gladly joined me for the adventure. I didn't tell them the whole truth, of course, that I would never leave behind vengeance, that perhaps there was nothing else for me. Only Rebekah sensed what I was hiding, and she loved me too much to pick apart my reasons.

Our new boss, Holger, a sometimes likable but mostly dull misanthrope, enjoyed my predilection toward picking pockets and expert knife-work and had, at first, put our ship to work on small smuggling jobs in small port cities. The meager coins and modest swords I swiped were easy work but hardly the daring adventures I thought the Order would be involved in.

During our first four years aboard *The Wasp*, we ran many such small jobs for the Order. I needed time to get used to running a ship and a crew, but a few years for a revenge-minded young woman felt like a few decades. Plus, my induction into the Order happened so swiftly, I wrongly expected that my next several promotions would happen rapidly as well.

The Order of the Labyrinth was purposefully opaque, and our lack of upward movement was starting to dull the thrill of our adventures. "Revenge ages like wine," Edmond wrote me once in a letter. "The longer it waits, the richer the taste."

Edmond had also expressed reticence about me and my friends joining such a ruthless and unstoppable organization, and my desire to bring down the Order of the Labyrinth from within. But I was no longer a child. My choices were my own to make, and my consequences were my own to face.

But four years into our employment, we had yet to meet

anyone in the Order, save for Holger and my initial contact with Bover. I had grown wary of Holger's influence and felt that if I were to impress the leaders of this secretive organization, I would have to take action myself.

One stormy night in the port of Estepona, we spotted a Spanish gunboat. Under the noisy cloak of thunder and massive undulating tides we boarded the ship, disarmed the two guards, and stole nearly four tons of black powder and cannon shells. A week later, in Oran, I happened upon exactly what I was looking for: another ship bearing the labyrinth emblem upon a black flag. I was proud to bring my fellow Order members a gift, and what better gift for a violent and powerful organization than violent and powerful munitions?

We sailed alongside the Order ship, but it did not slow. I waved and pointed to our matching flag. Two sailors on the deck of the ship noticed us. One was not tall and the other was not short. They stared at us, or at least I felt they were staring at us. Their faces were completely covered by dark hoods.

"We have a gift for you," I called, but the men did not react. I could not tell if they were suspicious of or annoyed by us. Would they thank us or kill us for attempting to board their ship with a gift?

Eventually, the one who was not tall signaled to the other, and they turned their attention away from *The Wasp* as their ship sped away. Before they left, I had gotten a good look at the stacks of brightly lit crates on the deck of their ship. The sun was hidden behind clouds that day, and I had seen no lanterns lit. The light emanated from the crates themselves.

This transaction with the unnamed, inscrutable ship, and its unnamed, inscrutable sailors, had befuddled me. I was without a clue how to ingratiate myself to the Order of the Labyrinth.

So my only path upward through the Order remained with Holger. My crew and I had just stolen tons of Spanish munitions—a much greater accomplishment than the pick-pocketing and produce smuggling we had previously been assigned—so with that I hoped to convince Holger to give us more responsibility and larger missions.

Unlike Holger, I recognized the immense talents of my friends and crew, as well as their taste for action regardless of its purpose. For instance, Vlad, our boatswain, who was a medi-ocre administrator but a fierce and almost unstoppable fighter. He had a haunting laugh when he smelled blood that sounded like a dog being let out for a long-overdue walk. His energy and appetite for violence were boundless, and he soon took over Lora's role of subduing anyone who needed to be subdued in the course of our business. She was bigger, but he had a true believer's enthusiasm for it.

"That boy is dangerous," Lora whispered to me, after one particularly brutal job.

"Just be glad he's on our side," I whispered back.

Before our voyage back to Ca'Savio, we stocked up on goods to inspire Holger. We emptied a bank vault in Monte Carlo (a three week adventure that saw Rebekah playing two separate bank employees and a minor noble from Finland), stole fine silks from a storehouse in Tripoli (in the process of charming our way in, André had so smitten the man who owned the store-house that he flat out offered the silks in exchange for a lifetime of companionship, but it felt wrong to take advantage of such a heartsick bargain, so we stole them fair and square), and lifted dozens of Renaissance paintings from a mansion in Rome (this was less exciting than it sounds, the place was empty due to a festival in the countryside and Lora simply put a rock through a window). We developed a taste for bigger heists, gleefully and successfully raiding larger merchant ships and well-guarded inland fortifications.

It was the artwork from Rome that finally changed Holger's mind. He originally wanted to burn it all, but André convinced him to sell three of the minor pieces to a dealer in Sicily, and when the payment was finalized, it was the most profitable work we had ever done for the Order. Initially, I detested Holger's limited aspirations, but I grew to love this about him, because it made him easy to impress.

After the lucrative art sale, Holger told us he had never been prouder of an Order of the Labyrinth crew. He thanked us for our adventurous spirits, and more importantly for our good business sense and after nearly half a decade in his employ he would put word in to his advisers about our talents.

"Maybe the other Order ships will finally speak to us," Lora said.

"Why do we not wear hoods?" Rebekah interjected. "All others under the labyrinth flag wear dark hoods. Are we underdressed?"

"You could wear hoods if you'd like," Holger offered.

"And what do they carry in those crates?" André jumped in.

Holger's face sank, a sour frown uncommon upon the face of anyone André spoke to. Holger took a swig of wine, then muttered, "Ships carry many things in crates."

"But these crates are different," André protested. "They radiate like stars."

"And who's in charge of the Order?" I added. Holger did not answer.

I began to think Holger was not as high up in the complex hierarchy of the Order of the Labyrinth as I initially thought.

He seemed to know less than us about the organization. I felt I had barely come closer to the vengeance I sought. I wasn't interested anymore in the low-level life of a flunky. I wanted to find the heart of this faceless monster and tear it out with my own hands.

At least Holger was true to his word about recognizing our talents, authorizing bigger jobs like bank and casino heists. Rebekah infiltrated these operations, disguised as employees. André played the part of a charming nobleman, moving easily through whatever crowds to scout out our entrances and exits. Lora loaded stolen cargo quickly onto our ship. Vlad broke noses when necessary, and often when unnecessary. He would return to the ship with bloody knuckles and bruises all over his body and salute me with a bellow: "Best captain I ever had!"

These greater assignments kept us energized over the next five years, as Holger also allowed us to seize cargo from much larger ships than ours. *The Wasp* was too small for ramming and had limited munitions for full on attacks, but its compact size made it possible to slip in behind less agile ships and board them before they could get a shot off.

After each mission, we would return to Ca'Savio and pay Holger his cut, and then set back out to plunder vulnerable cargo ships in accessible ports. Like any reasonable human, I do not like harming innocent people, but like any reasonable human, I do not consider the wealthy to be innocent people. Holger did not, at first, differentiate between economic classes when he sent his band of thieves to a job, so that left me to the task of getting to know who was who. It was important to me to know who we were stealing from.

As we traveled, Rebekah embedded herself in temples, churches, banks, warehouses, and so on, learning who were the wealthiest of each region, and who were the poorest. Who was generous, and who cruel. André got similar information just by chatting up people in bars. Truly André's onyx eyes and ivory smile transcended class. They all would tell him anything he wanted to know.

We cultivated a list of wealthy slobs, ruthless companies, and murderous criminals to harass and rob. And we found hapless villages, poor city families, and victims of the ruling classes to donate some of our spoils to. There's no such thing as a good pirate, but I could at least strive to be a pirate who did good.

This is how, nine years into my captaincy of *The Wasp*, I had ended up with five hundred pounds of pomegranates. André knew of an orchard in Malta owned by twins named Cesare and Luka Bennetto, low-level bosses in The Duke's Own who were notorious for monopolizing all sowable land and then hiking prices on the poorer population. The Bennetto's produce and shipping business put them among the ten wealthiest men in Malta.

As we anchored next to the Bennetto's cargo ship in Valletta, I told André, Rebekah, and Lora my plan to sneak in at midnight. André would distract the two guards as Rebekah, disguised as a stevedore, would redirect fruit onto our ship. Lora would be our muscle, helping move the larger quantities of cargo and also the guards if André proved insufficient. Then we could take that food to the west side of the island and give it to the villagers who toiled twelve hours a day in the Bennetto orchards and vineyards, for a salary that made them unable to afford the fruit they picked.

Lora, hearing my plan, said, "Only two guards? Let's do this now." Before I could object, she was striding toward the dock, in open daylight, her gait much longer and thus quicker than even our sprint. Vlad was following fast behind, howling with laughter. Rebekah called out "Lora, Vlad. Wait!" But the two guards were already separated from their swords and plunged into the charcoal water below. Lora stretched her impossibly long arm up toward a crane holding a sagging net filled with pomegranates. She yanked it off the hook. With her other arm, she reached down and tucked a crate full of lemons against her hip and ran back toward us. With no faces to punch, or bellies to stab, Vlad kicked in deck doors and hacked away sail lines until Lora called back after him.

"Let's go!" she shouted, running full speed past us, and we all hastily followed.

In addition to the succulent pomegranates, we had a hundred pounds of lemons, which maybe the villagers would have some use for. If we had been more organized in our raid, we could have gotten eggs, maybe honey, definitely some milk. I don't know what to do with lemons. It hurt my teeth to think of them.

"They're quite good in tea," André said. "A healthy drink, too, especially with ginger."

"We could have taken their ginger," Rebekah said. "If we had stuck to the plan."

"They didn't have ginger. I would have smelled it," Lora said unapologetically. "Eat the lemons. They prevent scurvy."

On the other side of Malta, the good people of Manikata appreciated the pomegranates, but didn't really care for the lemons. Lora, however, had developed an appetite for them, and we kept those for her.

After leaving Manikata, Lora handed me half of a lemon. Even though I despised the tooth-meltingly sour taste, I bit into the edge, taking skin, pit, seed, and pulp into my mouth.

The lemon was sweet. It was a flavor I remembered from my youth, but tasted again decades later, the juice was a crisp sugary redemption.

I held fast to my desire not to harm poor or small operations. This was not something I bothered to share with Holger, but I wrote regularly to Edmond on the subject and recounted our adventures to him. I missed him greatly. I wanted him to be proud of who I had become. If I had to waste my time reporting to a low-level nobody like Holger, then I was determined to spend my time developing patience with myself, discipline of body and mind, and a moral center upon which my soul could steadfastly balance.

2

In late summer of 1824, it appeared that our patience was paying off.

"I have something new for you," Holger said. "Higher priority. Higher stakes. The bosses think you're up to it."

The details of the orders bothered me greatly. He wanted us to go inland to Augsburg. A young man named Max, the nephew of someone quite important within the Order (Holger would not tell us a name) had been stabbed by the constable. Max and his friends had apparently been robbing carriages. ("Such a minor little thing," Holger sighed. "But these constables think they are little kings of their little kingdoms.") The constable and Max got into a scuffle, during the course of which the constable had pulled Max's knife from its hip sheath and drove it into Max's thigh. The ensuing infection led to the amputation of Max's right leg. ("Oh, the boss was not happy about that," Holger said. "I've never heard such language from them. Usually so solemn, you know.")

"What do they want us to do to him?" I said.

"Him?" Holger said. "Not just him. The leaders of the Order are clear. The constable and his family must die. Every person in that house is to be offed." He shrugged. "Oh, and a finger from each body returned as proof. Sorry, I trust you, but this is how these things are done."

I felt dizzy. I tasted lemon, bitter and sharp. Could I do this? I could. I had to. I just had to look at the bigger picture.

Leaving Lora to keep an eye on the crew, André, Rebekah, Vlad, and I traveled through the Alps and into Bavaria. I also took along Samuel, our navigator, a smallish and smart young man. He never said much, but I could always see thoughts tumbling behind his eyes. It seemed good to have a steady thinker with me on a mission of this magnitude.

The constable lived in a modest home, tucked away from the village at the edge of the forest. We spent a few days watching from the trees. He had a wife and two children. There were no guards or other security. They were just a family, like any family. Lemons again on my tongue and in my throat, the taste repeating and repeating on me.

Vlad, giddy at the potential for physical combat and murder, suggested that we set the house on fire and then kill each one of them as they ran out. André shook his head. "What are we even doing here?" he said to me, but I refused to meet his eyes.

"We enter the house," I said. "We do this cleanly, we do this simply, we do this quickly."

"Then we burn the house down," Vlad said with a throaty laugh. I thought of another burning house. I thought of another father. Was it another low-level captain, just trying to prove herself, that had destroyed my life once upon a time?

"No," I said. "No fire." One of the constable's children ran out of the house, and was called back in by his mother. I made a decision. "Or you're right. We burn the house down, but as a diversion for our escape."

André shook his head with disgust. Rebekah looked away. The tension between my dear friends and me was palpable to Vlad and Samuel.

"Rebekah, Samuel, and I will execute the constable and his family, while Vlad and André stand guard," I said.

"But I'm the murderer," Vlad whined. "I'm very good at it. Have I not been good enough at murdering?"

"You're very good at murder," I reassured him.

"You got to murder that banker last time," André said, his hand reassuring on Vlad's shoulder. "Remember, in Florence?"

Even Vlad was not immune to André. He nodded, placated. "You are right. Fair is fair. Others can do the murder tonight."

After nightfall, we left behind Vlad and André, and slipped into the house. We woke the family and moved them at knifepoint into the parlor. Rebekah went from one to the next gagging them. Only she knew what I planned to do next. I couldn't have hidden it from her if I wanted to.

I considered Samuel, the only member of the team I did not usually bring ashore for these kinds of things. He was Holger's man, most likely. Samuel was slight, sly, and wickedly smart, but he had a softness to him. I did not suspect him of being a high-ranking official of the Order, but then I had not suspected Señora Bover, either. I would need to be wary of anyone who was not André, Rebekah, Lora, or Edmond.

"Samuel," I said. "Help Vlad gather brush for the fire." He saluted and left.

I waited until I was sure he was gone. "If you want to live, listen carefully to what I have to say, and don't argue," I told the terrified family. On my instructions, I placed each of their left hands on the kitchen table. I took a hatchet from the corner, looked the constable in his eyes, and took off his pinky finger. I can still hear the dull thud of the blade against the wood table and the strained screams of him and his family. The same for his wife. The constable groaned as I moved to his children, but it couldn't be helped. The older sister bit down so hard her teeth tore through the gag and she nearly choked. When I went to cut her younger brother's hand, the girl weakly gestured with her good hand and whispered, "No. Take another of mine instead."

And I did. I hated myself.

Rebekah untied them, as I stood ready with the axe in case they gathered their wits to fight. "My men are behind the tree line in front of your house," I said. "You will need to run out the back. Do not do it until you hear me slam the front door. If any of us see you, we will kill you. Run out the back of the house toward your neighbor's barn. You are no longer constable, and you are no longer welcome in Augsburg. Rebekah will lead you to your new home in Innsbruck. It's not safe for you here."

I yelled the okay for Samuel to light the fire and ran out the front, slamming the door hard behind me. I could see the shadows of the constable's family and Rebekah through the smoke. Behind them was another figure. The figure lurched stiffly, slowly. I could only see a silhouette, but I knew that familiar face twisted into an unscreamed scream, that shirt covered in blood, that dry mouth muttering "Why? Why?" A figure I had seen since I was a little girl. Who was this phantom that had haunted me my whole life? I turned away, grabbed Samuel, and we ran toward Vlad and André.

"Let me see!" Vlad demanded, and I showed him my satchel full of fingers. He cooed like a child seeing ice for the first time.

"We've got to go. Now!" I shouted.

"Where's Rebekah?" André asked, truly frantic. It was better with him to not tell him the plan. He could charm, but complicated plans bored and irritated him. I would explain to him later so that he would not have to carry any fabricated murders on his conscience.

"She's guarding the rear door, making sure they don't escape," I said. "She'll catch up. Go!"

It's too complex to save every innocent life, but when we could, we did. Revenge superseded Samaritan deeds. I sought to find the heart of the Order and pluck it out. If I did harm along the way, then I would have to take that up with whatever god would be waiting for me after I died.

When Vlad, Samuel, André, and I arrived back at *The Wasp*, Rebekah was already there, as I knew she would be, playing cards with Lora. In lieu of a cribbage board, they were using knives on a plank of wood Lora had crafted out of a tree trunk.

In our absence, Nathan, the first mate, had whipped the rest of the crew into a cleaning frenzy, and the ship shone like a royal jewel. Señora Bover had insisted that Nathan was one of the brightest young men in all of the Order, an admiral in the making. Nathan was rigid but dutiful. I disliked him, but some evils are necessary. During downtime, most of the crew took to laziness and booze. First mate Nathan was an exception. He took care of his body, ate healthily when he could. His shirts were smooth and white, his boots polished. He kept detailed notes in his log, of meetings, of dinners, of activities.

I had teased him years earlier that writing down everything we do in such detail could get us arrested if not outright executed.

"It could, couldn't it?" he had said, and kept writing. I can only presume he wrote our conversations verbatim. Nathan paid close attention to minor details like uniformity of clothing and careful cleaning. He noticed missed spots on seemingly pristine galley counters, or the pale tongue of a partially tucked shirt. If Señora Bover had been the Order's spy on the ground, Nathan looked to be their spy on the sea. I was meticulously careful around him.

The crew had grown a touch restless while we were gone, and Nathan had prevented them from spending too much time on land so that they would not waste all of their money and mental acuity on drink. Upon my return, a few pointed out local fishing ships that could be quick jobs with easy pay. I surveyed the port, but most appeared to be small fishing operations, not worth the effort, and more importantly run by honest families I did not want to harm. As when I was a child, I had taken to memorizing familiar ships in familiar ports. We had stopped in Venice enough that these same little fishing boats had become regular sights for me: *The Vineyard*, *The Wanderer*, *The Pelican*, and so on. Knowing the names of these boats personalized them to me. I grew attached.

There was only one vessel that day that I did not recognize. It was a larger brig circling the port. Atop its mainsail, a black flag with white labyrinth emblem. We would certainly not engage this ship, although I longed to. A ship that large surely must carry men of great significance in the organization. *Someday I will captain that ship,* I thought, *and I will sail it directly into the black heart of the Order.*

Before heading back to Ca'Savio, I went to my quarters to lie down and clear my head, but really I only cluttered it more, thinking about what I had done to the constable and his family, how thankful I was for Rebekah's cleverness in getting them out of town. I made up a story that the constable was a vile man, that he had a mistress, that he took bribes from the wealthy to keep their kids free from the law, that he murdered the homeless and pinned it on his enemies.

Since I did not know a thing about him, he could be any kind of man. He was simultaneously good and evil, deserving of salvation and of damnation. In my head I chose the latter and thus solidified my moral obligation to deliver justice. The constable, after all, used deadly force to subdue a petty crook. A good lawman would arrest such a derelict, but he attacked this boy, using the boy's own knife against him, crippling Max forever.

"This kind of excessive power cannot be tolerated," my thoughts became daydreams, "and I am happy to have helped the people of Augsburg out from under the boot of this madman. My vengeance, though, remains my own. Avenging others' ills is not something I have time for. I do others' work to learn how to do my own."

I had the determination to find my father's killer and not only claim what is owed, but also collect interest on the debt. I did not know yet my method of revenge. Slicing the throat of those responsible for the Order would feel wonderful in the moment, but I am certain I would regret their lack of prolonged pain and torment.

I could try to ruin the leaders the way I did Lady Nora. Her elaborate embarrassment and death were a huge professional satisfaction for me. But the Order of the Labyrinth is a much more powerful organization than a single wealthy noblewoman, and far more elusive at that. Plus, it would be hard to ruin the reputation of the most notorious (and mysterious) pirates in the world, if such pirates even existed. Perhaps, like the Duke of

The Duke's Own, the leadership of the Order was only a story, and each part of the Order acted on its own accord. How would I ever take revenge against something so amorphous?

No, I would have to believe there was some single man, the decision maker behind every crime the Order perpetrated. Chopping off his hands would be good. Straightforward mutilation is always a good start if pain is what you're after. Maybe cut out his tongue. I could cook it and feed it to him. Or slice open his gut and let him watch as his innards uncoil from his belly. How ghoulish. That wouldn't do, either.

Planning was important, but it could certainly lead to disappointment. My opportunity may be brief. I might not even have time to tell him my name and his crimes before I pierce his heart. I needed to prepare myself for all possibilities. Would I be okay with his death if he did not know why he died? No, I thought. The revenge wasn't in the death, but the moment of dawning realization just before death.

Who even was my mark? Perhaps if I were to someday join the inner circle of the Order, I could find the man who destroyed my family. And that man would know his sins. He would know me. He would hear my name, my story, and my victory. He would bleed out along with the whole Order of the Labyrinth.

With my eyes closed I could see him. I could not make out his face, nor discern his voice. Yet I knew that this evil man was waiting for me. Perhaps the future lives inside the eyelids as well. But how to get to that unknown man, if he existed as a single person, was still unclear. At this point, I was lying flat on my back in my narrow cot and cramped berth where I had lain each night for nearly a decade.

And as focused as I was on destroying this imaginary man,

this leader I had conjured for the Order, I could not reach him. Even in my own daydream, I could not say anything that he could hear. He watched me struggle to act, and he laughed. I gritted my teeth and I could taste the metallic salt of my own blood. I could not wake myself up. I could only listen to the laughter grow louder.

3

I heard a soft rapping at the door, and opened my eyes. For a few moments I could not move. My mind had awoken from its failed dream, but my body had not. Another gentle tap on the door. A soft voice, "Captain? Are you in there, ma'am?"

My legs finally twitched. I arose and opened the door.

It was clever, sweet Samuel.

"We have some wine left. You want a glass?" he asked.

I invited him in and offered him the chair at my desk, seating myself on the edge of my cot. He poured us two glasses of wine and spoke while staring into his own. "I have a friend, a cook on an Order ship in the east. He came to see me when we returned to *The Wasp*, and he brought me highly interesting news. There's an envoy of spice ships moving out of Persia, toward Spain. My friend tells me that his ship is one of many that the Order is sending against it."

"Against it?"

"A heist, but also a war. The Order isn't in the business of stealing spices. They're in the business of stealing businesses. They're going to lock down the Mediterranean and control the entire spice market."

I grunted. Samuel studied me. "Bad dreams? Drink your wine, captain."

I did. All of it. It was tart and dry. My mouth felt full of fur, and my throat swollen. My head felt lighter, though, like someone had removed my heavy skull from my tender neck. My shoulders loosened and my back straightened. I wished I had cold water instead of this fetid wine, but for all the discomfort my mouth was in, the rest of my body was grateful.

He filled my glass again.

"I'm not built for combat," he continued. He was honest in his assessment. Samuel had a thin frame, but more importantly his expression was one of kindness, or maybe it was a kind veneer covering a firm sense of self-preservation. I couldn't imagine him plunging a blade into another young man or being forcibly enlisted into battle to protect the wealthy from the desperate.

"But combat is not the totality of war," he said. "I know you want to play a larger part in the Order of the Labyrinth. You're ambitious." He leaned toward me, dropping his voice although we were alone in the cabin. "I am too."

I studied his face closely. I could see the ambition in his eyes, or perhaps it was the drink that had loosened him up. I wanted desperately to join this war, to be noticed by the highest command of the Order, but they don't tend to send gilded invitations to join in their deadly festivities.

"Samuel, what led you to join the Order?"

He hesitated to answer, sipping his wine and looking at his delicate hands.

"I always knew that I was smart enough to be part of great things. But where I am from, there are no great things. There are the crops and the animals. There is feeding yourself and your family. That is the limit of the horizon. I couldn't accept that limit. A man came to my village, passing through on his way to the coast. He stopped at the inn and he asked me to take care of his horse. We started talking, and I suppose he saw something in me. He asked me to join him. The next day I rode out of town on the back of his horse. I haven't seen my family since, but I have seen so much that I would not have otherwise seen."

"Ambition has a deep price," I agreed.

"But ambition has a vast reward. What of this news I bring you?"

"It will take some consideration," I said.

"More wine?" he asked, with a conspiratorial wink. I accepted, and we turned our talk to lighter subjects, the weather in the nearby sea, the frantic eagerness of our newer deckhands freshly picked up from the ports of Europe.

We returned to Ca'Savio. Vlad was cradling the satchel of fingers in his palms and smiling. I almost thought I heard him singing to himself, or worse, singing to the fingers. He was reluctant to hand over the bag to Holger, but with a sad nod, he did.

Holger winced like a person who had just had a blood-stained bag full of body parts thrust at him. He accepted them, opened up the bag and counted the fingers.

"The constable really did have a family," Holger said, surprised. "My god."

"Holger, *The Wasp* is your best crew. We have successfully— and easily, I must add—plundered, swindled, and killed for the Order. My crew and I could do so much more."

"I'm sure you can," Holger said, not looking the least intrigued as to where I was going with this conversation.

"I hear the Order of the Labyrinth has engaged in a full-scale war on the Persian spice traders." I had rehearsed this speech so many times I could have given it while napping. "This conflict could mean complete control of all Mediterranean shipping routes for the Order. *The Wasp* offers its excellent service to this cause."

Holger didn't say anything. I wished I had let the silence linger, had let him finish his thoughts, but my impatience compelled me to continue.

"You challenge us with bigger and bigger jobs, and every time we not only achieve your expectations but exceed them. We have yet to meet anyone in the Order except you. We cannot improve our status, unless we join our brethren in their endeavors."

Holger considered me for another moment and then said, "If we're going to undermine the trade ships coming from the east, we need to undermine the markets in the west. Livestock and vegetable farmers, dock owners, all the way down to small produce markets who buy from the wrong people. No more banks or casinos or large shipping conglomerates. We must remove the weeds so the flowers can grow."

I did not like where this was headed.

"You and your crew will stay close to the coast. Intimidate people," he said, "until we know they'll buy our spices. Kill them if you have to. Kill them even if you don't."

Vlad clapped his hands vigorously at this.

I was crushed. My victims were moving down the hierarchy, not up. For the sake of the bigger picture, I agreed. I tried to picture my father's face, but the memory was less clear every year, and I couldn't quite recall it as it was.

"Report back to me," Holger said. "Bring proof of what you've done."

"More fingers," Vlad interjected with delight.

"Fingers, legs, ears. Whatever," Holger said, clearly regretting having asked for more severed body parts to be dropped in his lap. "But take their goods too. Think of it as a tax for the Order."

I thanked him and we turned to leave. When I was nearly to the door, Holger shouted after me, "I made it up."

"Excuse me?" I said, turning back.

"I visited Augsburg a few years back and met that constable at a tavern," Holger said. "Nice man. Didn't have a thing against him. Just someone I remembered. Poor fellow. Did you burn his house down? Members of the Order just love burning down houses."

I could taste the bitterness of lemons again in my throat.

"The Order is pleased to know you're willing to kill," Holger said. "You've passed the test. But you can keep these."

Holger lobbed the fingers back. Vlad cackled as he lunged forward to nestle the falling bag in his thick, dirty palms.

"I'll make a necklace," he squealed.

I didn't speak as we returned to the ship. What were words against what I had done against an innocent man and his family? Searching for some excuse to think about anything else, I invited Vlad to my cabin and asked him a question that had been plaguing me for some years now. Vlad truly loved murder and I wanted to know why.

He cocked his head. The question "Why do you like to murder?" was to Vlad as the question "Why do you eat food?" was to any other person.

I decide to start with something simpler. "Vlad, have you ever been in love?"

"Azra," Vlad said, a sudden smile across his sun-wrought face. The thick lines about his eyes and cheeks disappeared, as his face brightened. "She is in Chișinău."

"Is that where you were born? Is that your home?"

"Those are two very different questions," Vlad said, sadness drawing over his face like curtains at the end of an opera.

Vlad and Azra were both born in Chișinău. Vlad's father had been a cobbler in Kursk, but a devastating fire shortly before Vlad was born sent the family south to find work. They had heard of a thriving city in Moldavia, and they moved to Chișinău. The Greek governance in Chișinău was friendly to Russians, for a while. But by the turn of the century, when Vlad was a teenager, political tensions grew between the Ottoman and Russian Empires.

He saw his father begin to struggle to find work. Vlad's Greek, French, and Turkish friends began to shun him and his family. The only exception was Azra, the daughter of a wealthy Turkish banker. Vlad first saw Azra in a park, sketching swans and flowers. He noted that her pictures were not realistic, as was the classical fashion. She drew absurdly long necks on the birds, and silly faces that sometimes placed the beak above the eyes or trees in the background with human-like arms.

Azra's pictures made Vlad laugh, and Vlad's laughter made Azra feel understood. Azra's father hated that she "did not take art seriously." Vlad did not understand the history of classical painting. He only knew what he saw, and what he saw was funny and compelling. He loved her for it. And Azra loved Vlad for his honest admiration of her.

But a push by the Russian Empire to secure their land against the west led to a confrontation across Moldavia. Vlad, fifteen years old, and thus a grown man, was pressed into military service.

He fought the Turks, pushing as far south as Bucharest, quickly gaining the reputation of a madman, a fierce warrior who would not relent until all enemies were vanquished. The other soldiers in his unit encouraged his behavior by telling him to make earrings out of teeth or small bags out of scalps. He even tattooed tick marks for every soldier he killed, using a white-hot knife on his arm. His unit was the first time that anyone outside of his family, except Azra, showed him friendliness and acceptance. The more vicious he became, the more well liked he was by his comrades.

When the war ended in 1812, he returned home. Azra's family remained in Chișinău, but the city was divided into Ottoman and Russian sides, and she was no longer allowed to speak to Vlad. He tried visiting her home and knocking on the door, but he was turned away by servants, never getting the chance to plead his love. He tried calling to her from below her window, but was arrested by Turkish police and sent back to the eastern, Russian part of the city with a stern warning of unmarked cells in unnamed prisons if he was found loitering again.

After a year back in Chișinău, he could not stand it anymore. He missed the war, but there was no war, so he left for the Mediterranean, where he heard shipping conglomerates were looking for security against pirates. He found plenty of work, but it was dull. Eventually he met people from the Order of the Labyrinth, who recruited him, using the promise of constant adventure and violence as incentive.

I thought about my childhood friend Albert, who I had

never made any attempt to contact. This wasn't for my sake but for his. I didn't want to intrude on the peace of his life. And it made me feel a little more stable, imagining that somewhere there was someone who had once been a part of my life who got to live in simple happiness, where no one was killed, where nothing was stolen. Still, I asked Vlad, "Have you ever written to Azra?"

He looked down at his hands.

"Do you know how to write or read, Vlad?"

An almost imperceptible shake of his head "no."

"Vlad." I placed my hand on his hands, folded meekly in his lap. "I will help you write a letter to Azra."

"I want to write it in my own hand, my own words," he said.

"And you will," I said, and his rough hands squeezed mine in agreement.

4

So another three tedious years stopping in ports, doing Holger's busy work, as the great war over the spice trade was fought somewhere else.

At each town, I would send Rebekah inland ahead of the crew, whom I had told to take an evening to get some drink and some rest before beginning the intimidation of mostly poor farm and dock workers the next day. I needed to give Rebekah time to do her work.

Rebekah had crafted a hood, matching the Order of the Labyrinth men we had seen on countless ships in our years of pursuing higher membership. She would advance onto farms ahead of Nathan and the crew, in order to protect these innocent people. Rebekah could carry herself in a way that suggested someone tall and broad-shouldered, her voice deepening into a disaffected baritone. This mysterious pirate of the Order would advance on unsuspecting dock owners and warn them that they had to relieve all of their workers for the next day. Her associates would approach in the morning and claim a "tax" of food and merchandise. Failure to obey would lead to the abuse and possibly slaughter of many of their employees.

André and Lora would go with *The Wasp* crew and try to mitigate any situations that could result in death, or uncontrolled violence. André developed a friendship with Vlad out of necessity, and a soft word from him could keep the Russian's murderous urges at bay while Lora would offer to crush any dock owner who dared to protest the tax. Lora had exquisite control over her own body, so she could grab a man into her chest, leap, and slam him hard to the ground, an act that would appear, due to her size, to snap the man's spine. But she would skillfully do this in a way that kept bones intact, if leaving the person unconscious and a little sore. This was the best plan we had for showing the Order we could brutalize the weak while still minimizing real harm.

Between these stops we would occasion upon other ships of the Order with their black flags and white labyrinth emblems proudly extended in the wind. I did not know what I would do should one of these ships join us in our attack on the coastal farmers and merchants. It was one thing to fool Nathan and the Order members on *The Wasp*, but it would be an impossible task to con an entire brig of hooded men.

But these ships never docked in any of our same ports. In fact, these ships never seemed to dock at all. Save for Holger, Señora Bover, and whatever crew had murdered my father, I had never heard of any members of the Order spotted on land. I had never seen them board another ship, or even engage in combat. My only knowledge of these other Order sailors was that they were all the same height, neither tall nor short, and that they wore hoods.

By spring of 1828, my crew had wounded thousands of innocent farmers, merchants, and traders. The number of dead had to be in the dozens, and I was no closer to the inner sanctum of the Order of the Labyrinth than the day Señora Bover brought me to this ship. I had encountered at least a hundred other vessels that shared our flag, but I had never meaningfully spoken with any of their crew, let alone captains.

We approached southern Spain, and I ordered Samuel to take us to Barcelona. When we docked, I told Nathan to give the crew a full night and next day off. No more intimidations. We would return to Ca'Savio in two days with our current bounty, which was more than enough for Holger.

"You tell the crew to take some time to enjoy ourselves, captain," Nathan said, "but you and your friends never join us. You should come have drinks with your men, so they do not feel you dislike them."

"I have a someone I must see tonight."

"Who is this someone?" Nathan said, a touch of suspicion in his tone.

"It is none of your business," I said. Then I said, "It's my uncle," and hoped to leave it at that. I did not want to explain my close relationship to Edmond, a longtime member of The Duke's Own, which rivaled the Order for control of the continent. This nearly familial kinship with an enemy could do more than get me blacklisted by the Order of the Labyrinth. "Unless stories of me playing checkers as a child is information you are required to be filled in on, I believe you are done here, first mate."

"Yes, ma'am," he said, in a polite and even tone, and we parted ways till morning.

I called on Edmond at his home, and he welcomed me in with a long hug and a glowing smile. His face was more worn than the last time I saw him some three years before, like a parchment that had been wadded up and smoothed back out. Edmond had always felt much older to me, because I knew him as a child, but fourteen years at sea with the Order had put me in my mid-thirties. Edmond was fifty-one. He was ten years younger than my father, which did not read to me when I was a girl, but age gaps dwindle over time, and given my friendships with men even older than Edmond, I only now realized we more resembled close colleagues than a child and guardian.

"You're a damn captain, you are," he said in our embrace. He pulled back, his hands on my elbows.

"I am," I managed.

"You don't seem happy about it."

"Let's get some ale first." I sat, allowing myself to feel the years of exhaustion.

"Sounds like we need something finer than that." He excused himself, returning a few minutes later with a bottle.

"Svitzian wine usually tastes of fortified treacle, but this," Edmond held up the dusty bottle with an ornate label emblazoned with a sketch of a dragon devouring a ewe, "is like black pepper and honey but with the body of a beef broth."

We sat at the great table adjacent to the parlor, and a servant brought us goblets, opened the wine, and poured.

Edmond and I touched glasses, and I sipped the stolen wine—no doubt pilfered from peasants by The Duke's Own. He was right about the taste, at first savory and thick, like soup, but as it washed over the tongue, there was a pinprick of spice underneath a sweet nectar. It wasn't cloying, more like tea gently dabbed with sugar and blood.

"How is Señora Bover?"

"Who?" He looked genuinely puzzled.

"The old woman—your neighbor—always out on the stoop, outside your home."

"Ah," he said. "Yes. I'm sorry. I don't think I ever spoke a word to her. She was an old woman, wasn't she? I fear in the many years you have been gone, she may have passed."

I was certain she was neither dead, nor an old woman. I told Edmond as such. I filled him in on Señora Bover and *The Wasp*. He set down his wine in astonishment.

"I certainly knew you had joined the Order. You have written me about your many adventures, but I had no idea I had been living over a spy. A spymaster who cannot spot spies at his own doorstep is a poor spymaster indeed."

"Edmond, I'm worried that the Order already knows about my relationship with you. Señora Bover watched your work for years. My first mate, who was assigned to me by the Order, fills journal after journal with the details of every day at sea, and, I think, the details of my every move. If they knew you were . . ."

"Sshhh," he said. "I am your uncle, child. I am your guardian. My work has nothing to do with yours, and we will not talk about business here."

Suddenly aware of how many corners a person could hide in within a room that big, I nodded and sat completely silent.

Edmond laughed and said, "Oh, just keep your voice down and tell me what you have been up to."

I told Edmond about our adventures, and about Holger. I then told him (quietly) what I heard from Samuel about the war the Order was waging on Persian spice ships out east. I told him how desperately I wanted to join this war.

"Your little ship doesn't sound like it could handle being that far out at sea," he said, "let alone engage in full-on naval battles. My spies tell me the fighting has been vicious. Neither side is willing to relent even a little."

"Edmond," I leaned in and whispered carefully, "you know what I want. I need to move up in the ranks. This organization is as shadowed as the faces of their sailors. For fourteen years, I have not had my position brighten at all. I have tried to impress Holger, to communicate with the other vessels of the Order, but nothing is different. I have grown wealthier but angrier, and I am no closer to my true purpose."

"A job that brings you wealth is nothing to be ashamed of." As he said this, he snapped his fingers and the servant returned to pour us more wine.

He was attempting to mollify me and change the conversation, but this only made me more determined. "I'm torn because of Nathan, my first mate," I continued, still in a low voice. "I must impress him, as I am certain his journals are being sent off to those above Holger, but he does not want me to deviate from the small jobs assigned to us, even though it was my initiative in bringing down Lady Nora that earned my role in the Order in the first place."

The wine had gone to my temper instead of my stomach.

Edmond placed his hand on the table in front of me. "Do you remember what I told you about the art of persuasion?"

"When I was a child," I said. "You told me that if you made me go to bed, I'd rebel. But if you could manipulate the situation so that I believed the idea to go to bed was my own, then I would happily go."

He nodded. "A first mate, a spouse, a friend, anyone in this world, is no different than a child in this matter. You must not tell Nathan what to do. Nothing must ever be your idea."

"I must make him arrive at the idea on his own."

Edmond raised his glass to me. "You were always the bright one. Now can we talk about something else? I'm tired of whispering."

We talked about smaller things. Edmond had taken up poetry. I told him about Rebekah teaching me how to sew, which I think was just Rebekah's ploy to get me to mend Lora's clothes, a task too much for any one person. As we were finishing our meal and last drinks, I thought about asking Edmond if he remembered Albert, but save for those few final moments as we left the estate, Edmond would never have met Albert.

I spent the rest of my life thankful that I did not bring up Albert in that beautiful room, over those glasses of beautiful wine.

"It's late. I must get some rest," he said, the lines in his face deepened by the candlelight below us. "Stay here tonight. I'll have a room readied for you."

I agreed, and that night, on the largest, softest bed I had experienced in decades, I dreamed.

My crew and I were boarding rival pirate ships, taking their gold and executing each sailor, one by one. I walked down the line of men, each one on their knees, hands tied behind their back, and I looked them in their eyes. I told them my name and that they should remember my face in whatever world was next. And I cut their throats. One after another I repeated this.

Then I came upon one man. He looked up at me and he had Albert's face. Not whatever Albert looked like as an adult, but the young face of the boy I knew and loved from childhood. I stopped. Vlad yelled, "Execute them all!" He was floating several feet in the air, his red-lined eyes matching the ruby blood pouring from his mouth. He wore a necklace of fingers and each finger squirmed, beckoning me upward to Vlad's strange place in the sky.

I could not execute the man before me. Albert's face was so innocent, I could not kill this beautiful sailor. I said, "Albert." Not a question, a confirmation.

"Albert," I said again. "Remember when we swam together in the cove?"

But he did not respond.

André put his hand on my shoulder. He looked like Lora, in every way he was Lora, but in the dream I knew it was André. "He is not who you think," André said.

I looked back at the sailor with the face of Albert. The face seemed to be melting, it looked fake. Just then I realized he was wearing a hood. He was neither tall nor short.

Vlad, in the air, was changing, and I realized it was not Vlad but Rebekah disguised as Vlad. The fingers moved obscenely on her necklace. "It's not him," she called. "He's not who you think he is."

When I looked again at Albert, I could no longer see his face. I tried to move back, but found I was paralyzed. The man with no face who was not tall and was not short watched me struggle to move and laughed. I knew that laughter. I had heard it before.

Then Rebekah as Vlad swooped down, opening her mouth and screeching like a bird, and grabbed me. I flopped awake. I was alone in my bed in Edmond's Barcelona home, listening to the screeching of birds outside. It sounded a little like laughter.

Not able to return to sleep, I cleaned and dressed myself in the lavender glow of predawn.

I wrote Edmond a note thanking him for his kindness, but before I left, I went to his study, only two doors down from my room on the second floor. I lit a lantern and looked at the hundreds of leather-bound books I saw along the walls. There were histories of empires, most of which began with a rise, and ended with a fall, although some ended with a transformation. There were Greek classics of reason, logic, and philosophy. There were Christian Bibles written in dozens of languages. There were odes to something called the Brown Stone Spire written in archaic language and with what appeared to be blood instead of ink.

I had no particular book I was looking for. I was a woman with questions, and no answers. Books can help with that, but only if you know what it is you seek. I wanted only to learn something, anything, about the Order of the Labyrinth. For an organization as large as theirs, there must certainly be books, histories, something written on them, but I found very little. In a book about the history of pirates of North Africa, I found a mention of ships bearing a Labyrinth emblem, but it read as rumor or conspiracy. The ships had no history of combat, only that they were often seen along the coasts.

Another book about the Turkish textile trade, I found the phrase "the labyrinth flag." The book referred to the group of ships which bore the labyrinth flag as a peaceful private business. "It is uncertain what goods this organization brings across shipping routes, only that they carry unmarked crates that seem to radiate light," the book said.

I could not even find the phrase "The Order of the Labyrinth," only passing mention, and unattributed lore about boats that share a fondness for glowing crates and black flags. People feared and fled from these ships, but I found no accounts of interactions, nor a single name of anyone who had ever been aboard one of these ships. I despaired at the thought that I might never penetrate this organization, that my life would run out without ever getting to see the face of my father's killer. I could not keep following Holger. In fourteen years, I had moved no higher than when I first set foot on *The Wasp*. I had to get Nathan to convince himself to join the Order's war on Persian spice traders. It was the only chance I had.

I left Edmond's and hired a carriage to take me to the port. Along the way, I saw a small vegetable stand burned to the ground. A hundred feet on, a market with all of its windows shattered. Inside I saw a woman hunched over a body, her face pressed into her blood-stained hands, as she heaved great gulping sobs.

A crowd had gathered, each person talking quickly and loudly, trying to piece together every account of the violence on this street. I began to slow the carriage, so I could help in some way, or find out what happened. On the rooftop above the scene, I saw a man lurching, stumbling and clutching his chest. It was the man, the phantom, who had followed me my entire life. His eyes bulged obscenely from their sockets, only a slight tilt of the head away from falling out completely. He clutched his blood-soaked chest as he mouthed silently, "Why?" No one in the concerned crowd noticed him. I did not know who this man was, or what he wanted from me, but he had become as natural a part of my life as the passing of years. And like the passing of years, I feared him terribly. I told the driver to hurry, and I left.

There were more destroyed shops and vendors at the port. I reached *The Wasp* as dawn became day to find our whole crew cleaning the deck. Nathan, in his finest silk shirt and perfectly polished boots, saw me and smiled.

"You are up early, captain," he said. "The crew and I were too, so we got some work done."

"What have you done?" I said, my voice breathy and desperate.

"You don't look happy? Why would a captain not be happy with an overachieving crew?"

I looked around for André, Rebekah, and Lora.

"Your friends are in the galley. For some reason, they seem disappointed too. Have I not done a good job, captain? I could send our men out to do more, to really pave the way for the Order. I know you would like to impress the Order of the Labyrinth." I wanted to punch him, but I needed to keep him and his journals reflecting my best intentions for the Order if I were ever to lift my status higher than captain of *The Wasp*.

"First mate, I ordered rest and relaxation. You deliberately disobeyed me," I said loud enough for the crew to hear. "Your work, and the work of this crew, is of the highest quality. I thank you all for your dedication. But when I give an order you follow it. Is that clear?"

Nathan smirked. "Yes, captain."

I went below deck to my cabin and talked to Rebekah, André, and Lora. They were caught unaware by Nathan's early morning attack on the workers of Barcelona, and they had done nothing to prepare the people of this city.

I called for our navigator, Samuel, and he joined us shortly.

"Nathan smells weakness," he said.

"Forget Nathan. What else do you know of the war on the Persian traders?" I asked.

"I bought Persian maps which show their Mediterranean trade routes. I also met an Egyptian merchant in the bar who told me the Persians often stop in Cyprus where taxes are lower, and they can hire gunboats for escorts. I've been trying to get hold of my friend on the other Order boat, but there has been no word from him since they left for war."

"I'm impressed with your enthusiasm," I said.

"Captain, we should be in the east, taking over spice ships, instead of roughing up poor Catalan farmers."

I knew Vlad would be up for a war as well. I had been teaching Vlad to read and write for the past four years. He began sending letters once a month to Azra, finding messengers in ports and paying them gold for a promise to carry the letters overland. Sure, some of these messengers might discard the letter and keep the gold, but we hoped that with enough letters sent some of them would feel obligated to make good on their promises, especially with the possibility of running into someone so enthusiastically violent as Vlad again in the future.

The early letters had a stilted, childlike charm ("Hello. I am Vlad. I am fine. How are you?") but by late last year, he had begun to incorporate some more advanced poetic elements ("Hello. I am happily Vlad. I am like a dog who is happy but lost. I want to hear your laughter again. Your laughter is like a rose that can laugh in a nice way.") I didn't edit Vlad. He insisted on writing his own letters. Sadly, no messages from Azra had ever made their way back. Vlad had begun to think she did not love him anymore, or worse, did not remember him. I reassured him that it's possible her parents were hiding the letters from her, and maybe she had never seen them, or none of the messengers she had sent back had bothered to find *The Wasp*.

But Vlad grew despondent. He kept up his monthly letters,

but his demeanor aboard *The Wasp* had become more blood-thirsty, less disciplined. We could not always control his violence in altercations. Getting him more involved in this greater conflict would assuredly focus his energy.

Nathan, however, was a problem.

I approached the first mate in his berth. He was, as usual, writing in his log.

"First mate," I called, with Samuel behind me. Nathan stood at attention. "I have been made aware of the Order of the Labyrinth's war on the Persian spice traders."

Nathan's face contorted, preparing for an argument. I continued, "*The Wasp*, of course, is not built for naval conflict, so I do not believe this is a tenable mission. Not to mention Holger has not authorized such an action. The crew is restless for greater battles, so I seek your opinion."

"Captain, it is with only great respect that I caution you that—" Nathan began smugly, but he was stopped short by the sound of a loud crash from above deck.

We heard shouting, surrounded by cheering as the three of us scrambled up the stairs.

On the main deck we saw Vlad standing over one of the other crew, a slab of a boy who worked in the kitchen. The boy's thick, round face was marred by a deep purple welt that was oozing blood at an alarming rate. The rest of the crew was cheering on the battle. The boy scrambled to his feet, but Vlad barked while dancing around him in a semicircle and waving a broken barrel stave. Vlad had fully lost his mind.

Nathan broke up the fight, and the galley boy stumbled away, clutching his forehead. Lora grabbed Vlad and held him in place. Nathan ordered the crew back to their stations and then dressed down Vlad, held firmly by both shoulders against

Lora's torso. Vlad literally growled at Nathan. Perhaps he was playing his part a little over the top, but Nathan seemed to buy it, stepping back with a twinge of fear on his face.

"He is growing restless," Lora said. "He's a great fighter being made to pick pockets."

"We're not attacking those spice ships," I glared at Lora. "This crew is just not equipped for that."

"It's all about wealth and status with you," Lora roared. "'We can't disappoint Holger,' you say. 'I'll never get promoted,' you say. What about us? What about those of us who use our bodies for your living?"

Nathan put up a hand to Lora, saying "Sailor, I won't have you—" but she drove him aside.

"You don't even want to fight with the farmers and merchants on shore," she said. "We all see it. Our captain doesn't have the stomach to fight!"

Even though we'd scripted this altercation, I'll admit, Lora's words hurt.

"Stand down, giant!" Nathan shouted. He turned to me, "Captain, I apologize for this disorder and I will deal with it personally. Navigator!"

Nathan and Samuel retired to Nathan's room. I hoped Samuel's performance skills were half as good as Lora's. A few minutes later, they returned to the deck. Nathan said, "Captain, we have discussed the options, and I believe we should engage the Persian ships."

"This would be a big decision. It doesn't seem wise. Navigator, what do you think?" I asked. Samuel made a show of hesitating, then nodded thoughtfully.

"Yes, Captain, I believe it may be the right choice."

I sighed, bit my lip, and looked over at Vlad who was panting and sharpening his wood plank with a small knife. I pretended to search my conscience.

"Every person on this ship needs better discipline than they've shown to this point," I proclaimed. "That is your job, first mate. We sail east tomorrow."

"Yes, ma'am," Nathan and Samuel said in perfect unison. I did my utmost to maintain my face in an expression of steady worry, but I felt a surge of elation that made me feel like I was ten feet in the air, looking down at my busy crew. Finally, we were moving forward.

The sea was clear of storms and ships. I was pleased with the former, dismayed by the latter. By the time we had reached Malta, I had seen almost no traffic. Samuel referenced the trade route maps he purchased in Spain, but we did not happen across any Persian ships. Nor did we see any of the familiar Labyrinth flags.

We docked in Valletta for two nights to sell stolen goods, clearing space in our hold. The crew was given two days off in preparation for a long journey with few stops.

I approached Samuel about our lack of contact with a single Persian ship.

"It's possible an engagement with the Order of the Labyrinth has slowed their travels, Captain." Samuel looked perplexed, possibly near panic over his failure to locate a single ship.

I accepted his explanation because impatience had tipped the scale of my judiciousness. Single-minded fervor to join the Order in combat was my sole focus. I had only the excitement of movement after these years of purgatory.

Samuel routed us to Cyprus. A fortnight of no traffic and unusual rain, culminating in a storm two nights before we arrived. Two of our sailors on the mainmast fell overboard, and I mourned the first loss of life *The Wasp* had experienced in my fifteen years as captain. Men are a formidable force worthy of our full attention, which is why nature must remind us that it is an immortal god, capable of ending any of us in a moment.

We limped into the Cyprian port of Lemesós, under the cool glow of a full moon against clear skies. In the port, I saw a ship bearing the flag of the Qajar lion: a golden beast holding aloft a sword, behind it a leering sun, poking up only halfway behind the lion, suggesting the sun was either dawning or hiding.

As the actual sun mounted the eastern horizon in fantastic animation of the Persian emblem, we scanned the port for potential attack points, as well as vulnerabilities. On the back of the trader ship was the lettering: دلفین. A Cretan crew member translated this for us as "The Dolphin." A smaller gunboat docked on *The Dolphin*'s starboard had no distinctive marks, outside of side-mounted cannons. But otherwise, no flags or titles. Samuel suspected it served as an armed escort for the valuable cargo.

I sent Rebekah and André on reconnaissance to the other side of the port, where they could size up the crew and potential weapons on the smaller ship. I knew *The Dolphin* would have tight security and arms of its own, even with the accompanying sentry vessel, but Nathan had a plan for that. We could use *The Wasp* to blockade the larger *Dolphin* while subduing the smaller ship. If we could overtake the gunboat, we would have *The Dolphin* completely surrounded.

The ships were docked at the far end of the port in Lemesós, which if we could keep any cannons from firing, would buy us more time before police or Cyprian military showed.

André and Rebekah returned with a report of eight men on the gunboat armed with swords or small blades. They did not see rifles, but there was a single cannon both port and starboard. Rebekah estimated around three dozen on *The Dolphin*.

"That will exert every last member of our crew," I told Nathan. I knew I could not convince him to convince himself to engage in an all-out attack on two ships. I could not even convince myself of this, but I knew where I wanted him to go. Edmond had taught me well on how to manipulate another's decision-making.

"Without a larger crew," he began, "a full assault would be impossible. We need to board *The Dolphin* under a false pretense. I believe we have a member of our crew who is quite adept at that."

"Yes, of course," I said. "Our objective is to let them know the Order of the Labyrinth owns these waters. A minimum success is to turn them back home. A greater achievement is to remove their cargo and destroy their ship. Can we do this with our small crew, first mate?"

Nathan thought we could, and we set to work devising a plan.

Rebekah, dressed as a Cyprian tax collector, would board *The Dolphin*. She would demand an extra tax on the Persians' goods. This would draw the captain of the ship into a complicated conversation. This ruse could buy us up to an hour. Meanwhile, Samuel would steer *The Wasp* directly behind *The Dolphin*. Lora, having attached hooks to the ends of ropes, would cast those to the ship's stern, and our crew could climb aboard. Caught off-guard and without attention from their leader, the crew would be off-balance, easier to push back. We would then hold the captain at knifepoint as André led the crew down to the hold to take *The Dolphin*'s cargo.

Lora would enter the gunboat on the far easternmost slip. Her goal was simple: attack anything that was in the path of the port cannon. Upon André's command, she would fire the cannon into the hull of *The Dolphin*, thus incapacitating it, as the rest of *The Wasp* crew escaped.

It was not a foolproof plan, but it was a good plan.

My hopes were raised as I saw two large brigs sailing into port. My heart raced when I noticed the familiar black flags with white labyrinth emblems proudly whipping atop each mast. I had never felt anything like patriotism or pride in a nation until that moment. I forgot that my goal was to destroy this Order, and instead felt for a moment that us members of the Order were perfectly united against our common enemy. We had perfectly timed our approach. If anything were to go wrong on board *The Dolphin*, the Order of the Labyrinth ships would arrive momentarily, bolstering our forces and our confidence.

Samuel maneuvered *The Wasp* behind *The Dolphin*, as Lora hurled hooked ropes upward. André and I led the climb, with the rest of the crew coming behind us. Above us was quiet, which I took as an auspicious sign—no alarms, no shouting, only the dull muttering of people being confused over taxes.

I was halfway up the rope, and I stared out over the open water. The two Order brigs were still there, moving slowly, like a fog, toward the docks. I was tempted to wave to my pirate mates but refrained from such silliness. As I neared the top of the rope, ready to climb over and draw my weapon, I looked once more at the brigs. A doubt had crept in, and I wanted to revisit it.

The brigs were pointed slightly askance of a port-bound trajectory. They were not stopping here. They were ignoring us. In a crystal moment, knowledge bubbled up from deep in my subconscious. The Order was not in a war with the Persians at all.

A lump formed in my throat as I crested the deck of *The Dolphin*. We had prepared for a stealthy entrance onto the deck, at which point we would quietly disperse throughout the aft, catching *The Dolphin* crew completely off-guard. What we encountered instead was the captain of the ship, only fifteen feet from us, holding a dagger at the throat of a Cyprian tax collector.

"Drop your swords, and bring me your captain," the man with the blade said. Surrounding him were two dozen or more armed men. André and I turned back toward our crew to order them to do as instructed. But our crew had not emerged from atop the ropes. A quick glance down and I saw two dozen cowards gliding back down the ropes to *The Wasp*. On *The Wasp*'s deck was Nathan calling them back. I counted only eight of our crew reaching the deck of our ship before Nathan cut the ropes to *The Dolphin* and ordered the sails raised. The remaining dozen or so men on the ropes, no doubt as surprised as I was by Nathan's betrayal, swung back toward the great cargo ship, slammed hard into the hull, and fell limply into the water below.

My gut spun, and I felt my knees try to give. I wobbled in place as *The Dolphin*'s men surrounded André and me.

We dropped our swords, and I turned toward the man threatening Rebekah. "I am the captain," I said, and stepped forward. The Persian sailors took our weapons and two of them grabbed André by his arms.

"I am Captain Iraj," said the man with the knife at Rebekah's neck. "Your friend here is a convincing Cyprian but not a convincing tax collector. My ships bring more money to this island than anyone. My closest friend, Mirza, is the head of collections for the city of Lemesós. I know every man in his office, and they would not haggle me over a few thousand piastres."

"I dropped my weapon. Let her go," I said. And Iraj did. Rebekah stepped calmly away from him and stood next to me.

"Tell me. Why do you raise that flag above your ship?" he asked.

"We are the Order of the Labyrinth," I began, but he laughed.

"Enough with your unconvincing playacting. The Order of the Labyrinth does not involve itself in thievery or barbarism."

"You are at war—" I stammered, not believing the explanation I was about to give.

"I am not at war. I am in business," Iraj said.

"This is a misunderstanding," I said, more to myself than to Iraj. The truth articulated itself for me horribly. Nathan's mutiny, the deliberate ignorance of our efforts by other Order ships, Captain Iraj's honest declaration: I was not a member of the Order of the Labyrinth, and neither was anyone I knew. Nathan had betrayed my trust in this assignment, and there was no doubt he had betrayed me much more deeply. "We mean your ship no harm, then," I added, convinced that we, in fact, did not mean to harm a ship that had nothing to do with the Order of the Labyrinth.

Iraj laughed again. His warm charm was second only to

André's. "You confuse intention with preparation. You meant great harm to me."

Waving lazily to his crew, he concluded, "Kill them."

As Iraj's words came out, André had already grabbed the two men holding him at knifepoint and swung them into three others. He grabbed one of the dropped swords and tossed one to me.

A sailor swung directly toward the back of André's head. He ducked as it passed. Whirling, he kicked the man's legs out. André disarmed him and threw the other sword to Rebekah, who was already running to assist. Captain Iraj and I engaged our blades. He was smiling, with soft, joyful divots deep into his round cheeks. I could tell he had left the young man's world of soldiering to become a business owner. The spice trade was more lucrative, but nowhere near as thrilling. He looked giddy at the nostalgia of returning to his old fighting form.

As André and Rebekah battled back his sailors, less competent than their captain with swords, Iraj and I danced about, tapping occasionally but each waiting for the right moment to strike.

"Keep on your toes," André shouted. "Reinforcements!"

I looked over Iraj's shoulders to see two dozen more of his men, fully armed, charging into the fray.

"Shit," I exclaimed, and in my moment of distraction, Iraj lunged.

I was not prepared. My sword was low and not balanced. I did not have enough time to parry. The sharp tip of Iraj's blade plunged toward my heart. I had a split second to reconcile my entire life to this point. In the slowing of time, I could hear André shouting Lora's name. An immense boom jostled the ship and hurled us nearly off our feet. Iraj's sword veered off-target and I was saved. Everyone tumbled sideways as the blast from the cannon to our starboard side violently shook *The Dolphin*.

I ran for the ropes. "André. Rebekah. Down. Go. Go." The ropes were no longer connected to anything below. *The Wasp* was well on its way out of the harbor.

As *The Dolphin*'s crew scrambled to understand what was happening to their ship, I rushed my friends down the ropes. We were twenty feet above the water. I remembered another time I had been pursued into a position like this with André, and I considered how I was living my life. My head spun with fear, dangling so precariously over the water. Our only hope was to dive into the harbor below, and swim to shore. Iraj's men would be able to catch up with us, but we would at least be on open land, rather than trapped on that tiny deck. As we neared the bottom, I thought of the days I spent with Albert, jumping into the cove. I was always afraid to jump from the highest rock. It was not the water I feared, but the fall. Well, I would have no choice this time. I saw the rear of the gunboat. I saw Lora waving up at us. When I closed my eyes, I saw Albert encouraging me to jump, telling me not to be afraid. Memory lives inside the eyelids.

"Swing!" I shouted, and using our legs against the hull of *The Dolphin*, we rocked the ropes back and forth. Once we had gained enough momentum, we let go, and together we dived. The water made everything go silent and blue. I tasted the sea. Albert would be proud. I closed my eyes and saw my childhood friend. I opened my eyes and saw the surface of the ocean breaking around me, and Lora's enormous hands scooping me up out of the water.

The three of us crunched onto the gunboat deck in a heap.

I tasted splinters in my mouth and heard gunshots from above. A line of men with rifles along the deck of *The Dolphin*. We were easy targets. André and I scrambled to the masts and Lora steered. A fortunate wind caught our sails, and soon we were clear of immediate danger.

Out in the bay of Lemesós we watched *The Dolphin* begin to list portside. The ships of the Order of the Labyrinth were long gone. No other ships followed us. I turned and faced front, as we set out to pursue *The Wasp*.

6

The gunboat we had stolen was fast, much faster than *The Wasp*, but it was bereft of the money and provisions we needed to survive. Lora wanted to fire the cannon once again and end Nathan and his insolent crew. But we needed our ship and its supplies to get home. Nathan also abandoned more than half of his men during his escape, and I believed the four of us could handle the remaining men aboard.

Two hours later we had caught up with *The Wasp*. Using ropes, and ignoring thrown trash and jeers from the crew above, we yoked our two ships together. André, Lora, and I hung by all fours from the ropes and scampered up them to our deck, where we engaged immediately with our former crew. For all of the discipline they had learned under Nathan, and all of their experience assaulting unarmed farmers and merchants, they had learned little in the way of combat with an experienced gang of thieves.

The remaining crew appeared to be in the dark about Nathan's ultimate plans. They clearly had been ordered to fight if we should return, but their faces showed bewilderment at the reasoning behind this. We were able to disarm the four men on the top deck and haul them tied up aboard Iraj's gunboat, where Rebekah watched over them.

I opened the hatch and was immediately greeted by the sinewy, round faced boy from the staged fight with Vlad. His immense leg muscles propelled him up the steps, and I fell back into a defensive position. Still, it was one man against three. Worse for him, he didn't see Lora behind him with the slop bucket. Lora rang the wooden pail hard down onto the young man's crown and he collapsed immediately.

One more unlucky (or unskilled) sailor followed, succumbing to the same bucket. Then two more, who saw what happened to the ones before them, and managed to dodge Lora's attacks. But not the subsequent attacks from me and André. By my count, we had only Vlad, Samuel, and Nathan remaining.

André and I climbed below. The suffocatingly narrow passageway was empty. I made way immediately for Nathan's berth while André rooted out the others. Lora remained on deck to stop any potential escapees.

Nathan's tiny room was empty. I peeked under his bunk to see if he was hiding. He was not there. But he had left his log book, which I opened and read. It was not a normal log book, detailing our journeys across the sea. I knew that already. But it was also not a journal recording my actions for the upper ranks of the Order of the Labyrinth.

A small involuntary croak burst from my throat as I read. Again I tasted lemons, sharp and sour and awful across my tongue. From behind me, I heard, "Captain! You made it."

It was Samuel. He was nervously looking over his shoulder. Down the hallway, perhaps even below in the hold, I could hear fighting and shouts. I drew my sword on Samuel.

"Captain, I had no part of Nathan's mutiny," he whined.

"Nathan plans to use the gunpowder in the hold to blow the ship. He's going to light the fuse, and jump to your gunboat, leaving you and your friends to die."

I eyed Samuel carefully. I had always liked Samuel, but I could not trust him here. Did Nathan betray the entire mission by abandoning us in Cyprus, or had Samuel known since the beginning? It was Samuel, after all, who had navigated us to our doom.

"Why are you telling me this, Samuel? Undermining your superior is mutiny."

"Nathan's gone mad. Follow me. We have to get to the hold to stop him."

I dropped Nathan's log book and the horror it contained. "You're a good one, Samuel," I said, placing a compassionate hand on his shoulder and my other on his waist. "Thank you for always looking out for me."

I followed Samuel down the narrow passageway to the hatch leading to the hold. From behind me I heard a loud thud. I turned to see the door to my own cabin at the far end of the hall, broken open. Lying in the shattered wood, bruised and bleeding, was Nathan. Standing over him was André. "The coward hides in the captain's quarters," André said with a laugh.

Samuel, of course, had lied. I knew he would lie, which was why I had taken the opportunity back in Nathan's berth to slip his dagger off his belt.

Samuel reached for the scabbard. In doing so, he simultaneously recognized that, one, his blade was gone, and, two, he had confirmed his own deception. He asked with a defeated sigh, "Captain, what else was I to do?"

I threw his own dagger into his eye. I was still an excellent blade thrower. The knife went in smooth and rattled sharply as it cracked through the bone of his socket. He wheezed and was on the floor, done but not dead. Death would take another ten minutes at least.

If the hold was Samuel's trap, then there was only one person who could be waiting for me there. I opened the hatch and climbed down. The hold was dark, save for a single lantern by the narrow, steep stairs. I pulled it from its mooring and walked slowly.

"Vlad?" I called. No answer.

"Vlad, you're the only one left. I know Samuel wanted you to kill me, and you, of anyone on this ship, are capable of doing that."

I heard a breath, or maybe just a draft from the open hatch, to my right. I turned the light in that direction, but saw no one. The hold had mostly been emptied out, but it was still so dark.

The breath again. I walked cautiously toward it, continuing to speak. "Vlad, I care for you greatly. I hope you care for me too. I think you do. We grew so close, writing letters to Azra."

The breath sounded like a sob. It was coming from behind the stack of sacks to my left. I stepped carefully around them and shone my lantern in the corner, illuminating Vlad, shivering and tentatively raising a long knife.

"Vlad, you stopped taking writing lessons from me. I hope you were not discouraged by Azra not writing."

"No," Vlad said through a quivering lip.

"Why then?"

"Embarrassed."

"I never wanted you to feel embarrassed. I'm sorry."

"Not you. Azra. She wrote me back."

"Vlad, that's wonderful. What did she say?"

"She said she misses me too, and wants to see me again." His knife trembled a little closer to me. "And I was scared to write again, because her letter was so smart, so easy to read. I read it over and over, and it was perfect, but mine was. . . . It was not good. She cannot love me, because I am a monster. Because I am not smart enough to read her books."

"Vlad." Tears came to my eyes, and I tried my damnedest not to let them, because I needed above all to be able to see. There was still a good chance that Vlad would lunge at me. "You are the most beautiful man, so sincere, so loyal. You know what you said is not true. Give me the knife and tell me about her letter."

Vlad wept too, but he held his blade tight. I twitched apprehensively toward the hilt of my sword, but before I could take action, he turned the knife, handed it to me, and leaned forward to hug his tutor, his captain.

I held him tight for a moment, and then pulled away to look into his eyes. "Oh, Vlad," I said. "Please forgive me." I swung the lantern across the side of his jaw, knocking him unconscious.

We sailed both ships to Malta. Once there, we loaded all of the munitions, weapons, and provisions from both ships into *The Wasp*, and left Vlad and the others with the gunship in Valletta. We took Nathan with us. I waved good-bye to Vlad as *The Wasp* pulled away, but he did not reciprocate. Once to sea, we sailed directly for Barcelona.

Rebekah stayed on the quarterdeck, looking thoughtfully back to land.

"We've left Vlad with the faster ship," she said.

"And nothing else," I said. "By the time he raised weapons and men in port, we'd be out of range."

"You could have at least taken their sails."

Ah, when Rebekah was right, she was right. On our long trip west, we took turns on lookout, but in any case, we never saw that gunship again.

Upon arrival in Barcelona, I sent a messenger into town with an urgent letter for Edmond, telling him to meet me at my ship. That dispatched, I gathered Lora, André, and Rebekah.

"Thank you, dear friends. You fought for me and would have died for me. Please know I would do the same for any of you. But I am through now. The Order of the Labyrinth is a foul trick played upon us, and I cannot have you risking your future families, future wealth, future loves, or any other kind of future anything for me when I have been so wrong for so long. I have one final thing I must do, alone."

There was the solemn silence that follows heartfelt words.

"Don't be stupid," Lora said. "We're staying."

"This was your big speech?" André said. "You used to be better at this stuff."

Rebekah folded her arms.

They were the best friends I could ever have had and I did not deserve them. "Please," I said. "If you wish to show me loyalty and love. If you wish to stand behind me. Do it by listening to me here. It is not cowardice or distrust. I can only do what I do next alone."

Now the silence truly had weight. And it was Rebekah who finally nodded and embraced me. André, seeing her give in, shrugged. "I won't force my company upon you. But do drop in someday, please. I feel life will get so boring without you." Finally Lora swept us all up in her arms and we were lifted from the floor, our gang of thieves, saying our good-byes.

"We will see each other again. I am certain, but for now our adventures are at an end," I said. "Lora, please set us down, I can hardly breathe." André gave a muffled grunt of agreement. "Weaklings," scoffed Lora and let us go.

And so my friends departed *The Wasp* for the last time. I had no idea if and when I would see them again. It seemed to me that perhaps I never would.

Edmond arrived forty minutes later, and I greeted him at the gangway. He was smiling and soft-eyed as usual, holding open his arms upon seeing me. I stepped back, refusing to touch him. I expected confusion in his eyes, but what I saw was cold knowing.

"Your crew is on leave, I take it?" he asked, even though he already had his answer.

"Who are the Order of the Labyrinth?" I asked, even though I already had my answer.

I didn't let him respond. "They carry crates," I continued. "They are not tall nor short. They do not interact with us unless they have to. They are as part of the world as the wind and rain."

The words fell out of my mouth effortlessly. I had known all of this ever since I left my father's body at our burned estate, but I had stashed it away. I had poured this knowledge into a bottle, and let it age and collect dust deep in the cellar of my conscience. And now the vintage was uncorked, its bouquet opening up, bitter and sharp.

"They do not steal the crates," I said. "The crates belong to no one and everyone. Perhaps there are entire worlds inside the crates. Perhaps there is nothing, and the transport of the crates is its own purpose. The Order does not steal anything, nor have any interest in other activities. I was never in the Order. They are a fog, a storm, a breeze, a forest. They are true to their name. They are a labyrinth, bigger than human greed or power.

"I read Nathan's journal. I read the notes he made for you.

You staged all of this. Over two decades of my life. Why did you do this?"

I tasted the hot salt of sweat and tears on my dry lips. When I thought of all those wasted years. My father hadn't wanted me to spend my life this way, and yet I had foolishly stepped into the trap, like a child. And even though I had reached my middle years, that is what I felt like. I felt like a child, a foolish little girl tricked one more time by her uncle Edmond.

There was a moment where Edmond did not react, and then he gave a short laugh. I knew that laugh. I had once dreamed that laugh, as my sleeping mind had desperately tried to warn me of what my waking mind hadn't yet realized. When he spoke, it was with an airy casualness, as though we were chatting in his parlor.

"I'm getting old," he sighed. "Before I die, I want to have a son. I want to settle down someplace nice and enjoy my wealth and my wine. You pushed my hand, but perhaps it was time anyway. And this fool," he indicated Nathan, still beaten and tied up on the deck, "couldn't keep you in line."

"Edmond, the Order has no interest in human affairs. And so it had no interest in our little smuggling operation."

Edmond looked bemused and tolerant, the same face as when he mock cheated at games when I was a child, and let me catch him doing it.

"And so the threat you brought to us was false. And so the Order did not kill my father." There had been a slow awareness over the last weeks, a dawning of understanding. But even still, as I put it together out loud, I felt the shock in my teeth, and tasted it in my saliva. I took a step off the gangway, onto the dock. "And so the Order did not burn the house, or watch me for years, or send me to do random acts of cruelty up and down the Mediterranean. You did all of this to me and my father." I took another step closer to Edmond. "You had him killed." I could barely voice the words.

"It really did take you a long time to figure that out," he said. "And you used to be so clever as a girl."

The world went fuzzy behind my tears, and I wiped them away so I could look that devil in his eyes. I voiced the question that had plagued me as soon as my doubts had come to the surface of my mind. "What did we do to you that caused so much damage, so much pain, that you needed to destroy not just my father, but his daughter too?"

"Your father betrayed me." Edmond dropped his causal air and showed for a moment the real malice beneath. "He betrayed my trust, my friendship, my livelihood. We were small time. We were nothing. Unless we joined The Duke's Own, we'd spend the rest of our lives doing the same tiny nothings for the same tiny no ones."

I wanted to lunge at him, drive my sword into his neck, and it is with great regret that I did not, but my mind was spinning madly. I only took another step closer. Far beyond him, at the city gate, I thought I saw a familiar man lurching stiffly along, blood running down his shirt, mouth open in his silent scream.

"Again and again I begged him to allow us to join The Duke's Own," Edmond said. "But again and again he refused and for the same reason: you. His family. His legacy. My fortune held up for a proud man's legacy."

"My father vowed never to allow me to become a criminal, or a pirate, or a smuggler."

"And yet you became all three," Edmond said. "I killed your father, yes. It needed to be done. If he wouldn't join The Duke's

Own, then he was a competitor. So killing him became my ticket into their ranks. Proof of my usefulness to them. A nasty necessity."

"Then you blamed the Order so I wouldn't know."

"Yes, it gave a rather large target for your revenge. A life lived for revenge, by any means necessary. Needless to say, your father would have hated that. So perhaps it was sadistic, that final twist of the knife. Taking away his precious legacy. But we are," he shrugged, the airy act returning, "all allowed our vices."

I was within striking distance. Just do it, I told myself. Just do it, I say to myself centuries later.

"You manipulated me."

"I told stories. I surrounded you with my spies, Holger, Samuel, Nathaniel, Señora Bover, all playing different parts in the play of your life. But it was you, child, who chose. Every choice, it was always you."

My stomach twitched, acid again burning my mouth. I had thought I was doing this for my father. It was love, I had thought. And in doing so I had allowed myself to betray his memory. I felt almost as though I were the fraud and the monster, not Edmond. After all, Edmond was right. It was always me making the choices that betrayed my father's memory. Somewhere there was a version of this life where I walked away from the estate with Albert instead of with Edmond. But I hadn't, and every choice after had been mine.

I took one last step closer to Edmond, my sword pointed at his throat.

"Sadly, I could only stretch the story this far," said Edmond. "I am in my fifties. Still so much time left. It is a shame to end it all so soon."

"You have no time left," I said, as I finally swung my blade.

But two burly arms crashed over mine, and my sword tumbled out of my hands. Edmond stepped back, unharmed.

"I thought you might react this way," he said. "So I arranged for a friend of yours."

I heard heaving thick breaths behind me and I knew who it was. The man I had left with a boat much faster than *The Wasp*, and I hadn't even taken the sails.

"Vlad," I cried. "Vlad why are you here? Are you not returning home to Chişinău? To see Azra?"

"Shut up," Vlad growled, then laughed. I kicked my legs and tried to bite his arms, but he was so much bigger than me.

"Finally got her," Nathan said, through sunburnt chapped lips. "Let's get out of here."

"No. You'll stay," Edmond said politely, stepping around Vlad, climbing up the gangway and in a balletic, single motion pulling his sword and plunging it into Nathan's neck. Nathan gurgled a final unintelligible word and flopped like a bag of lentil beans onto the deck.

I screamed, but Vlad held me tighter.

"Vlad. No! I'm sorry I struck you. I'm sorry I abandoned you. I had to get home. How much did he pay you? Is it worth killing the only person who ever believed in you? Believed you could find your lost love. Vlad!"

I kept talking, and kicking. Vlad was standing right at the lip of the pier, holding me over the cold black edge of the sea. I no longer hoped to live. I only hoped that Vlad's sword completed the task swiftly. I was a child again, standing on the high rock, not wanting to jump. It is not the water I feared. It was the fall.

Vlad lifted me by my collar and let out one final coyote howl of a laugh as he stuck his sword deep into my gut, deep enough that I could feel the sharp rip of the blade's exit from my lower back. Edmond nodded and said something. I couldn't understand quite what as my senses were failing. I tried to call out, to say one final thing to my father's killer, to my life's undoing. But Edmond was already walking away, back toward his elegant and elaborate city home, afforded by betrayal and murder. As he went, Vlad dropped my limp body, and I splashed down into the choppy water below.

I sank, my muscles rigid with shock and panic, the weight of oceans upon me, pressing my body down, down, down. I could not calm myself enough to patiently await imminent death. My vision left me. I was alone underwater, in a void of my own making. But then something was pulling me up, and I felt annoyed. It was peaceful in my void. Let me stay there. I would have waved away Vlad's hands if I had the strength. He pulled me from the water. My vision returned with a blear of sunlight. I gulped and wheezed and spit a pint of saltwater from my nose and mouth. My belly and chest burned intensely. I could not move.

"He is gone," Vlad said quietly into my ear. "I will take you to a doctor now. I must do what Edmond said. But you will live. I am good with the sword and know how to avoid heart and lungs—a lesson from the master torturers of Bucharest. I studied there many years. Best student they ever had."

"Why did you do it, Vlad?"

"He is paying for me to return to Chişinău with enough to buy a home, you understand? I will see Azra again. You understand." And I did understand. I understood doing terrible things because you believe it is your life's greater good.

"Then why not kill me?" I managed.

Just before my vision faded again, I saw Vlad put his hand on his chest in respect.

"You are my captain."

CRAIG

2016

It's hard to smile without a face, but on rare occasions I do.

When Amaranta kissed you, and Orlando, your officiant, pronounced you husband and wife, I smiled.

You honeymooned in Luftnarp. I had mixed emotions about returning there, but it is a beautiful country. You found a modest chalet nestled in the Alps. You drank zesty, sparkling red wine. You went to the Museumos dus Modernias Artim—world famous home to Leonardo da Vinci's "Dogs Playing Bloodborne." You rode horses. (Did you know horses were invented in Svitz in the sixth century?) You went sledding, which the locals called, for some reason, "sledging," and nearly broke your neck at the end of the run when you realized you didn't know how to stop and so went flying down the middle of the little town's main street. That scared me. What would become of your burgeoning family if you died doing something as silly as "sledging," Craig?

I had not been there in so long. I was afraid to go. I almost tried to cancel the trip on you, force you to stay here, because of my own unresolved feelings. The abandoned mine shaft outside of town has king beds, free wifi, continental breakfast, heated pools, and HBO. I know it's a prison used by the Sheriff's Secret Police, but it's also a top-rated resort, receiving an average rating of four stars on TripAdvisor. Plus there are weekly laser light Pink Floyd concerts at nearby Radon Canyon.

But I trusted you. It was mainly Amaranta I trusted. But I trusted you both. Trust can go far, Craig. Trust me on that.

Luftnarp was bright and cold. You two made love as the sun set over the snow-cloaked mountains. I didn't watch. I'm not a creep. But honestly, it was hard not to hear, even with the shower door closed and both of your passports rolled up and shoved into my ears.

I took some time to myself on that trip, too, leaving you two alone as I traveled south to the coastal cove where I was born. The countryside is so different now, with its vehicles and shopping centers and wifi and tourists, but also there is much about the countryside that is undeniably the same. The hills, the shape of the coastline, the orange trees, the white-blue of the sky at noon, the purple-blue of the ocean at dusk. Where my father's home had burned down was another estate, this one more luxurious, albeit less inviting. A famous movie actor lives there three weekends a year, and it is otherwise only occupied by staff. Sometimes he forgets that he owns it, and when he remembers, he feels afraid, because he knows that his wealth and fame have taken something from him that he will never get back. The weekend I was there the house was empty. I found the hill where my mother was buried and where my father's body last laid and I watched the luxury yachts coming into port, knowing none of the ships' names. I tried to remember every choice I had ever made, not out of regret, only merely cataloging what I had done, what I am doing now, and what I will have to do next.

I knew a man named Vlad who loved a girl named Azra. Vlad's path led him away from her only to bring them back together. Vlad made choices to come back to Azra, but many of the choices were made by the path he had to take. Vlad knew who he was and where he needed to be. He did not always know how to get there, only that he would.

I thought of Vlad as I stood atop the hill where I last saw my father, and I knew there was so much more of my path left for me to follow.

When your honeymoon ended, I was ready to return to Night Vale. On the first night in your brand-new home, shortly after you fell asleep in the soft crescent of each other's arms, I thanked you both for the gift of your life together. I did this by painting your kitchen cabinets. Those maple veneers were so 1990s, and I prefer a cleaner, brighter color. I chose Arctic Fur. It really opened up the room, I think.

You knew something was different that next morning, and you told Amaranta, "Those aren't the same cabinets," but she disagreed. You pressed the point, but she kissed you just under your right eye and said, "Our new home is perfect." You thought about a figure standing behind you in the mirror and about how unreliable your experience of the world has become and you stopped arguing.

Your new home *is* perfect. I know there are still countless boxes to get sorted and unpacked, but you have a tiny guest room, with its own en suite. There's even two separate living spaces: one for television, one for a more traditional parlor. A fireplace you won't ever use, even on the windy nights of the desert winter, but it's cute. And a small third bedroom, for a child.

I don't know what clicked. I can't get inside that mind of

yours, but you took action. You admitted to Amaranta you were dragging your feet, and that it wasn't because you didn't love her or had nerves. You listened to her questions about your career and what you want out of your life, and became worried that you might not be a good enough husband. You're bad with money, content to stay in the same job, and happy living right here in Night Vale.

Amaranta wants to move up in her career, maybe she'd even want to move away, you thought. But she said, not at all. She wants a life with you. She wants you to be happy. Your happiness was key to her happiness, and she hoped vice versa.

She gets it.

And you said you were happy living a life with her. Growing. Slowly, but growing as a person, as a human, as a family. And you wanted that more than anything. You didn't do that sniveling get-down-on-one-knee thing. You asked directly if she wanted to marry you, because you wanted to marry her, and you both discussed all the things this could mean. Or at least all the things you could comprehend that this could mean. Which, to be fair, is almost nothing.

Mutually, you both agreed this was right. And it was. And it is. And I'm smiling again.

I've already picked out the wallpaper for the baby's room. Lavender bears holding golden fleurs-de-lis. Or maybe they're knives? Hard to say. It's in the catalog I put on your night stand. I left it open to the correct page, so you'll order it.

One thing that came up the other day was Amaranta's career. She mentioned applying for a promotion at the bank. She wants to move into human resources and do personnel training courses, which she's perfect for. She's so confident and likable. She's great with people.

Plus, it would be a significant pay raise, and that's wonderful.

But I read up on that position, and it's going to require a lot of travel. She didn't really mention the travel part to you, which I bring up now only because you've already picked out the wallpaper for a baby room, and if she's traveling a lot, she may put off getting pregnant, for how long? Forever?

Just something to consider.

I know you're planning on staying at home, so raising kids isn't impossible. Plus, I saw you opened an IRA. Excellent work. Putting money away, saving on taxes. You're paying off your Amex each month. You're growing up, Craig.

You're so content in your job writing press releases and online copy and the occasional slogan. (I know your marketing team voted you down, but I thought "Ford: You Never Chose to Be Born, But We Chose for You" was your best work yet.) With the people skills you have, you could be a manager, or a director of marketing. Someone with the power to hire and fire. Copywriters are some of the first to get laid off in hard times. We can't have that.

Plus your friend—I forget her name—quit for no reason at all. People come and go so often there. The management at that dealership is not to be trusted. By the way, interesting that you and what's-her-name did not keep in touch, which oh, well. You're married now. You have lots of friends. I guess it all worked out for the best.

You've read my messages I know. I crafted a needlepoint skull on the inside of your windbreaker. I left a skinned squirrel in your glove compartment. I wrote a letter, which I saved as DATE TIME AND DETAILS OF CRAIG'S DEATH.docx right there on your desktop. I knew that file name would get your attention. It wasn't about your death, but about your life.

It said: "You should try sleeping on your side. You've begun snoring. It's keeping me and Amaranta awake. And it'll keep your future baby awake. By the way, here are some helpful resources for best practices of parenthood and family planning."

And then I linked to a few interesting websites about the joys and practicalities of raising a child.

It disturbed you so much that you immediately deleted the file, which is frustrating, because there were some really enlightening think pieces in there. Also the last link took you to a website I built that gives the date, time, and details of your death. I'm full of interesting, omniscient factoids. Sorry you missed out on that one. Maybe you're right. Maybe it'll be better as a surprise.

You also changed your password after you found my letter, but that didn't work, because I can stand over your shoulder without you seeing me. You could try crouching under a blanket or a towel next time, but then you run the risk of actually seeing me. You will be seeing more and more of me as you get older, but I promise I have good reasons for all of this.

Thursday, after I filled all of your jeans with warm, damp leaves, you yelled at me. You didn't know who I was or anything about me or even for certain that I was there, but you yelled at me.

I deserved it. It was rude of me. But we can't communicate in a healthy way if you're going to lose your temper. And it's especially not good if people hear or see you, because they can't hear or see me. As your PR director at Ford, Donovan Lewis, would say: "Bad optics." (This coming from a man who writes deer erotica under the username yougotcervidae.)

If you want to talk to me, try writing a note. I created a folder called "Fantasy Football" in your Documents. (Your wife's never going to look in a folder called "Fantasy Football.") Just save anything you have to say to me there.

Oh, who am I kidding. Keep digging under the bed and looking behind clothes in your closet. Maybe check the attic. I heard a story on my favorite podcast, *Criminal*, about a guy who secretly lived in this woman's attic for a year. She seemed pretty cool about it, given the circumstances. I think you should listen to that episode. You could learn a lot from that woman. I'll link to it in the Fantasy Football folder.

So obsess all you want, but don't let it get the better of you. Take care of yourself, so that you can take care of others. How is Amaranta supposed to feel if she comes home to find her husband screaming at no one?

Especially when she's so stressed out from her recent interviews for the new position with the bank. Unfortunately, she didn't get the job. She hasn't told you this yet, because she's only now finding this out.

I listened to Steve Carlsberg's call with the Regional Director yesterday. Apparently Susan Willman, a good friend of his, applied for the same HR job as Amaranta. This surprised Steve because Susan's been running her own management consulting business, and he never thought she would be interested in leaving such rewarding, independent work. He never even bothered to send the job announcement to her because of this.

But apparently someone helped convince Susan that a stable job working for a stable bank, alongside a stable old friend, would be a better career path than the uncertainty of entrepreneurship. Who even knows what unknown emailer would have told Susan about that job, or if that emailer was the same person who once put a Honey Nut Cheerios box full of tarantulas in Susan's pantry.

Like Steve, I was surprised. Susan's not nearly as friendly or assertive as Amaranta, but never discount the bonds of friendship. Nepotism is a powerful persuader. But also, Susan has over twelve years' experience in corporate training, so I think it was the right pick.

Amaranta deserves better, but the Last Bank of Night Vale needs to do what is best for the business. As much as I love and respect your wife, Susan is simply more qualified. Steve is making the correct choice.

What I'm trying to say is conserve your energy. Limit your frustration. Amaranta needs your fullest emotional support tonight.

Oh, look she's home. She's crying. Remember to listen more than talk, Craig. She needs you.

No. Don't yell.

You can't help her by being mad at forces neither of you can control.

She doesn't need your empathetic rage. She needs your comfort, your compassion.

Craig.

Stop yelling. You're yelling at me. You're upsetting your wife. She's confused.

I'm going to touch your shoulder to try to calm y—

Ow!

You hit me.

And you know it.

You hit me.

It was pure accident—a wild, hopeful swing—but I can't believe you did that. Craig. Sit down.

Sit. Down.

I'm going to whisper something in your ear now.

"Shut up, you obstreperous little imp. Sit down and listen to your wife."

You heard me?

You heard me.

Okay.

You're sitting now. She's sitting now.

Good.

Put your arm around your crying wife. This moment isn't about you.

Focus, Craig. Oh, Craig. You're growing up.

I'm proud of you.

Look at that. I'm smiling again.

THE REST

1830–1862

1

Albert woke before dawn, partly because he had a long day of work ahead of him, and partly because he liked the color of the sky when the light was just coming up on the horizon. The solemn blue calmed him, and the first thing he did was go out into the cold morning air and look at that sky and the ocean beneath it. Then he returned to his cottage, and cut himself some bread for breakfast.

His morning routine, such as it was, done, he went out to examine the orange and lemon trees growing along the hillside down toward the water. Despite the cold, there was little chance of freezing in this climate, although the Year Without Summer fourteen years earlier had badly damaged that harvest. Ever since then, he had learned to not take the weather for granted, and so he walked through the trees, eyeing them carefully.

This was the earth his parents had worked, until they had died a decade before, both of them to the plague. Since then he had worked it alone. It was not a rich plot, but it was his, and it was fertile, and he could eat from it, and sell enough for anything else he needed. It was a self-contained world. He had learned long before about what the outside world could do to a family, having his closest friend disappear from his life after her father was killed and her estate burned. He took that lesson with him. It was a fence he built around his life. He had no ambitions, but without ambition came safety. No one noticed him, and in not noticing, they did not harm him. Along with his own crop, he also regularly harvested from the remaining orchards in the estate next to his small plot of land. The estate house was still a charred ruin. No family had claimed that land. Perhaps it was too obscure a location, and so had slipped the attention of the squabbling aristocracy. Or perhaps the viciousness of what had been done to the inhabitants was still a stain upon its reputation.

Not even the smugglers landed in its cove anymore. Ships steered well away from its shore. This suited Albert well. He would take a haunted reputation if it left him in peace. And so he walked the forty minutes or so through the woods into the lower slopes of my former estate, where the orange trees that had survived the fire hung heavy with unripe fruit. There wasn't much to do at this point in the growing cycle. The trees had enough water from the damp air, and it was too cold for them to grow enough to need pruning, and so he just kept up his steady inspection. Once done, he started back toward his cottage for his midday meal, and then he froze. A figure, standing at the end of the row of oranges. The first other human being he had seen in this estate since . . . Since. "Hey!" he shouted, even though he had no more right to be in that abandoned orchard than anyone else. "Hey!" he said with bravery he did not feel, as he had not felt bravery since . . . Since. But still he walked forward, and the figure turned. It was a woman, his age. He knew who it was, even with all those wasted, vicious years between us. Mine was not a face he could forget.

He smiled at me, and I shook. "I didn't know where else to go," I said. He reached out, and I stepped closer, and he touched me and said, "You're home," and in the moment of him saying that, I knew he was right.

I had never seen where Albert lived. He had always hid it from me. And so there was an aspect of mystery, a crossing of a threshold I never thought would be crossed, when he led me back through the woods to the small orchard he worked.

"Is this where you always lived?" I said, looking around me at the neat line of trees and the cottage, small but, like the trees, carefully tended.

"Yes," he said, with a dip of his head and a twist of his hands. "I know you always thought I lived on one of the other estates, and I was too ashamed to tell you the truth. But I'm a farmer, with only a bit of land. A son of farmers. We've worked this land since before there were any great houses on this coast."

Ashamed? I could have laughed, if there was anything like humor left in me. "Oh, Albert, your family made something. Your family brought food into the world. Our estate was fed by thieving. You were too good for us." And then I stumbled, and realized just how hungry I had become in my long journey back to the place I had been born.

Albert took me into the cottage, and I studied with interest the sturdy planks and beams, the way the light darted up the walls with the movement of the fruit trees outside, the way the window by the hearth was perfectly situated to look over the sea below. How wonderful this room was. I regretted every year I had spent not sitting in this quiet room, with this quiet man, who at this moment was cutting bread and cheese

THE FACELESS OLD WOMAN WHO SECRETLY LIVES IN YOUR HOME

and placing it with some pickled vegetables on a tin plate. I ate greedily, then laid back on his bed without asking permission, because I did not have the strength to ask, and I slept soundly at last.

There weren't many questions the first week. He fed me. He let me sleep. He went about his work. His work was simple but exacting. It required his entire attention, but there was no betrayal, no unintended consequences. Every year the trees grew a little more. Every year they bore fruit. It was a natural rhythm that I had forgotten could exist in a world with so much subterfuge and deception.

Sometimes I would join him for his rounds, but often I would sit by his cottage and look at the ocean. It was never the same view from one moment to the next, the exact formula of ripple and froth and cloud rearranging itself into infinite possibility. I would hold my small hand up against the view, and feel calm in its stillness against the moving background. I loved the calluses on my palm. I loved the dirt under my nails.

I began to understand that there never needed to be questions from Albert, not if I didn't want to answer them. And for this I was more grateful than I was for the food and the shelter. A space where I didn't have to explain myself. Where nothing was required of me. That is what I needed more than anything. Quietly, that is what Albert gave me. As a child, I had loved him. And deep within, under the layers of self-protection that years of survival and revenge had necessitated, I started to find that emotion again. Over yet another dinner of bread and cheese I stopped eating and I watched him.

"What?" he said, after he noticed I had been staring at him for several minutes.

"This is the only nice thing to happen to me since the last time I saw you," I said.

He laughed and shook his head. "You've gone soft," he said, but he kept grinning as he went back to his food.

We established a pattern. I started to help him with the work. Especially during the harvest, he needed a lot of labor. Usually he hired some men from a nearby village, but I convinced him we could do it ourselves. I phrased it as a challenge, but really I just didn't want anyone from the outside world to break the fragile bubble we were living in, and I think Albert recognized that. He agreed, even though he shouldn't have, even though every day became an exhausting race to get the fruit off the trees before the birds did. He couldn't seem to say no to me. I wouldn't have said no to him either, but he never asked.

An entire year passed like this. The two of us working the farm, and never talking about where I had been since I kissed him and rode away from my charred home, and never talking about what his life had been like all this time, or what was happening here between us, or what would happen next. It was so easy to merely take each day as it came, and deal with that present, and then shuffle the day away with the setting sun until the sky took on its predawn blue again. And I thought: *Could I do this forever? After years of traveling all over the continent, and sailing through the seas. After all of my adventures and all of my crimes. Could I wake up and go to sleep and push my hands into the earth and against the leaves of the trees, just a few miles from where my mother and father had died?* I thought I could. If we never talked about it. If we never questioned, I thought that perhaps I could live like this for however many decades until I died, basket of oranges in hand, on a slope that was visible from my bed.

So one night, after dinner, as he retired to his mattress and I turned to sleep where I usually slept, a cot in the corner, I stopped. I took his arm. We looked into each others' eyes, not saying anything, each waiting for the other to start.

"I think," I said, and then didn't know what to say next.

"Oh, god, me too," he said, and shifted his arms so I could enter his embrace if I wanted to, and I wanted to. I kissed him for the first time since we were children, and it was so different. Then, that had been the limit of the possible, and now it was merely the start of the unfolding of our bodies.

I had wondered if I could do this forever. That night I knew I could.

From that night, many nights. We settled into each other, the way a house settles into its walls. Through a simple repeating movement of dawn and dusk and harvest and pruning and eating and kissing and sleeping, another year passed, and I found that I was able, in certain moments, to let some of my past go. I let go first of what I had done when I had thought I was on a ship belonging to the Order of the Labyrinth. I let go of my blindness, my foolish trust in Edmond. I let go of the mistakes, of the crimes, of the pain.

"It'll be harvest again soon," Albert said, as a question.

"Yes," I said, "we can hire some workers this time." He breathed relief.

Another year, and I wondered at how much I had aged, and I let more go. I let go of André and Lora and Rebekah. I let go of the final screams of Lady Nora, and Lord Fullbright's frozen face as he fell. I let go of Vlad holding my wounded body above the water. I let go of the pain still present in my belly. I let go of every moment back to that first moment, a moment I could only approach as a white light too bright for me to look into.

"You didn't have to be ashamed," I said up into the silent dark one night, knowing that Albert was awake too just by the subtle pattern of his breathing. "You could have told me where you lived. I didn't care."

He said nothing for so long that I began to think that I had been mistaken about his being awake. And then, "That's easy for you to say now." His voice carried the pain and shame of having to hide the basic fact of who you are even from your childhood best friend. I put out my hand and found his. We didn't talk about the subject after that.

A fourth year, and now this is where I lived, and where I always would live. I thought about what it would be like to die so close to where my mother and father died, whether that would in any way make up for the years we never had together. But I was starting to realize that there was no death that could make up for any amount of life. When I thought about my fruitless years of revenge, I shuddered. I had chased after death, and in doing so, squandered life. I would never do that again, I vowed to myself.

So I finally approached the moment that was so difficult for me to approach. I looked at the memory of my father's death. And I looked at the knowledge of Edmond's guilt. I sat alone, tucked away a little from the orchard, on a rock with an expansive view of the sea. Almost everything in front of me was blue, but almost no patch of it was quite the same shade of blue. I marveled at how many forms of blue could exist, even in this little corner of the rapidly growing known world. As I thought about that, I let go of my father. And I let go of

Edmond. I could not stay with Albert if I continued to hold my revenge, like a flimsy mask that stood in for all that my face could express. I let slip that mask. It was just me now. I stood and returned to where Albert was working and I wondered if he could see the difference in me, but I didn't suppose it mattered.

Once I had reached that first flame of revenge deep within myself and stomped it finally out, I felt free, as I had not felt since I had smelled the smoke that terrible night so many years before. I fully embraced the long-dormant person I had once been. I let myself love Albert, and I accepted his love in return.

And so:

"You've hardly touched your oranges."

"Albert, I love you, but I can't eat any more oranges."

"I suppose you're right, I suppose they're better used . . . for throwing."

"Hey! Stop it! Okay, well you started this."

And so:

"I miss you when we're asleep. It feels like all those years you were away and I lived here all alone again."

"Well, let's meet in our dreams."

"Where should we meet?"

"You know when we jumped into the cove as kids?"

"I could hold my breath way longer."

"Quit bragging. Let's meet in the moment when you first jump in the cove, and your entire body goes underwater, and you haven't yet opened your eyes so you can't see the water around you, but you know it's there."

"You want us to meet inside that one second?"

"Yes. Don't be late."

And so:

"We should get married."

"Why would we need to get married? You came back to me. You live at my farm. Who cares about what it looks like to anyone else?"

"But that's exactly it. It's your farm. I want it to be our farm."

"That's sweet."

"I want property rights, buddy."

"Still sweet. Okay, let's get married."

"Okay then."

And so.

Two nights later, I thought I saw a man in the distance, a man I had seen so many times throughout my life, lurching stiffly in the moonlight, but when I looked closer it was only the branch of a tree, moving innocently in the Mediterranean breeze.

2

It might seem strange, living so close to my old home for so long, but I never went and looked at it. What was there but pain and memories, and didn't I have enough of those? But having finally let go of the idea of revenge, I found that I could now walk through those woods and look at the corpse of my childhood, that stone and wooden wreck, and feel nothing but the smallest twinges of pain. The pain felt as though it belonged to someone else, as though it sprung in someone else's chest, and all I was experiencing were the faint twinges of sympathy.

Walking into the house was a transition of light, the Mediterranean brilliance of outside becoming the dusty dim of inside. I was surprised by how much of the furniture had survived. Here was the table where my father and I had eaten dinner, blackened but still standing. Here was my bedroom where I had sat at the window waiting for my father's return. My bed was mostly undamaged. From there I went into the rest of the house, the parts my father never really visited after my mother died. We didn't often discuss my mother's family, and as a child I had never thought about it much, but she must have come from extremely wealthy nobility, because the estate was huge. Room after room that my father and I had ignored. Some of the rooms were bare, but others held the remains of well-made furniture and rich household items. I wanted to understand my family, because in that moment I knew that I had never known the shape of my history. And so I went carefully through the estate, room by room. I found a silver necklace, and I have no way of knowing if my mother ever wore it, but holding it felt a bit like touching her. Perhaps my father had given it to her, but my father had come from a merchant family, and wasn't likely to have the money for a gift like this.

Then I found the most precious treasure in the estate. In a writing desk that had been merely singed, I found a locked drawer. I allowed an aspect of my criminality to stretch its legs again, as I quickly and easily picked the lock. Inside were a stack of letters. They were love letters my mother had written to my father. They were kept in this study that no one entered after she had died. It was the ghost of my parents I was holding, in crackling, yellowed parchment. I took the letters with me, but didn't tell Albert what they were. He didn't ask. He respected that there was much about myself I wouldn't tell him yet, and much more I would never tell him, and he accepted that he had my present, and so he didn't need to have my past.

I savored the letters, reading them only one every week or two. There weren't many, and I knew I would all too soon run out. They were sweet, slight things, but each revealed an entire world of my mother that I had never known. Funny, full of love for her family, especially my grandmother who organized the house while my grandfather was off handling diplomatic matters or whatever it was that nobles spent their time doing when they traveled. I also learned from these letters that my mother had a younger sister, who, at least as my mother told it, followed her around at all times, imitating my mother in that kind of worship that can happen between siblings on good terms.

And of course there was my father, who she clearly loved so completely. She found my father deeply attractive, and at times I had to jump ahead in a letter, flushing as though I were a child peeking at them around a doorframe. Perhaps these were not my letters to read, but what else did I have left of my parents? Didn't I deserve at least this? I wasn't sure what I deserved but I read them anyway. Because, more than anything, there was the language. My mother turned from concept to flesh as I discovered her sense of humor, and the words she regularly used when she was searching for the right turn of phrase, and what she liked (dogs, bread, sunlight reflecting off water onto the leafy canopy of a tree) and what annoyed her (rats, celery, the short days of winter, her sister sometimes, but that last one with a tolerant love). I was, for the first time, getting truly acquainted with the woman who had died so I could live, although I'm sure if she was given that choice before they had conceived she might have rethought things. Certainly I would not have held it against her.

Meanwhile Albert and I talked through our wedding. It would have to be in a church so that it could be official, although neither of us had much patience for that. His worship had always been around cultivation and soil, the feeling of palm on earth, the drift of pollen in the air. Mine was around the complications of the human mind. I had seen too many permutations of what we are capable of to believe in the necessity of someone else waving the baton. We were far too busy with the harvest to get to the wedding right away, and we decided on six months from then. I don't know why that amount of time. It's not like we had family and friends that needed to be arranged. My friends surely thought I was dead, and let them. It was better that the woman I had been stay disappeared. She had little relationship to the woman I was now, I thought.

We were wrapping up the harvest when I picked the next letter from the pile and realized that it was not from my mother at all, but was in fact addressed to her. It was written by her sister and was full of family gossip and stories from the royal court that she was visiting in neighboring Luftnarp. I smiled at the fondness in my aunt's words—how delightful to get to know my mother's sister, whom only a few months ago I had no idea even existed. I noted in my aunt a fiercer streak of independence than my mother had perhaps given her credit for. She was a woman who would do fine in the world. I thought maybe my mother's sister was still alive, and that I may visit her someday, to try to see some of my mother's face—my own face—in another person. But then I reached the end of my aunt's letter and saw her name: Nora. Nora who was visiting Luftnarp as part of a marriage arrangement, because the family would not stand for both of their daughters married outside of nobility. Nora, who would become Lady Nora of Luftnarp. My mother had a sister, Nora, whom I had ruined and then murdered.

I felt Vlad's knife once again piercing my stomach. I had let my old life go, let Edmond go, let the Order of the Labyrinth and The Duke's Own go, let it all go for my life with Albert. I did not cry upon seeing Nora's name. I only sat silently with the pain.

3

Harvest passed in a daze. The physical labor was a blessing. The heft of the oranges, and sight of them, clusters of green and orange in these huge stacks, bundled into the brown sacks and loaded onto carts to be taken to the docks and cities. I welcomed these distractions. Because any time I had to myself, I went over and over what I had known about Lady Nora. All of my information had come from Edmond. It was Edmond who told me of her reputation and her crimes. Edmond who reported on her violent responses to what we had done. Edmond, always Edmond. And the men who had acted in the name of Lady Nora? When had I ever seen proof that they were Luftnarpian soliders? Had I paid close attention to the accuracy of their uniforms? Or had I seen men who were paid by an evil man to come after me and my people and claim to do so on behalf of my aunt, so that I could be used as a tool against my own family.

Edmond wasn't content with my father, or even with me. My father had threatened Edmond's ambitions in the name of my father's family, and so it was that family that Edmond had set out to fully destroy. First he made me into his creature, a weapon of criminal intent, exactly what my father always feared

I would become. Then, as an act of pure sadism, he had turned that weapon upon my mother's sister, a noblewoman whose true reputation and personality perhaps I would never know, because I had so fully believed the vile woman that Edmond had created for me. I was a fool. And I was a monster, for what I had done to my own family, as credulous and cruel as a child.

The months passed, and harvest was over, and the summer months were a series of sunny days that I considered blankly, lost in the darkness within myself. Albert surely noticed my brooding and introspection, as he often brought me cheese or fresh pomegranates and sat to talk with me when I was alone and quiet for too long. By that point, he knew so much of my life, my crimes, my adventures, but I could not tell him about Nora. I could not tell him how I tormented and killed a family member out of blind vengeance. Because I could let go of my father's death, and the loss of our home, and the betrayal of someone we trusted, and the years I wasted as a criminal. I could let go of my need for my revenge, and my ideas about what justice might look like. But with all of that behind me, I still had this guilt upon me. Did I deserve happiness after what I had done to Lady Nora, to my mother's little sister? I couldn't let go on her behalf. It wasn't mine to forgive. I wanted nothing more than to marry Albert, to live out this life around the soil and the sun, but I didn't think I deserved that. My face burned with anger at myself, at the world, and at Edmond. All I had let go over many years, had returned to me at once. There had to be consequences for my crimes and for Edmond's. Or else, what hope was there for quiet, simple lives like Albert's?

On the night I knew I would leave, I made dinner for Albert. I slaughtered a chicken, cooked it with orange peel and wine.

Summer vegetables. Bread. I tried to communicate to him through the food I made. Usually he was the one who cooked. He accepted this turn around in our duties without question, simply letting me go about the actions that frankly I was not as practiced at as him.

"This is delicious," he said.

"You're kind."

"I am kind. But also this really is quite good."

We sat on the porch and watched the last of the sunlight drift off from the sky as the ocean turned from a deep turbulent blue to the silver of night. The evening was cloudless, and we looked at the stars in silence. I considered what I knew about the stars, which was nothing more than navigational markings upon a black ceiling, and felt a fluttering in the pit of my stomach at my ignorance. Now, all these years later as I tell you this, I know everything about the stars, and the flutter is even worse for my knowledge.

"It's been better," he said, "since you came."

I didn't let him see my tears. "You did fine without me."

"Fine is not enough, sometimes."

On the night I knew I would leave we had sex twice, once early in the evening, and then again after hours of sleep, when we both found ourselves awake during the long wait for dawn. It was tender, and felt like we were both reaching for something beyond ourselves, something like the stars we had been looking at, something impossible to ever reach, and yet we strained for it together, and the pleasure made me sad, sadder the more intense the pleasure became.

"What a lucky man I am," he said into his pillow.

"What lucky people we are," I said, folding him under my arm, onto my chest.

"You're beautiful." It was the last time anyone would call me beautiful.

On the night I knew I would leave, I left. It was as simple and brutal and awful as that. I got up from the bed in the early morning. I went gently so as not to wake Albert. I took only a few possessions, those things that I had come with nearly four years earlier. I had no right to anything else. What I was doing was unforgivable, but it was precisely because I had already done the unforgivable that I needed to do it. Turning to get one last look at Albert, I saw that his eyes were open. He did not sit up from bed.

"I knew this day would come," he said.

"I'm sorry," I said.

"True joy never lasts. We are lucky we had it even for a while."

"I wish I could explain."

"Don't."

"Okay," I said.

"No," he said, sitting up. "I mean don't go."

His dark eyes searched mine with the desperation of loss. He was beautiful. I never really appreciated how beautiful until that morning.

"Whatever it is you think you need to do," he said, "decide not to do it. There is still time. Stay with me instead."

I almost did.

4

The years on the sea did not let me down, and it was easy
enough to get work on a ship. I cut my hair short, and convinced the crew that I was a merchant from a maritime family
to explain my apparent experience. Mostly I tried to keep to
myself, which was easy enough as my sorrow was so complete
that I had no interest in human company, and anyone looking
for companionship could feel that I was not the place to find
it. I did not have a specific destination in mind, since I had no
idea where Edmond even was, and after my years away, I certainly did not feel prepared to face him. So I moved from port
to port until I found myself stepping off the ship in Cagliari,
on the southern coast of Sardinia, and for some reason not
returning. There was no thought process behind the decision,
I just saw the buildings climbing their way up the hill from the
water and knew that it was time for me to leave the ship behind.
I didn't speak the local languages, nor did I blend in very well,
but since I had no interest in communicating with anyone, that
worked out fine.

The island shone a path, an invisible and incomprehensible path, but one I chose to follow. From the port I quickly

moved north, coming to the great wilderness of Barbagia, in the Sardinian mountains. Here I built myself a shelter, living off foraging and setting traps. I stopped paying attention to the passage of time, so I don't know how long I stayed there. There were a few villages nearby, close knit. Many of the inhabitants were shepherds on the mountain fields. I got the feeling that more than a few of them were also bandits, but no one in those villages would ever talk about it to an outsider. They distrusted me, avoided me. I was a little afraid I'd be branded a witch, but the villagers were too busy dealing with the practicalities of survival to worry about that nonsense, and gradually I was even able to trade with them, picking up bits of their language as I went. I would never be a local, but as the months passed, I got the feeling that I was gradually slipping under their cloak of silence, and that if anyone asked about me, not one of those villagers would talk. This gave me some feeling of safety, even though I was sure that Edmond would have no reason to be looking for me.

In order to open my arms to Albert, I had let go of Edmond and his many betrayals, but alone once again in the mountains of central Sardinia, I embraced revenge. I practiced the fighting and survival skills I had let lapse, and taught myself new skills. I worked on my strength. I worked on disguise, not only in clothing, but in physical movement and voice. I would take long rides back to Cagliari at times, to listen to any news, and hopefully to steal a book or two from wealthy travelers. I began to study things that I had been too impatient and restless to learn before. But anytime I felt myself grow tired and stopped for even a moment, I thought of Albert, and felt a physical pain shoot through my body, and so I didn't give myself a minute of free time. My mind had to always be occupied.

I lived in those mountains for at least as long as I had lived with Albert. Probably a little longer. And then one night, alone in my hut, I heard footsteps outside, slow and stiff. I did not look outside to see who it was, because I knew who it was. It was a shambling man, blood down his shirt, face pale, mouth contorted into a groan. I still did not know who he was or what he meant, but he had returned to my life, and I knew that my time in Sardinia was up. It was time that Edmond paid his debts. I took one last trip to Cagliari, and boarded a ship heading for France.

Paris was a different world than the one I had last visited, during the height of Napoleon's reign. There were more people, for one, and the streets swelled from the surge. Modernity had touched our world at last. Gas street lights brightened the night, making darkness a little safer for the people. The flickering of the lights gave an unreality to Paris. It felt like I was telling myself a story about the city rather than walking through it. But then Paris is a city that has always been more story than place. The lights were only installed on the wealthiest streets so far, but those were exactly the streets I was heading toward.

The house on Rue de la Chaussée-d'Antin looked as tall and impressive as the first time I had seen it. Any signs of the violence from our last visit had long since been repaired and painted over, as distant now as the memory of it. Had we once been so young and stupid, running from soldiers paid by Edmond to impersonate the men of Lady Nora?

The servant at the door squinted at me to see if he recognized my face, and when he didn't, his squint settled into a sneer.

"No visitors today, I'm afraid," he intoned, and looked past me with the solemn expression of those who are paid to be difficult.

"André will want to see me."

The man's smirk returned slightly, but still he did not deign to acknowledge my presence. So I kneed him in the balls and walked into the building. I figured I could sort it out with André once I saw him.

The entrance hall was even more lavish than when I had last visited. André had always had expensive tastes, but in his older age, he had really let himself indulge. He had taken over his family business, and it was thriving better than ever. There were silks from China, depicting landscapes and incredible creatures. I didn't know enough about the world yet to know if they were fanciful or the actual flora and fauna of the region. There was porcelain from the Dutch. From Luftnarp, there were large granite bowls. That was what Luftnarpian craftsmen made, and no one knew why, or what exactly one was supposed to do with a large granite bowl, but they did make them perfectly, and so people bought and displayed the useless things. André had eight. From Svitz, there were beautiful figurines of people screaming, which the rest of Europe found unnerving but which Svitizians reportedly found quite cute. And from Franchia, mysterious and vacant land of arches, there were several lovely paintings of dogs and other domestic animals. No one knew who made these paintings, since not a soul lived in the entire country, but occasionally these paintings of undisputedly Franchian origins would show up in the finest shops for exorbitant prices, and the rich and foolish would snap them up. I admired the five that André had acquired.

"My god," I heard behind me.

"A truly stunning collection," I said, before André had swept me into a hug.

"I thought you were dead. My god."

He had grown older, as had I, and a little heavier, as happens with age, but he was absolutely himself. I started to cry.

"Now, there, there," he said, sweeping me back against his shoulder and letting me ruin the expensive material of his jacket.

The front door banged open, and the man who had finally recovered enough to walk came limping in. "That's her," he shouted. "There's the criminal."

"Gérald, we've all been criminals at some point in our lives."

Gérald took in the affectionate way that André was treating me, and I saw his world crumble before him. "But sir . . ."

"That'll be enough. Please shut up and go keep the actual riffraff out."

"I . . . Very good, sir." He moved painfully back outside.

"I did get him real good. You could have been nicer," I said.

"Ah, Gérald has always been a fool."

For a few silent seconds, André considered me closely.

"What?"

He frowned. "You look a little less like yourself."

"We all look different," I said. "Time is unforgiving."

"No." He stared so long that it made me uncomfortable. "Your face is . . . less so."

"It's less my face?"

"Yes." He shook his head as though to wake up from a dream. "Come, let's have a drink."

The living area was as lavish as the entrance. In the years since, André had returned to his family, and despite the tenor of their parting before, he had been accepted back once he had made clear he was no longer working on the left side of the law. Despite their fears, the family had quickly regained their status in the social upheaval following Napoleon's defeat.

"I hope you will be staying for some time," he said, as he poured us glasses of the kind of wine I had not been able to afford since I had spent my last stolen coin.

"Unfortunately not," I said. I felt heavy bringing this burden to him, but it was his burden too. "I came because we have committed a terrible act, and now we must make right what can be made right."

5

I will not be caught unawares. I will not be unprepared. I will not fail. And I will take as long as I need in order to make sure that this remains true.

In Rome, I slip down an unassuming alley just south of the Tibor into the shop of a man who sells daggers and swords, deadly functional items, not intended for ornamental use. He looks at me over the thick lenses of his spectacles "What are you looking for?" he says, in the soft accent of the Romans. "Pain. Unbearable, unspeakable pain," I say. He smiles and pulls a wooden box from under the counter. "You have come to the right place," he says, and he shows me the most wicked knives I have ever seen. I buy two.

I age, and each year I am a little slower, but also a little better prepared. I would rather be older and have accounted for every possibility than once again face Edmond as a young and raw talent, and once again be easily swatted aside. Let my years pass. I gave up a life when I left Albert. Now life has no meaning for me. I am an instrument, as brutal and single-purpose as the weapons I have purchased.

In Stockholm I meet with a black market trader known as

The Shadow of Gamla Stan, who is perhaps more powerful and dangerous than the King that ostensibly reigns from that town. The Shadow's loyal subjects are invaluable for anyone looking to overwhelm a dangerous enemy. These men are mostly small-time thugs and thieves, but there are hundreds of them, and every one of them is indebted to their leader. He is happy to write off any monetary debts in exchange for a lifetime of loyalty and dedication. I do not wish to owe The Shadow of Gamla Stan anything. I wish for him to owe me.

The Shadow and I meet in a lavishly appointed home on his name-sake island at the heart of the city. Outside the windows, the harbor glitters in the mid-summer sun. I tell him that I will pay a fair price for the aid of his fighting men. "I do not need money," he says, indicating the decadent gold lamps and marble floors. "Money is not special. I need something special," he says. "Bring to me the Murderer's Mask, rumored to be in the vaults of Drottningholm Palace. It is the very mask worn by the assassin of King Gustav III. If you bring it to me, you will have the promise of my men." It is not easy. It takes me weeks to plan, and days to execute. It is not dangerous, but tedious. Many heists are in reality the result of hours of boring work rather than a few moments of great adventure. I retrieve the precious item, more out of patience and bribery than skill, offer it to the Shadow, and leave Stockholm with the promise that when I ask for them, a small army will be at my call.

As I live, Edmond lives. I hear of him occasionally. The Duke's Own is everywhere in Europe, especially in bars. Drunk men speak loudly, and drunk thieves even louder. I listen, waiting to hear the name of their legendary spymaster. His genius is in how little profile he takes on. Even as his power grows, and it grows massively, his name is rarely heard.

He governs by the nudge, by the knife in the back, by the threat from the shadows. Still, I know him well. Even in the darkness he surrounds himself with, I can see him.

At an inn in Sofia, I find three men who are members of The Duke's Own. I buy them drinks and ask about the sea, about their ship. They are drunk and forthright. Made unwise by my eagerness for revenge, I press further. I ask about Edmond, his whereabouts, his current dealings. Tell them I am an old friend. They stop speaking and leave. That night as I begin to fall asleep, I hear the familiar clicking of a lockpick. Whoever is attempting to break in is an amateur, and an impatient one at that. I have to scramble out a back window as the front door is kicked in. I believe Edmond still thinks I am dead. But he knows someone is sniffing around, and his protection of his privacy is absolute. I will have to be more careful.

That night I make my way to Palestine where he won't think to check and where his reach is unlikely to stretch. I hide out for a year. Jerusalem has no choice but to be a letdown. It is the center of so much myth and legend, and yet it is also a place where people live, and so has all the messy and unglamorous necessities of that life. The disconnect between the mythology and the physical reality of the place is disorienting. During that year, I live a quiet life. I eat, I look up at the hills, and sit in the sun. But it is not like my peaceful oasis with Albert. There is no joy in it. I exist, like moss exists, or the ancient walls of Jerusalem, or the soil that came long before those.

Between these sojourns, I vanish back into the wilderness of Sardinia, where the locals begin to know me by one of my many names, and are willing to trade me for food and look me in the eye. In this way, I grow older, as the years of preparation pass and pass.

6

In the village of Gwoździec, a day's ride at least into the Lithuanian countryside from any city, there was a rabbi of considerable renown. I had learned of him while in Jerusalem, and knew I must visit him immediately. He led his community wisely, kept up careful relations with the Christian neighbors to keep at bay the constant threat of pogroms and murders, and his command of Talmudic matters was already legendary after only a few years in his position of authority. I went to consult with the rabbi one cold winter's evening, as the snow drifted in great swells along the roads.

The synagogue was a tall, graceful wooden structure. I pushed my way in from the biting wind to the warmth spilling out from the brick hearth. It was like stepping through the gates into the Garden itself. The ceiling and walls were painted bright colors depicting plants and animals. It was immersive, and made me feel like I was floating up into the world it had created. It was a lovingly articulated masterpiece, and I still think about it regularly, long after it has been burned along with the community that had built it.

"What can I do for you?" said a gruff voice, and I looked

down from the splendor of the ceiling to see the rabbi approaching, a thin man with a storm cloud of a voice and thick expressive eyebrows.

He had arrived in town as a traveling scholar and quickly gained respect for his knowledge, while at the same time deflecting envy from the other young men of the village with his humble generosity and kindness. No one was quicker to point out when someone else was correct or faster to concede an argument. In this way, he had become the most well-liked man in the village, and no one thought it unusual when he began courting the rabbi's daughter. Marrying her had cemented his place in the community, and when the old rabbi had died, it was a natural and easy choice for him to take that place.

And now here he was, staring at me with his mouth agape. "My G-d," he said. "I never thought I'd see you again."

"You can't lose me so easily," I said to Rebekah, and she threw her arms around me. We embraced for a long time, and if any of her community had come in, there might have been some awkwardness in explaining the long embrace of a strange woman, but no one came in and Rebekah led me through the night to her home.

Her wife stood to greet her husband as we entered, then started upon seeing me.

"It is okay, Yemima," Rebekah said. "This is an old friend."

Yemima smiled tentatively and said a few gentle words in Yiddish. I smiled back, hoping my greetings would transcend my lack of her language.

"She and I were lucky to find each other," said Rebekah, as she started to remove the elements of her disguise and place them carefully near the bed where they could be quickly reached in case of unexpected callers at night. "I believe she would have faced an unhappy life here, unable to be united with someone she was able to truly love. But I provide the perfect middle between what she wants and what she is allowed to have. And in return, she has shown me love I didn't know was possible. I never thought such happiness was available to me."

She gave Yemima a long kiss, and I felt the terrible weight of my intrusion on this perfect life. I was a dark visitor bearing only revenge and regret.

"I am glad you have found this place," I said. "The synagogue is so beautiful."

"It is not a perfect community, but it is our community." Rebekah squinted at me. "I would say you have grown older, but that is not exactly what I am seeing. Instead you seem to have faded. It is hard to remember your face even as I look at you."

"You are not the first to say so. I look less like myself."

Rebekah nodded thoughtfully. "Yes, that's it exactly. You look less like yourself. But then I never look like myself." She shrugged. "You are my oldest and best friend. I am filled with joy on seeing you, but I also suspect you have come to tear me away from this life I've lived." She touched my face that was less and less my face, and she frowned. "I hope I am wrong. Please tell me I'm wrong."

I looked at her and at Yemima, smiling up from the hearth, unable to understand what we were saying.

"You have never been wrong in your life," I said.

Rebekah exhaled, long and tired, and it was only then that I felt both of our ages. "That's not true," she said. "I befriended you, didn't I?"

After two decades, and how the years did slip away so completely and quickly, it was time to make my move. I had heard that Edmond would be holding meetings in a rural area along the Adriatic, a stretch of emerald lakes and misty waterfalls in the Hapsburg Empire that was just starting to be known to the wealthy travelers of the continent but for now was still a quiet area of beauty, a playground for local children. I went several months early, to learn the surroundings and make connections with the farmers in the area. I got along well with farmers, having lived much of my life among the growing of things. They lived a life that I had almost lived, and so I felt a perilous longing among them that I did my best to suppress. Through a careful combination of asking them for advice, genuinely listening closely, and generously showering them with any number of ill-gotten gains, I was able to turn the population into my allies, and they provided me with regular updates about Edmond's progress toward the lakes, rumors filtered through far-flung family members and trading partners.

Mine was a blunt plan for a blunt hatred. He was meeting deep in the woods around the lakes, and so would need to travel by a series of boats as there were no paths to that part of the forest. I called upon my ally in Stockholm, and, as promised, he provided a number of dangerous men to back me up. Together we would attack the boat, capsizing it and hacking Edmond to pieces. As I said, a blunt plan, but I became convinced that trickery would never outdo violence. There are times when simply reaching for what is needed is the only way to grasp it, and what I needed was Edmond dead.

We waited in an inlet along the lake. The water was a luminous green that looked like a painting of water more than it looked like water. In other places, the water was so clear that the fish seemed to be suspended in the ether, moving by mystical means through the nothingness. It truly was an extraordinary place, and I wish I had been able to enjoy the beauty of it, but instead I clutched my Roman knives and waited to murder a man that I had decided needed murdering.

The plan worked, as far as it went. We saw the boat and came along it, having sprung from our hidden inlet to offer them little time to avoid us. But I had to call a halt to the wholesale slaughter of the passengers because looking into face after face, I realized that Edmond was not among them. Edmond, I would later learn, had cancelled his business in the Adriatic in order to take his young son to King's College in London. He had a child, a smart and charmed boy, like his father. More happiness for Edmond. More disappointment for me. I sent the Swedes back north, and my revenge was foiled for many years more.

Edmond no longer lived in Barcelona, and my inquiries there gave me no information on his whereabouts, but I did hear a story that led me west to Madrid, on the trail of one last friend. The brightly painted banner that read SEE THE GIANT was the first indication that I had found the right place. Crowds pushed into the little tent set up in a field east of Madrid's walls. Flames licked at huge spits of meat, and the tent was a perfect green that popped invitingly against the brown of the hills around it. I paid my money and was ushered into a circle of wooden benches. First a man came out and sang a love song that, as far as I could tell, was about a horse. The horse had died, and the man didn't think there would ever again be a horse born that could match that horse. Although he did eventually have other horses, still his one true horse would always be that first horse, who had died. Anyway, that was the gist of it. By the end, half the crowd, mostly the men who looked as though they likely didn't allow themselves to express emotions in any other venue or capacity, were dabbing at their eyes about the horse.

Then a couple of lithe acrobats twisted and toppled all over the place. The crowd now oohed with delight. Finally the main feature. The giant. I wondered how I would feel, seeing her in this context, exhibited for the delight of strangers. The giant appeared, and the audience was suitably impressed. The master of ceremonies waved her hands extravagantly and bellowed: "We present, Ivan, the Russian wonder."

Ivan? For what it's worth, Ivan did not appear to be anywhere near as big as Lora. After the show I stuck around and asked one of the acrobats about what happened to Lora the giant.

"Are you a friend of hers?" the acrobat asked, and to my shrug she added, "I loved her. I was so sad when she went. But she said that this wasn't the business she was meant to work in and I think she was likely right about that."

"Do you know where she went?"

The acrobat looked at me closely for the first time, and her smile faltered. "Your face . . . It . . ."

"Tell me where she went," I said again, and this time I let every drop of innocent blood I had ever spilled seep into the words. Her own face went ashen and she told me.

I didn't have far to travel, fortunately. Toledo was a day's journey, and I climbed up the steep path to its walls and into its winding streets, a dusty knot of a fortress in a dusty expanse of land. There I found Lora at her new job, keeping the books at an importer and exporter of religious icons and other sacred items, which, in a place like Spain, is a thriving business. When I stepped into the dim back room and found her hunched over a desk that was far too small for her, she coughed in shock, and it took a minute or two before she found her breath and her voice.

"You look . . ." she said.

"Don't tell me. I've heard it enough."

And then I was swept up into her hug, and it was my turn to lose my breath.

"Well, you still have your strength," I managed.

"How did you find me?"

I told her and she snorted. "Those circus folks. I hated being looked at in that way. I would rather sit here, and have no one see me at all. The numbers never stare at me."

"As a younger woman, I seemed to remember a joy in what your size could do."

"Joy belongs to the young," she shrugged, without any visible sadness. "I never thought I'd see you again. Now that I see you, I fear it is because my life is about to change in difficult ways."

I fell into the chair across from her, which was quite uncomfortable. "I'm so tired of bringing bad news. I feel as though my entire life's purpose is to cause harm to others." I twisted, trying to find the position in the chair that didn't feel like a part of it was jabbing into me.

Lora nodded at the chair. "When you are a bookkeeper, you don't want to make things too inviting for your guests. Otherwise they might get the urge to check in on you more often."

She rubbed her face, stood and looked out her little window to the dry hills outside the city. "I don't know what to tell you. We all don't get happy lives. Maybe a happy life doesn't exist, at least not as some complete, discrete entity. We get what we get and we sort through how we feel about it moment by moment. So." She turned back to me. "What do I need to do?"

If I don't exact my revenge eventually, time will rob me of it. Already I am old, and Edmond even older. Sooner or later one of us will drop dead. I just want to be involved when it happens. I realize that perhaps I have been avoiding this moment. That while I must be prepared, there is a limit to preparation that can never be surpassed by pure action. In other words, at a certain point one must simply do the thing, and yet I have avoided and avoided it, as the decades pass me by. My mother was twenty-six when she died on the water. Life is unbearably short. I have lived almost as many years since my discovery of Edmond's betrayal than I had lived up to that moment. Life is unbearably long.

Before I make my final move, I have one last bit of preparation that cannot be avoided, much as I would like to. It is torture for me, but I must know, and so I return to a familiar part of the coast, and stand atop a hill overlooking Albert's farm. My body thrums with nerves and grief, as I watch the sun glitter its way over the sea and the land until it has fully risen, and there he is. He steps out on the porch, the same way he always did, as though it were as easy as that, as though that kind of life were attainable. He is older, of course. Old, one would say. My breath is gone. I gasp against the pain. He surveys his farm, squinting at it with the gentle habit of decades. And then the door opens again, and she comes out. She looks a little like me, although more and more I have forgotten what I look like, and anyway, people tell me I look less like myself. My identity has been subsumed by my mission. The other woman is as old as he, and they stand together with the quiet intimacy of a lifetime spent together. He turns to her and the smile he gives her breaks my heart completely, but it also answers a question I needed answering. Albert is happy. He found someone and lived a life worth living. That is enough for me. I leave the two of them on the farm that they work together. As I travel, I pass a cart moving the other direction. When I look, the man driving it is pale-faced, and stiff. Blood runs down his shirt. "Why?" he mouths at me. I cry out, but now it is only a puzzled farmer looking back at me, alive and well and nudging his horses to put some distance between us.

Not a week later I meet with André, Rebekah, and Lora. Their faces are grim. I don't know what my face is.

"We do it now, or we do it never," I say.

Lora breathes out through her nose and nods. André gives me a confident smile that doesn't quite make it to his eyes. And Rebekah takes my hand. They are each loyal friends, and I know exactly what Rebekah is about to say.

"So we do it now," she says.

7

It was the long northern summer in Nulogorsk, Russia, and even in the late hour the water still glinted back up at the little bar on the dock at which we would make our final stand. The sun, low on the horizon, stayed close to its twin on the sea, and looking out over that double sun was a squat building with no name, no history, and few customers. Nulogorsk was a no-where town in a nothing region of a sprawling territory. I chose this little corner of the world as my battlefield because I wasn't looking to hurt any bystanders. I was only looking to hurt one person very much.

From the back of a carriage, I watched the bar for a long time. I'm not sure what I was looking for, as we had spent months in this town, planning every moment of this night, but still I stared at it as though I could see my future in its rough wooden walls or the queasy wavering of light reflected up from the water. Finally I stepped down from the carriage. I didn't tell my driver, a reliable Swede provided by my friend in Stockholm, a schedule for when to come back. Either I wouldn't come back from this, or I would, and if I did then the last thing I would care about was my transportation to the rooms that André had rented for us on the edge of town. If and when I stepped out of that bar, it would probably still be daylight, and my life's work would be done, and after that I did not care. I was old now. I could walk with no possessions onto a road to who knows where, and that would be fine. Finally, after seventy odd years, my life could begin.

But first this evening. And first this bar. I took a breath, and checked in on myself. This was me. I was here. I could hardly find it in myself to step forward, yet I stepped forward.

As I did, a crowd of people shuffled out from the bar's front door; André led the way, laughing and patting one of them on the back. He had done his part in this. The years passing had only firmed up his looks, so he seemed less like a flighty, beautiful creature and more like a gorgeous granite rock face, as solid as the earth itself. And age had added to his charm. The selfishness of youth had long since dissipated to be replaced by the grace of giving, which is sometimes actual generosity and often merely a more tactful selfishness. But André truly was a giving person. Perhaps that was easy when he had lived his entire life in plenty, exempting a few adventurous years in my company.

That advantageous childhood had also left him in command of a number of languages, most usefully amongst them Russian, which he had been using at this bar for some weeks now, introducing himself as a Parisian merchant with an interest in investment in the fishing trade. There were, after all, preservative techniques that might allow him to take the bounty of the Arctic ocean to the more discerning diners of France. The best lies are mostly truth. He changed nothing about his biography, and while the excuse was just that, in developing it he found it was a sound business plan and made ready to act on it.

Of course, he didn't need weeks to completely win over

the fishermen of this village, and, most importantly, Venedict, the owner and sole operator of the bar. The bar had no name over its door and was referred to by locals only as "Venedict's." André found Venedict a truly welcoming host, charming in a way that felt as sincere as his own charm. In this way, they enticed each other, and while André had never developed any interest in romance or attraction, he had as much interest in human bonds as any. "My good friend Venya," was the invariable formula by which he referred to the man. I did my best never to be seen by anyone in town that did not need to see me, but I found myself drawn to Venedict as well. There was something warmly familiar about him, like an old friend that I had once known but had since drifted away from.

In any case, when, a few days before, André had suggested that his employer needed a place for a quiet meeting without bystanders, Venedict had practically begged him to take the bar. André hadn't even needed to offer the gold, but of course he did, because he didn't want to take advantage. The bar owner had been so delighted, he had even allowed us some time late the night before to decorate for the festivities. And so we had, although the results were not visible to the casual eye. Or I hoped they weren't.

Lora was holed up in a village a few miles down the coast. We thought it best that there be as little connection between her part in this and our machinations in Nulogorsk, on the chance that Edmond's spies might start to piece together even a vague outline of our plan, or realize that I was still alive and coming for him. He had a powerful organization of crime and wealth. We had the element of surprise and a sincere desire for his complete destruction. This was the evening where we would find out if it was enough.

Lora's job was simple. Get a boat, whether through hire or sale. Then row the boat the few miles to the bar at the right time and wait, floating in the darkness beneath. Her massive arms would eat through that distance in little time, and so she had been the most obvious choice for the job. Also her size would have made her conspicuous in such a small town, so it seemed best to give her a role that did not require her to stay with André and I.

The bar had a square gap in its floor looking down on the harbor water. It was a convenient place to toss trash, and a miniature underwater mountain had formed underneath. The mound of debris was a point of pride for Venedict and his regulars, a monument to the time spent diligently drinking the nights away into squinting, bleary mornings. The hole was also just big enough for me to step through and fall into Lora's waiting arms when the time came. Yes, I was hoping to survive this revenge. I didn't see much point in a vengeance I didn't get to see carried through.

I approached the bar slowly, keeping an eye down the shoreline. Edmond wouldn't be arriving for some hours yet, but timing was never exact, and I couldn't afford to be surprised. I also glanced under the pier but there was no sign yet of Lora. That too was good, she was to wait outside the harbor, only slipping in after Edmond had come. I didn't want any evidence of our plan to come to Edmond's cunning notice. As I crossed the street, I prayed to no one in particular for Rebekah's success.

Rebekah's role had been to lay the groundwork for our confrontation with Edmond. She had insinuated herself months before into Edmond's social circles within The Duke's Own, playing not one but several different men, and so in this way was able to bolster her own reputation. Rebekah committed treason against the organization as one man, only to catch herself and then have herself brutally disposed of as another man. At one point she offered herself a promotion, and while no one was quite clear who this man announcing a promotion for the (unfortunately not in attendance) junior level member was, all of his connections checked out and the news was accepted with bored equanimity. All of this work, tireless and thankless, to achieve one impossible task for a man as invisible and stealthy as Edmond: to put him in a specific room, in a specific place, at a known time. At a bar with no official name, in the harbor of a town that no one over fifty miles away had ever heard of.

From her senior position in The Duke's Own, Rebekah had been staging a number of attacks with my army of trained and dangerous Swedes against her own underlings, all falsely attributed to the Green and White. The Green and White, once a sweeping rebellion threatening the monarchies of Europe, had, in truth, devolved into a disparate collection of thieves and bandit gangs. But Rebekah brought glory and fear back to the name. The mercenaries from Sweden, clad in those familiar colors, overran dozens of Edmond's ships in the North and Baltic Seas, cutting off his financial gains entirely in the region. Rebekah then staged her own execution at the hands of the resurgent Green and White, and later, speaking as a representative of this uprising, called for a private summit with Edmond to discuss terms to regain his ships and territorial control. Should he wish to retain a single crown of income there—which I knew, thanks to information from The Shadow of Gamla Stan in Stockholm, was the bulk of his wealth—he would need to meet with this man at a specific time and date at a certain bar with no name in Nulogorsk.

Rebekah could be quite convincing. Or I hoped she could.

For obvious reasons, I had not been able to talk to her since she had embedded herself, and so I walked toward the empty bar without any assurance that I would meet anything but another frustrating failure within.

And my role in this plan? I had traveled to Dubrovnik, to the man known as the Seagull, whose hut sat below the walls, next to the placid gray of the Adriatic. He was ancient, but alive, and he remembered me. "What now?" he said, and I told him.

"Simplistic. I expected more interesting from you," he muttered. "But I can see how the looming specter of death might make you value efficiency over artistry. I can have it for you tomorrow."

I spent that evening sitting cross-legged on a slab along the water, just outside of the walls, watching the sky and sea shift through the night. It was a long and perilous journey bringing such delicate materials all the way north, but shortcuts cannot be taken in this life.

It all led here, to this moment. I opened the door to Venedict's and walked into the small tavern. For all the importance it held in my life, this was the first time I had been inside it. It smelled sour, like ferment and acrid water.

I sat at a table in the corner with a view of the entire bar, such as it was, and prepared to wait. I wouldn't have to wait for long. A quarter of an hour later, Edmond entered and my vision swooned at the sight of him. My hatred was a second entity, sitting next to me, a hungry old creature with no eyes, no mouth, no face at all, only the quiver of rage. It was an inhuman thing, and it urged me on, but I sat, and did my best to ignore it, considering Edmond not as a plague that contaminated my life, but instead as what he was, a man. Merely a man. Older than me by fifteen years, and moving quite slowly, but still with the recognizable trace of the swagger he had carried his entire life. It was the swagger of a man who considered himself beyond the possibility of being touched. He would soon feel the cold digits of the invisible creature next to me, the creature already coiling itself to pounce. I would let loose my hatred upon him. I would get my revenge.

But first. "Hello," I said. My voice sounded weaker than I wanted it to be. I had reached an age where unless I drank water regularly, I got this wispy rasp to my throat that made me sound helpless and it infuriated me. He saw me and smiled, showing none of the shock I knew he must have felt, seeing a woman he had thought killed decades before. His career as spymaster was built on a careful performance of emotions.

"What a pleasant surprise. After all these years," he said, and I was glad that his voice was equally weak. Time had worked the two of us over, and in that way we were both no longer who we had been when we had last faced each other. This added some uncertainty to the equation. Who was he now? And who was I?

"Sit," I said, gesturing across from me, trying to take some control of the situation, to feel an authority that, if I were to make the mistake of being truthful with myself, I did not feel. Edmond chuckled, a warm, honest chuckle that reminded me of when I had loved him, when he had taken care of me and guided me into the life of crime my father had always wanted to shelter me from. His love had felt so genuine, but poison sometimes tastes sweet. And perhaps he really did care about me, even as he guided me toward my family's ruin. He crossed the empty bar, and obligingly sat.

"I didn't think I would see you again," he said. "Not in this life." His words were disturbingly tender.

"I knew I would see you." I kept my voice steady and cold, because otherwise the faceless creature next to me would crawl out upon him, and that wasn't the plan. I had to stick to the plan. Under my feet was the potential destructive energy of a lifetime of hate, and I could picture the flames even as I looked into his placid eyes. They were the same flames that had burned down my home, so many decades before. I would enjoy seeing the fire touch him, the widening of those damned eyes as he understood for the first time what I had done.

"Don't suppose it would come as much comfort to know that this had nothing to do with you," he said. "It was always about your father. His precious family."

Ah, if I could do what needed to be done with my hands, but those years were past me.

"There is no difference between my family and me," I told him. "His blood is in my veins."

"His blood is on my hands," he said, holding them up and smiling. This was all a joke to him. I was a joke to him. Or no, step back. Look at the situation more clearly. He was trying to bait me into doing something stupid. I would not do anything stupid. I would follow the plan all the way to the dirt on Edmond's unmarked grave.

"Where are your guards?" I jeered. "Where are all those young and strong folks you hire to make sure no one can see if you're actually as strong as you like to pretend?" Now I was baiting him, and I could see it work a little. Despite his airs of superiority, he had a deep pride inside of him. It was what had turned his hatred upon my father. A seething anger. A deadly pride. I knew where to scratch him.

But he too found some placid spot in his mind and settled

there. "I gave them the day off. It seemed to me an old woman was not a good use of my guards' blades."

Then he had known it was me, despite the extent of Rebekah's subterfuge. His lack of shock upon seeing me was not an act. This gave me a slight spike of fear, but I suppressed it. What difference did it make, now that he was in this room with me?

"Strange," I said. "Because an old man would be the perfect use for mine." I reached toward my waist and saw him grow nervous for a moment. Then he smiled. What could I do to him? I pulled out one of my Roman knives and threw. The blade came to rest in the wall just by his head and his smile dropped away for good.

"Your old bones are not so accurate anymore," he said.

"If I had wanted to hit, I would have hit. I only wanted your attention," I said. I had wanted to hit. My old bones had missed. While the plan was a good one, if I could go ahead and skewer the bastard's head to the boards I would have. But my arm was not what it once was. Still, I wasn't going to let him know that. I took a second Italian knife out and laid it on the table. He was jumpy now. A little nervous. This was all going well.

"I came unarmed," he said, spreading his hands.

"Liar."

He shrugged, and pulled out a knife of his own, setting it neatly across from mine. "It's merely a wood carving blade."

"And your guards are all hidden somewhere on the waterfront outside. You don't take chances. Even with old women like me."

"An absolutely fair point," he said.

"So here we are. Shall we have a duel, you and I?"

"Oh, ho ho." He shook his head. "I think our days of dueling set themselves to rest some time ago."

"Then I suppose we could simply talk," I said.

"Ah yes. Talk. That's good. For I do have a few matters to discuss."

Glancing down through the hole, I saw the dark outline of a boat against the soft glint of the surface. Lora was ready. Everything was in place. And hidden beneath the floorboards of the bar, the explosives that I had placed, provided to me by the Seagull of Dubrovnik. I had not told André this part of the plan, as blowing up the establishment of a kind and dear man as Venedict would have alarmed and confused André, but I knew we could procure the funds to rebuild such a modest bar.

I shifted my chair, and in the process, seemingly by accident, tapped the wood twice to alert Lora below that it would only be a couple minutes now. When I tapped three times, that would be the moment.

"I'm listening," I said to him. Now that everything was in place, a conversation wouldn't make any difference. I was fine with letting him blabber his last breaths out.

"I imagine you hold quite a grudge against me," he said. "And it is understandable. But foolish. What benefit is there to a life spent casting yourself against me like a wave against rocks? The rocks stand. The wave dissipates into spray."

"And gradually the waves whittle the rocks away into nothing."

"If we had a thousand years, a fair point," he said. "But unless you have a way to give yourself endless time to complete your revenge, then it would appear you have only a few years left. What I have to propose is this: Why not spend those few years living quietly? If you will walk away, I will walk away.

Neither I, nor anyone in my organization, will seek you out. Surely one of your kind friends will take you in, busy as they are with their more productive lives. Surely Albert—although I do see he has married—would welcome in an old friend." His words, carefully and cruelly chosen, stung acid. "I'm offering you a chance here."

The stupid, condescending man. To think that I hadn't offered that same chance to myself years before, and come to the conclusion there was no moral way forward in that direction. No, both of our lives led only to here, only to this village whose name would be long forgotten, to this bar that was not even going to exist in a few more minutes. Just a tap. Three times. And then Lora would light the fuse. André already would have quietly barred the door on the outside as soon as Edmond had entered. I would drop down into the boat. And before it could even occur to Edmond to follow, the fuse would reach the barrels I had brought north from the Adriatic, full of a most efficient substance. The bar would be an inferno. This sad struggle that had entangled our two lives would end with the arctic winds blowing away the ash.

"Ah," he said. "It is as though I can read your thoughts. Speaking of your friends, how are they? Whatever became of that giant? Oh, what was her name." He mock-grimaced in exasperation. "Funny how her size is so much more memorable than her personality. Lora, right? That's right. Where is Lora for instance? Where could she be?"

I heard shouting outside. A crowd. I tapped my foot once. The lock on the front door was turning. I tapped again. I lifted my foot. Better to end this before whatever reversal Edmond had planned could occur.

The door opened and Venedict came running in. His face

was twisted in grief and again I felt some echo from earlier in my life. I knew that pain.

"André," Venedict managed. "It's André. He's been . . ." Venedict's face contorted into a sob before he could finish his dire statement. The expression was disturbing and familiar.

"What have you done?" I said to Edmond.

He stood and brushed his hands off.

"I'm afraid this whole ordeal has been rather an embarrassment for you. I would have expected better."

"Venedict, where is André?"

Venedict howled at the name. Edmond made an annoyed wince. "With the movement of tides, who can say, but it's possible his body is well on its way to the icebergs by now."

I took up my wicked knife and came for him, with all the skills that once my father had spent patient afternoons teaching me, but Edmond easily stepped away. My body was just not what it used to be. Those lessons from my father could not account for the simple fading of age. Edmond loudly and calmly said the word "Light!" And through the hole in the floor I saw a flame kindle in the boat. A torch. The light revealed its bearer not as Lora, but as some sallow-faced stooge of Edmond's, grinning up at me with the immutable sneer of a skull.

"Ah, I'm afraid you gave a job to a Lora too?" Edmond said. "Took eight of my men to subdue her. You should be proud. If I could have found the man who infiltrated my people to set up this meeting, I would have done him in too, but I never could figure out which one he was. Well, can't worry about every detail."

It was over. It was done. All that was left was Edmond. I lunged again with the knife, and for a moment I had one hand upon his face, and the other toward his chest, but Edmond, poised and balanced, took my arm, stepped aside, and used my momentum against me. He pulled back and I stumbled forward with the blade. I saw what would happen a second before it did, but I could not stop my fall. My Roman knife perfectly skewered Venedict, who let out a faint pop of air.

Venedict's face went pale, and his features contorted into a look of absolute shock and pain. The front of his shirt was wet with blood. He gasped at me, but couldn't seem to make words, leaning forward over the wound, hunching his back. In that moment I knew where I had recognized him from. Truly, I had known him my whole life. He had been my own failure, my complicity in all that would come, and he had followed me from my childhood all the way to this moment. A strange hunched man, bent with pain, lurching, mouth agape. The consequences of my rage had been given presage since my earliest years by this poor man's stumbling, dying body.

"Why?" Venedict said to me. His shirt soaked red. "Why?" And then he fell dead upon the bar floor, the last victim of my life of foolish failure.

But how is a child supposed to know what to make of prophecy? Truly, how is anyone? I cannot avoid what I cannot comprehend. It is only in Venedict's death at my hands that I can see the fault in my path. No. Not *my* hands. Edmond's hands. Edmond never needed to draw a knife to make decisions on life and death. He manipulated people into executing his every desire. I did not kill Lady Nora, nor Lord Fullbright, nor André, nor Lora, nor Venedict, and especially not my father. Edmond did. The faceless, hateful creature who sat beside me moments ago, perched upon my back and snarled as I knelt over Venedict.

"Venya," I said. I had moved too late to stop his fall. "I'm so sorry. I'm so sorry. I'm so sorry." An incantation for a man whom I had known since I was a little girl, although I had not known that I had known him. My spell was useless. I was not absolved. The creature on my back dug its sharp claws into my armpits, pulling me upward, but I held Venedict tightly.

"Well," said Edmond. "Hate to leave the party, but . . . listen. It was nice to see you. Really it was."

He paused for a moment, staring at me. "Your face . . ." he said. "You don't look like yourself." The creature's faceless head was right alongside of mine, gurgling and panting. Edmond took a little skip down through the hole in the floor. I heard his bulk hit the boat. I heard the crack of the fuse being lit. Venedict bled in my hands. The flame raced along the rope, toward barrels I had carried countless miles only for them to be used against me. The door to the bar slammed shut again, and I heard the thick bar fall across it. The hole in the floor was sealed from below, leaving me alone with the body of Venedict. The flame would be almost to the barrel now.

This was my failure. Not only of myself. But the death of my friends. And Venedict, sweet Venya, the last innocent to die in the wake of my revenge. I had no escape, no other plan. The faceless creature was gone now. With no vengeance left to fulfill, it had retreated back into my body as flames poured up the walls, a liquid in reverse.

I smelled smoke and alcohol and gunpowder. I heard a savage roar as the explosives from Dubrovnik, efficient as promised, ignited. I tasted salt and charred wood. I saw the walls burst outward. I felt the man whose body I was holding torn from me.

I was in the air, and then I was in the deep water. It was freezing. I thought that perhaps I could swim, but I didn't know how injured I was, and anyway I didn't have the strength I used to have.

They came to me one by one.

First came André, sweet André, who had disappointed his family with his embrace of my way of life. I wondered if all in all I had been a net positive or negative for him. Certainly he would have had a more peaceful life without me, but I wondered if he would have been happy. Of all of us, he enjoyed the excitement of it the most. I did not mourn his death the way I would mourn Lora's.

The pain here was heavy, because Lora found joy not in our way of life but simply in the expression of her massive body, which could have been found in any of several more salubrious means of living. To have brought her all the way to this seedy corner of this seedy world, and to have her die over something as silly as a boat, that was a heavy blow.

Then Rebekah, and here I had some solace, because I knew that she had disappeared. Her greatest skill was never to be seen, or at least not to be seen as she was, and so I knew that somewhere a tired soldier or an industrious merchant or a tattered peddler was making her way back to Lithuania, and to the wife that waited for her there. She, of all of us, would die at home, and I was glad of it.

The water grew colder, but I began to feel warm. It was as though my body didn't want me uncomfortable for this drift downward into the frigid darkness of the sea, and I was grateful for the wisdom of flesh. I moved my limbs a little, just to see if I could, and as I did, I saw suddenly one of those clear, mild mornings on the Mediterranean, when Albert and I would go swimming in our cove. The water was clean, the waves were light, and our bodies were so young and so strong. We darted through the water, beings of promise, as all children are, yet to become the beings of regret that we all transform into. Through that water I could see the face of Albert, and he smiled at me, and I smiled at him, and I would never see him again, not in this or any other life, because as Lora said, there is no whole, discrete entity called a happy life, only sometimes we get happiness but often we don't, and either way we must keep going. As my limp and bloodied body sank to the bottom, I saw my younger self in memory rising back up. I saw my head breaking the surface. There on the shore, I saw my mother and my father. They waved to me, beckoning me over, and my younger body moved toward them with strong sure kicks, touching the shore just as my current self, lifeless and torn, touched the sea bottom, and both selves felt the soft grit of sand upon their skin.

CRAIG

2020

Your father was a real shit, Craig. He was a good father, and he loved you, but that doesn't mean he wasn't awful in other ways. He didn't take care of himself, which was selfish. You know how I feel about that. If you don't take care of yourself . . . you know the rest. You noticed, I'm sure, that he left you and your mother no money. He drank a lot. Not stumbling through the daytime drunk. He always waited until evening to have a scotch or a beer, but until his cancer diagnoses, I don't think he had a single day in twenty years where he didn't have two drinks.

Plus, Donald had an affair. It was after you were born, thank goodness for you, but such a tragedy for your mother, Marina. She found out because of the rain.

Marina's sister, your aunt Eugenia, lived in Red Mesa, about a forty-five-minute drive down Route 800. When Eugenia broke her jaw playing chess (she took a brutal hit from someone easily two weight classes higher than she), Marina went to spend the week with her. Decent sisterly things: liquefying foods, cleaning up, taking care of bills, being good company, and so on.

The afternoon your mother left for her sister's, a storm rolled in. A rare storm for the desert, and the streets flooded. Marina knew it was coming so she left early, but after stopping at the Ralph's to pick up produce, she missed her window, and the rain was already coming down. Night Vale is not built to handle much rain, and the streets began to flood. The Highway Department blocked access to Route 800, and Marina gave up and drove home. There was a blue Lincoln in the driveway. When she came inside, she saw Donald standing in the doorway to the bathroom. A towel around his waist, his thick peppered hair matted to the side of his flushed face.

"You're back," Donald croaked. "Why are you back?"

"Donald, you're dripping all over the carpet. Whose car is that?"

"Probably a neighbor's?"

Marina headed to the bedroom with her suitcase.

"No. Hon. Wait." He blocked her path, and she saw the window was wide open.

"Donald! You left the window open during a storm."

"You're right. You're right," he said, relaxing. Outside, a blue Lincoln burped itself awake and drove off.

As Marina set down her suitcase, she saw a single earring, a dime-sized opal, lined in gold. It looked like a delicately painted fingernail. Marina did not linger long on the earring. She knew immediately the story of the shower, the window, the Lincoln, the opal, but she did not confront Donald about it. Instead she told her husband about the highway closing, and how she called her sister's neighbor to have them go check in on Eugenia today. That night, when Marina went to bed, she saw the earring was gone. She never mentioned any of this to your father or anyone else, save for an obtuse comment when you were eighteen years old and shopping for your first car. You liked the Nissan Versa, in cobalt.

"I'm not buying you a blue car. Pick something else," she said, and you were angry, and you still resent her (a little bit) for it.

When Doctor Hernandez told Marina that Donald's cancer was not only in his lungs, but also his bile duct, his colon, and his liver, she did not cry. She made him food, held him when he was sick from chemo, kissed his hair, read books to him, and bought him new music to listen to. The doctor's prediction of twelve to eighteen months stretched to four years. And when he died, she cried, not because her husband was gone, but because you were crying. You loved your father. And you wailed, and it hurt to see her child so inconsolable.

Marina said, "He'll always be a part of you, Craig. Dead dads are magic in that way."

You were only seven, and this comforted you. Dead dad is magic. That phrase stuck in your mouth like braces all through your teenage years. You still think about it to this day. Dead dad is magic. "He's living through me," you think. "*With* me. I can still hear his words."

Your mother never meant that dead dads have magical powers to remain with their sons. She meant living sons have magic and they waste it keeping dead fathers around. She wasn't trying to cheer you up after the funeral, she just accidentally formed a pithy, memorable phrase out of her bitterness.

The words you hear in your sleep, in your lost thoughts, in dark echoey corners of your home are not your father's. They are mine. You have long known I'm here, and that I'm taking care of you. That I want you to be healthy. To be financially secure. To be a good husband. To be good at your job. To raise a child. A boy, who looks just like you. And you are all of those things. You've inadvertently bested Donald as a man.

You put away money for your family. You've honored your marriage vows. You treat Amaranta as an equal. You finally even left your job with the car dealership and became an English teacher at Night Vale High School. It doesn't pay as well, to be sure, but the union-negotiated health plan is stellar. Plus, you found your true calling, inspiring imaginativeness in kids.

I heard Janice Palmer tell her boyfriend that you're her favorite teacher. She's begun writing short stories about an investigative radio journalist and his charming science-loving sidekick. You inspired Viqaas Bishara to write quaterns about space travel. And your greatest student of all, your daughter Camila, is already at age three beginning to read picture books. She knew how to read them but hid it from you, because she was afraid that if you knew you would no longer read to her. You assured her that you would always read to her, if she wanted. From then on, she's been comfortable reading the books to you, with your gentle help.

And while he's only nine months old, your baby boy Darius looks as bright and beautiful as you once did.

You're nearing forty, and you've accomplished so much, Craig. For yourself. For your wife. For your two children. I'd like to think I've helped, but I also tried with your own father, and his father, and his father. I try to help lots of people, but not everyone listens. It is the choices you make that get you where you are. And you have made excellent choices as a father and as a man. I'm proud of you.

But you're letting your paranoia get the better of you. I know you know I'm here. You listen to me. When you were a boy, and Davy Williams knocked you off your bike, right in front of your own home, you were scared. You crawled backward, belly exposed to that bully, as he advanced on you calling you "dickwad" and "fuckface" and other words only his most hateful of fathers could impress onto an already disturbed child.

But you heard something that day. Didn't you? You heard a whisper, "Kick his knee," and you did. You wouldn't harm anyone, but you did. You heard a sharp crack, and felt his leg bend in a seemingly impossible direction, and Davy shrieked and fell to the ground clutching his dislocated patella, and you don't know how you rose so quickly but you thought you felt a cold, shriveled hand yank your shirt collar upward. You raced inside, and when Davy's mother arrived, he was still shouting epithets at you.

You knew it was me that day. And years later you knew it was me who was texting awful things at women I didn't like so that they wouldn't date you anymore. I suspect you knew I even arranged that fateful meeting between you and Amaranta. Deep down you know I have been guiding you toward happiness and fulfillment, that by resisting me, you risk missing a positive choice in your life.

I watch you look for me when Amaranta isn't around, opening closet doors and taking a flashlight into the attic. You scan mirrors nervously.

But you have a curious one around now. Camila watches you too. She's caught you several times. "Who are you looking for, Daddy?" she asked when you were poking your head into the kitchen cabinets. What a disturbing question that must have been for you. "WHO are you looking for?"

Why would a child ask "Who" when you're looking inside cabinets? Wouldn't a normal child ask "What?" And you knew. She's seen me too.

Of course she has. Children are often the only people I can talk to. Adults are difficult, so judgmental about running into an old woman without a face who secretly lives in their home. Kids? I can talk all day to Camila. I once talked to you too, when you were Darius's age. You were delighted by me. And you began to talk back, not with words, but with demonstrative waves of your billowy fingers, and an articulated patter that suggested the shape of speech rather than narrative specifics.

Recently you've begun talking to me again. It's not delighted. Nor is it demonstrative. But at least it isn't yelling. Many evenings, you sit alone in the parlor and quietly, but forcefully, deliver a similar version of the same talk:

"I don't know who or what you are. But please leave our home. I think you have helped me in many ways, and for that I thank you. Thank you immensely for everything you have done, whatever that may be. But I'm losing my mind here. I can't tell if my daughter is talking to herself or to you. I can't tell if I'm talking to myself or to you. And I don't want this. I want to raise my children in peace. I've not always been the most responsible person, but I've changed. Am changing. And I can do this. I promise you I can do this. We can do this. Without you. Please leave."

And my feelings aren't hurt at all, Craig. You'd be surprised how often I've heard something to this effect.

Some people whose homes I live in, I just read their books and put the occasional dragonfly larvae in their coffee maker. Some people whose homes I live in, I have full-on conversations with. They love and accept me as part of their families. Some people whose homes I live in, I punish. Some I help. Most I ignore all together.

But I can't ignore you, Craig. You're special. I would never leave you. I will be with you for the rest of your life. Don't worry. That won't be much longer now.

I'm saying all of this but you can't hear me. You're too busy driving. I'm sitting right next to you in your passenger seat, and you don't even see me. I think you think you're alone. Oh, Craig, you're never alone.

I get it now. Your long drives out to the canyon or to the edge of town or down Route 800 till it loops back into Night Vale are an attempt at escape. This is your private time away from your haunted house. Away from the ghoul. The ghost. The poltergeist. Is that how you see me, Craig? As a poltergeist? A long dead soul determined to pester and annoy the living? I would not be insulted if you did. I suppose my behavior comes across that way.

This past Monday, you found a lucky rabbit's foot in your sports jacket. You didn't notice it until a student asked what that stain was on your coat. It was freshly removed from the rabbit. Then on Tuesday evening you went to go get pliers out of your tool chest to fix a loose bookshelf bolt, but you couldn't find them. You did find the rest of that rabbit though. On Wednesday you woke up with your tongue feeling around the empty space where one of your molars had been, just the night before. Losing a tooth is scary, right? In dream analysis, it's symbolic of feeling a loss of power. In the waking world, it's a literal loss of power. On Thursday night you found your pliers, and in their serrated steel grip was the tooth you had lost. I had the whole thing encased in acrylic and set onto an onyx plinth. (Most people don't realize just how long a human tooth actually is. They only see where the tooth stops at the gums, but that's not even half of it. Noting the look on your face, I don't think you knew this fact, either.)

You threw that sculpture away. You've never appreciated my artistic talents.

So yes, if you think I'm a poltergeist, then I would not be offended. It's not correct, but I see how you might arrive at that conclusion with your limited information.

When you drive you feel at peace, relaxed. Alone and safe. I'm glad you have a haven. I'm glad about a lot of things. Of any man in your family, at least for the past couple hundred years, you have done the most for yourself and others. I've told you all about your ancestors, but you don't remember, because I told you before you were even one. You just giggled and laughed all the way through it. It was cute. It was the last time you ever saw me. Truly saw me. You were delighted by me.

If you saw me now—right now—I don't think you would feel the same. But let's give it a go.

Hello, Craig.

No. No. Craig. Don't scream.

Yes, you are seeing me now. Stop screaming.

Silence!

Good. Now listen to me. I need you to know I'm here. I always have been here, with you. And I needed to say out loud that I'm proud of you. You have lived such a good life, Craig. You found Amaranta, so smart and magnetic. You created Camila, who's as full of wonder as a wizard's hat. And little Darius, as healthy and strong as a baby boy could ever be.

Craig. Are you listening to me?

You're too busy searching for my eyes, my mouth, my nose, any semblance of a face, to hear me, aren't you? I don't have a face, but you know me. You remember me from your crib. You remember what I told you that day. Oh, the breaking horror of familiarity is in your bulging eyes, on your quivering lips, Craig. I'm so happy about this. I'm so glad you remember our talks.

Your breaths are shortening, Craig. That won't be good for

your mindset. Concentrate on your breathing. In. Out. Good. Good.

I'm going to touch you, so you know I am real. Do you feel my hand around your wrist? Okay, keep breathing. Keep relaxing, Craig.

Anything you'd like to say to me?

You just want to go home?

You and I both know that's not going to happen, Craig.

No, I'm not going to let go of your wrist.

That canyon ledge is so close. I'm not going to take my foot off the gas pedal either. Keep breathing. It will help keep you calm as a faceless old woman folds her bony limbs around you. It's almost done now. We're almost there.

Craig.

Craig?

Craig!

Can you hear me? I'm amazed you're still breathing. What incredible determination you have. You're like Snowden here, Craig: You're cold and I can see your intestines. Did you read *Catch-22*? Did I already ask you that? A 120-foot drop into the ravine, Craig, and you're still breathing. Is that a choice you're making on your own, or the only thing your body knows to do?

Man, after all, is matter. Cells programmed to do what they have always done.

I'm glad you're not dead, Craig. I can see your windpipe is fully crushed, but you're a long way from anyone who could hear or see you anyway. Airbags and seatbelts save a lot of lives, but in this case, I think they've only prolonged your pain.

This is going to be a rough few minutes. Or hours.

Maybe days.

It gets cold in the desert at night, doesn't it? Are you cold? I bet you are, your insides uncoiling without skin to tuck them into the warmth of blood and body.

Eight hours, and not a single car has gone by. There might, if I'm honest, be a detour sign recently placed a mile back on the road, keeping any helpful traffic off it.

I saw your hand moving, so I think you're conscious. You were probably trying to find your cell phone. I put it in your glove box, so you wouldn't lose it out here in the desert. Your glove box is about fifteen feet over by those two boulders where you initially made impact.

Relax. You're getting upset. You're spasming, Craig. I think your body is trying to vomit, but it can't find your abdominal muscles, or an esophageal track. It's been a hard, hard day, hasn't it? But the good news is that day is almost over, and there will be no more days after it.

So let me say this: I've known you for almost four decades, and watching you right now has been a real highlight for me. I'm sure it's not been great for you, but we all have to pay for our secrets, Craig. And I told you when you were a baby. I warned you. You would one day pay for yours.

Good-bye, Craig.

You're gone now. I'm not sure if you heard all that, but I hope that you did.

I'd love to let your corpse rot indefinitely, but I'd hate to do that to Amaranta. Off to find the Sheriff then.

AWAY FROM THE SEA

1863-2020

1

This is what drowning feels like.

It hurts quite a bit. For quite a bit. Like a knife. Not a knife slashed swiftly, but a heavy knife lain point-down upon your chest, its gravity slowly piercing your lungs. Sharp but not brief.

For a minute or more without air, you think of the word *unbearable*, but you are only thinking of it figuratively. Your chest aches and you cannot inhale. There is no relief from the heavy blade of suffocation.

Eventually the weight of the knife against your breast is joined by heat, a white-hot steel searing black your heart, your guts, your very core. And then you think of the word *unbearable* again, and you still cannot mean it literally, because you have no choice but to bear the stifling agony of longing for a gasping gulp of an ocean breeze.

But you remember bearing pain is a choice—never a fair one, but a choice.

You smell salt.

You hear your heart churning like a locomotive up a hill.

You taste bile.

You see the flickering orb of the moon, a wavering, fading white glow above you in the dense midnight sea.

You feel water breaching your nostrils and your throat. The horde battering down your front gate to overrun the castle.

And you make a choice to no longer bear the pain. To no longer bear this pain. The pain of asphyxiation. You make a choice to bear a different pain.

You inhale.

I inhale.

I inhaled. This was then. I am now.

I breathed deeply the sea.

The pain seared. But only for a moment. Like a sharp knife swiftly slicing open my chest, and in the process cutting loose the iron binds that held my soul.

The cold water warmed. The midnight sun glowed brighter. I soared, even as I sank.

My muscles gave up their argument against gravity. A lifetime of debate finally settled. My body agreed to descend, and I floated down farther into the night sky below me.

I had feared the fall into deep water my entire life, ever since the high rock above our inlet with Albert. Now I realized that the fall was the only direction I wanted to go. Floating is tedious. Sinking is natural.

The moon was gone. The water was gone. I was gone. Everything was blackness and light. I was cold and warm. I was heavy and light. I was falling and flying.

And then I was not. And then I was rocks. I was sand. I was still.

When a whale dies, its corpse bloats with water. It sinks to the ocean floor and is eaten, not by sharks, but by tiny eyeless fish and crustaceans who take their share of fat and flesh, who make homes in jaw bones and who live lives waiting for the watery skies to rain meat upon them.

I was a whale. I was a corpse. What felt like larvae wriggled in my eyes and in my belly. They devoured me in millions of gulps each no larger than a droplet in a fog. I did not feel my body decaying, rather dissipating. Each molecule swallowed and digested and disseminated, millions of me repeatedly broken down and reassembled as a scale of a fish or a tooth of a shark or a branch of swaying coral.

I felt myself spread wide across the globe, my senses growing broader, less acute. It tickled, if I'm honest.

It is a slow process, perhaps years, for the world's smallest life forms to rend my body completely. But time is meaningless to the dead. It felt not like decomposition but like an explosion, a burst of confetti from a cannon in a victory parade, each slip of festive paper flitting in a different direction.

My life had measured itself in moments, in days, and in months, but my death measured nothing. I, like the universe, was cold, timeless, and ever-expanding.

Along the jagged, hard bottom of the sea, in no light, in no body, I was aware that I still somehow was. I could feel the water around me, dark and heavy, like mourning.

Sadness presses into you like a shaper of clay, sculpting your spirit into the form of a blighted tree, into the form of a dilapidated monastery, into the form of an empty hand. The depths of the sea, too, crushed me, pinned me down until there was nothing left of me for it to press against.

I lay there in the dark, immobilized by density and incorporeality. But, really, the reason I did not move was because I did not want to move. I was immobilized by defeat, by failure, by humiliation.

Like an infant, my memories were only emotions, untethered to narrative. I did not remember murder or betrayal, merely a kaleidoscopic swirl of anger, loss, and resentment. There was vengeance, as well, but I could not piece together its target. I could only feel water, at first upon me, and eventually becoming me.

I was as fluid as my thoughts.

gunpowder
E
dm
o
n
d
sw
eetora
ngehoney
stickysou
ronmy
lip

cool black blood of ocean brine in my heart arteries twisted back into themselves a closed circuit this is what i always was and will ever be a small boat born on the mediterranean furious splashes of oars as my mother exchanged her life for mine my father my screams under his screams as he taptaptapped upon my mother's ashen face our howls heard only by the sea her blood washed from my body an ineffective baptism

From whence I came so have I returned.

E
dm
o
n
d

I heard a name in my ears, but I had no ears. The word sliced me like a blade.

E
dm
o
n
d

I felt his throat in my fingers, but he was not there. He was with the living.

I felt my hair waving slowly about my face, enchanting throes of silk billowing around a graceful dancer. But I saw only sea. I saw only sun melting away the wet sky. I saw coral. I saw life I had never seen before, but I had no eyes.

I felt water in my sinuses, but I had no nose.

E
dm
o
n
d

I felt myself mouth the name "Edmond," but I had no lips, tongue, or teeth.

The reef swayed in shallow water. Sunlight unfurling the gauzy pink of its limbs, the gaudy stripes of its inhabitants, schools of fish who climbed and turned and dove in precise formation, like a military band.

My father taught me to fish using a silk string tied to a branch fallen from an orange tree. We caught bugs in the orchard and kept them in a lidded pot, which we carried to a narrow stream. The bugs were mostly beetles, sometimes worms, and occasionally a sluggish dragonfly. He would open the pot, and I would tentatively place my hand into the crunchy stew of bug corpses, but a few were still flickering and squirming, grabbing at my fingers, hoping to climb to freedom from this metal tub of a mass grave.

I would take a scarab and solemnly impale it onto the hook. I pierced the point directly through the middle of the bug. To have the beetle sideways on the hook would fail to look real to the fish, I thought. Best to have it symmetrical and upright, perfectly balanced in the water. Fish were aesthetes in my young mind.

The first few times I had fished, I caught nothing, because I became distracted by the fish themselves, the way they moved, their panicked darts away from sound and splash. My fishing rod lowering slowly as my attention turned toward the study of their movement, their expressionless faces belying their intense hunger and fear.

Now, floating in this reef, amid the schools of brightly colored fish waving like flags, I reached out and grabbed one. It was blue and yellow striped, flat with long, bannerlike fins. It wriggled before me. I could not feel my hands, nor could I see them, but I held the fish. I felt its whipping fright, and I stared into its eyes, hoping to see terror, to see a plea for mercy, to find an iota of emotion.

I saw something worse. I saw nothing. The fish's face was meaningless, an ornament. I imagined someone looking at me now in the same way I looked at the fish, gripped with fright as they tried to discern any level of humanity. They would find none. I let the fish go, and it did not even look grateful as it darted to another patch of coral.

I was moving now, but not swimming. Like a dream, space and time bled one into the other with no clear transition. There were no doors separating the rooms of my experience. The parlor is the bedroom is the kitchen is the cellar.

I had stopped asking myself if I were dead, if I were a ghost, if I were reanimated somehow. The idea of heaven or hell never appealed to me. What could I do with the peace and prosperity of Lora's Catholic heaven, or the Garden and Gehenna of Rebekah's cosmology? Heaven is not heaven if that which you love most is not there. I had come to love my rage the most.

And hell. What is hell but the life I had lived? Life had already taken my childhood, taken my dreams before I could even have them, manipulated and abused me.

E
dm
o
n
d

Life infected me with vengeance and it had wasted me away. By the end, I could barely move from sore joints, my weathered countenance, my hunched back, erosion from years of obsession. What could hell do to me besides?

Heaven and hell were one and the same, and perhaps this sea was it. Yet I had held a fish, and now I was touching sand. I was alive.

The gritty squish of beach sand beneath my feet, in my toes, up my calves. The feeling of being unclean until the cool sweep of another wave rinses you off and you glisten and shine like a burnished clay urn.

I was above the water now, standing. My wet hair matted across my brow. My chest heaved and I walked, but it was not the walk of an old woman. Nor that of a young one either. It was fluid, incorporeal. I looked at my hands. They were the hands of an old woman. They were my hands, dark and creased with wrinkles and scars. They were the hands that lunged at Edmond's face moments before he abandoned me to the fire and then to the sky and then into the sea.

gunpowder

I could not feel the elderly pains of my back or neck anymore. I did not feel good, but I also did not feel bad. I felt nothing.

In a blink I was not on a beach but in a patch of tall swamp grass, the sea no longer in sight, though I could smell putrid kelp and salt. I was crouched, close to the earth, and I saw a small brown spider, about the size of my thumbnail. I snapped my palm down quickly, a child gathering bugs for a morning of fishing. I pressed my fingers tightly into my palm around the creature, sealing it into my hand, but it squirmed itself out, squeezing its compact body through my knuckles and skittering down my arm back onto the sod.

My knuckles were as tight as I could make them, yet I was too weak to hold such a small thing. I did not know where I was, or what I was. All I knew was that if Edmond were alive I would find him.

And then do what, I thought. I could not even catch a spider. What could I do to a man?

But beyond where or what I was, the greater question was when. How long had I been below the sea? How long had I decomposed? I lifted myself from the ground. It was no struggle. I was in a body, yet not bound to a body. The humid grass clung to my toes and stained my knees.

I did not know where or when I was, but I was certain that I would not be treated with gentleness, let alone respect, if anyone saw me.

An entire day passed and I did not move from my spot in the marshy grass. What god makes this awful place? No homes can be built. No crops grown. Perhaps a god of something more than humanity. Perhaps a god of all things, great and terrible. Or perhaps a fool or a maniac.

From east to west, the sun passed behind two long gray wisps of clouds, arced and motionless in the sky. They looked like eyebrows, but painted onto a portrait before the rest of the face. The most expressive parts of the visage, but completely meaningless when removed from the context of eyes, lips, and cheeks.

Feelings came and went, and I did not know how to keep them. At the height of the day, I burned under the tropical sun. Yet moments later I felt nothing, neither cold nor warm, neither humid nor arid. The sun swung smoothly like a trebuchet crashing into the western horizon, destroying nothing but the light.

It would try again tomorrow. I was certain of that, but of little else.

2

I attempted to sleep, but I could not close my eyes. I could not feel tired. I walked but with no sense of where I was going. I tried to mark my path, but it changed constantly. First a sea, next a marsh, then woods, and never a person in sight.

I felt dead. Not dead. I felt nothing. Perhaps nothing is what death feels like, but I believe now that I have never died and may never die. Still, at that moment, I smelled, heard, saw, tasted, and felt nothing, which is to say I lacked all awareness of my own existence. Lucid dreams of a lackluster imagination.

Yet the nothing was eventually subsumed by sensation— the wriggling fish, hot sand on feet, the putrid smell of sea, the soggy marsh grass—I felt alive, living in the real world. No ghost can touch something real. No spirit would deign to put their feet to this rotten, imperfect ground. But where were the people? Was I the only one here?

I could wander until I found other humanity or I could stay still till I found my own.

Sitting atop a small earthen bulge, which dared to think itself a hill, I stared into the sky, as black and soulless as the eyes of that fish. There was no expression to be found. No spiritual meaning in the geometry of distant suns.

In what I now know to be St. Augustine, Florida, I walked from the marsh, through a field, and onto a beach. The full moon lit the sand like snow. Atop the low ridge before me, an orange dome of light, a city's dying embers. Nighttime had cooled the burning day of the unknown town before me, and I moved in its direction. I followed an invisible path, one I knew was there but could neither see nor comprehend.

I did not walk. I moved. One moment I was on the beach. The next I was in a hotel room. A woman slept alone in a four-post bed, tulle and lace formed a sagging ivory crown atop. I bent over the slumbering stranger.

Young. Distressed. She snored loudly, her face pressed into an eider pillow, each limb escaping in a different direction and angle. Her wardrobe was tidy and full with dresses, gloves, gowns. A perfect stack of matching hat boxes sat atop the armoire, like a pyramid, a religious monument to the doctrine of money and fashion.

Her name was Eleanor. She was American, a grandchild of wealthy English expatriates who had funded the fight for independence from their former motherland. I did not know this woman, yet I knew her. Eleanor's father owned tobacco farms throughout the Carolinas and Georgia. He was one of the richest men in this young country. He always kept Eleanor close to him, even as he traveled. She was beautiful and stylish, but with a lack of obstreperousness that would have disappointed her royalty-adjacent ancestors. Her refined speech and manners impressed the genteel Southerners who met Eleanor's father. These things I knew without knowing.

He was proud of his daughter. He was proud of her the way a man is proud of his home or his mustache. Her beauty and charm were his emblem, his flag. Only a man of God, a man of wealth, a man of divine accomplishment could own something so beautiful, so perfect. And only an equal or better man could be allowed to take her from him. This is why Eleanor had always traveled with her father, to be protected as a rare jewel, not left at home to be stolen away.

The year prior, she had finally been married to a suitable match, and was awaiting her husband's return from a three-month trip to Europe. Eleanor never chose marriage of course, but she also never considered free will a reasonable request. Asking for her own agency would have been akin to asking her father for the ability to fly or move objects with her mind. She did make some choices. She had chosen this hotel in St. Augustine, near the port where her husband would return. And there were other choices she had made that I did not yet realize.

I loved her like I would a sick child. I brushed her troubled head gently as she slept and snored. I could not feel her hair.

I began to wonder again if I was, in fact, a ghost, though I refused to be dead. I had always respectfully fought death. Death does not often play fair, to be sure. The rules of its game are clear yet lopsided. Still I rejected the unjust notion that I should be murdered by the man who killed my father, my aunt, my dear friends, and who raised me on the poison of lies and vindictiveness.

I could feel tears welling but none on my face. I felt my throat swell and breath shorten, even though I had no breaths at all. I whirled my body around toward the mirror atop Eleanor's vanity.

I grabbed at the ornate wooden posts holding the mirror, but I could not feel the wood in my hands. I shook the vanity, hearing my groans of panic and exertion. But the mirror did not move.

Exhausted, I quit. I sat on the mauve velvet stool before the small countertop and I looked at my reflection for several quiet moments. If I were alive, surely I must learn to control my physical self. I did not look dead. I looked old, but alive, and as healthy as I had been before Nulogorsk, before my lifelong dream of revenge came to an end, before I found myself drifting cloudlike through coral.

The lines around my mouth and eyes were deep, but aesthetically so, like the stylistic flourishes of a master sculptor's rasp. I pulled apart my lips. The teeth I had in that last battle with Edmond were all still intact. My tongue and gums still pink and my eyes dark and large. But when I tried to examine my full visage, it was impossible. I could see each part of my face, but I could not see it as a whole. I was somehow less myself.

I placed my fingertip against its looking glass counterpart. The mirror was cold to the touch. I pressed the rest of my fingers and then palm to the glass. There was a mild chill in my hand, which sent a shuddering chill across the rest of my skin.

I felt . . . something. I was not a ghost, I was certain of that. I grabbed one of the drawers of the vanity and pulled. It opened. I could move things, hold things, although not well, not consistently. (The drawer pull slipped out of my fingers several times, and I had to constantly grab at it to make full contact again.)

Elated by my success, I stood up and kicked the drawer shut. The sudden slam caused Eleanor to stir. She sat up in bed, and I stepped backward into a shadowed alcove just beyond the moonlight's reach. The light was a blue shard across her body and I could see her pupils growing large. She was still breathing heavily, but it was no longer from difficult slumber. She was afraid.

"Eleanor," I said. "Do not be scared. I'm sorry to have entered your room unannounced—"

"Is someone there?"

"I thought I had died at sea, but I managed to come ashore. I saw your room, and I knew it was your room. I'm certain we have never met, but I know you. How do I know you?"

She did not seem to be listening. She stood up, and it was at that moment I realized I hadn't known everything about her. Through her nightgown, I could see she was at least six months pregnant. She reached under the pillow and withdrew a single-shot pistol. She pointed it vaguely toward me.

"Whoever is whispering in the dark, if you do not show yourself I will shoot," she called out. I knew she was bluffing because as long as she could not see me, she could not shoot me. I loved her like an untrained dog. She needed discipline, guidance, not a hand raised in anger.

"Eleanor," I pleaded, lifting my voice, to let her know I was not a rapist or common thief or murderer. It was becoming clear though that my voice was not full. She only heard faint whispers close to her ears. "Eleanor," I repeated.

She jerked her body around over her right shoulder.

"Where are you?" she screamed. "Who are you?"

"Eleanor, I was killed, but something kept me alive. I do not understand what, but I believe it has something to do with you. The sea swallowed me only to spit me out here. And I knew everything about you. Your name. Your travels. The birdcage of a life your father keeps you in."

Eleanor stopped blindly pointing the gun straight out from her body, instead bending her elbows and relaxing the gun, barrel-up against her chest. She closed her eyes in calm concentration, steadying her breath.

I wanted her to think about what I said, to allow me into her world, to speak with me, to help me find out why I came here. She slowly opened her eyes and said coolly, "You know nothing of me nor my father," and then in a single quick rotation of her body she extended her arms and fired the pistol at me.

The muzzle was directly perpendicular to my body as the shot went off. The explosion was a golden spark and charcoal puff. If I was not dead before, I was certainly dead now. She was an excellent shot. Whatever I thought I knew about Eleanor, it was not everything. I failed to know she was as skilled and steady as a pistoleer. I wondered what else I had failed to know about her.

But in the moment following the shot, I felt no pain, no impact. In the corner in which I hid, I felt my neck and my chest. I was intact. I turned behind me. I put my fingers to the wall and felt a hole where the lead shot had gone through. The wall was buckled, sharply frayed, and hot to the touch. I do not know how the shot had missed me. Or if it had missed me after all.

Eleanor did not move. She stared in my direction, weighing her options: collect the dead body of her intruder, or reload the gun. I weighed my own options, which were either to flee or to confront. I heard men shouting from the hallways and I knew my chances of escaping this situation were narrowing. Even so I chose the latter.

I stepped forward, the moonlight revealing only a swath of embroidered jacket and still-wet trousers, the remnants of what

I was wearing in Venedict's bar. "Eleanor," I said, almost pleading. "Of all places on the earth, I arrived here. In your room, having never met you, but knowing exactly who you are. I need to know why."

Eleanor gasped. She wanted to step back, to run away screaming. I could see it in her raised shoulders and swaying knees. But her resolve was strong, and she stayed in place, a protective hand across her swollen belly.

"Show your face, coward," she told me.

I took one more step forward, the moonlight cold across my face and neck.

Eleanor's eyes widened. She drew in a slow breath. I waited for her response: a scream, a sigh, a conversation even. The door of her room buckled under the thumping fists of men outside.

"Miss Eleanor, open the door," came one shout, amid several similar others of frightened concern.

"I must go now," I said to the still frozen Eleanor, "but I will return."

The door finally gave way and three men stumbled inside, immediately surrounding Eleanor.

"Ma'am, we heard a gunshot," said one man.

"Are you okay?" said another.

The third man walked to the bullet hole and caressed it.

Eleanor said, "I thought there was someone in here, but it must have been the wind." She looked to where I had been standing, but I was not there.

I was outside the door, peering in on the action. My movement was neither human nor ghost-like. I did not walk with legs. I did not drift through walls or hover off the ground. I had gravity. I could feel the floor against my feet. I could (occasionally) hold things, but I was still learning how to do so consistently. My elderly body was an infant in many ways.

Underneath the feeling of skin contact, though, was something less tangible, more powerful. My connection to Eleanor.

I watched her stand stupefied and indifferent to the adolescent panic of the men who designated themselves her protectors. They were employees of her husband who had taken over ownership of the young woman from her father last year, on the day of their wedding. These men lived in fear and awe of Eleanor's husband, a European trader who had inherited great wealth from his father. They were chivalrous and noble men who would come to the aid of any white woman of a certain class, but their protection of Eleanor was entirely an act of self-preservation. She did not need them, and felt more irritated than comforted by their presence. Still they clucked about her, because should something have happened to the boss's wife they would face more than unemployment. There were frightened whispers about how powerful and dangerous her husband's family was. These are the things I knew without knowing, but what did I not know? My connection to this wealthy American woman confused me deeply.

Their wedding was a business arrangement between Eleanor's father and her husband's father. The European had arranged for his only son to marry the American's only daughter. Money and accounts had changed hands. Graceful stags and handsome alligators had been gunned down on chummy hunting excursions between the two old men. The wealthy protect their wealth by combining it into more wealth.

Eleanor's husband was set to arrive by ship on Thursday night, so that he might be present for the birth of his first child, a son. Arriving with him was his elderly father. And before I heard the name of Eleanor's father-in-law said aloud, I already knew it.

E
dm
o
n
d

"Theodore and his father Edmond will be here soon," said one man.

"He'll be glad to know you are safe," said another man.

"Do you want us to tell him of this?" grunted the third man, still gingerly touching the hole in the wall.

"No," said Eleanor, her expression unchanging, "let me rest, gentlemen."

They left the room. She remained standing.

Suddenly I was no longer in the hotel but sitting at the end of a gnarled wood fishing pier hissing his name.

Eddddmmmmoonnnnnd.

I inhaled the first syllable and exhaled the second, as I kicked my bare feet in the moon-dusted water. My feet were colorless and enormous beneath the surface of the sea, warped and wavering beneath restless ripples.

I knew Eleanor because I hated Edmond. The petty gods of my forebears were real enough to let me play this game of righteous vengeance, and I would not disappoint them.

I did not know what year it was outside of Eleanor's hotel, but Edmond was in his mid-eighties when I drowned in Nulogorsk, and still he lives. Still Edmond lives in the wealth, peace, and fatherhood he always desired, free from justice.

In the stars above I imagined dotted lines and arcs, trying to find a divine message, but it was folly. They were only stars, and even if they were something greater, they kept their secrets. Below the stars, I saw, at the edge of the dark horizon, a single sail ship. It was lit not by the moon, but by the radiant stacks of crates upon its deck, and atop it a flickering black flag with a white labyrinth emblem. Like the stars, the Order would forever remain immutable and beyond the reach of my influence.

I let my legs farther into the water. The cold water soaked into my trousers and raced up my hips. I no longer feared the deep and I dropped my whole body in. The trauma of temperature and atmosphere caused me to cry out. The chilly brine seared my skin, and the silence of the midnight air was replaced by the dull roar of the ocean. A low, loud thrum that undulated imperceptibly, each change in pitch taking place over hours as the tides shifted, neap to ebb, the heartbeat thrum of the ocean. I felt alive. I did not believe I was dead.

I stared upward at the would-be gods in the sky and saw only warped dots shakily drawn on a fake firmament, a theatrical set piece for the play of my life. It was here, under the water, that I felt most real.

Two worlds, top and bottom, dead and alive, land and sea. Maybe I belonged to both. Or neither.

My chest began to burn and my vision darkened. I could not breathe. Lost in my joy at Edmond's eminent arrival, I had drifted several feet down from the surface. I tried to swing my arms to get back to the surface, but I could not move. At one moment my intangibility saved me from a mortal gunshot wound, and at the next it doomed me to drown.

Edddddmmmmmooonnnnd, I hissed with my last usable breath. I wanted Edmond dead in my arms. I wanted him to cough his last blood-splattered breath right into my lap. From below the water, I looked back at the stars, wiggling like silver worms in the wavy surface of the ocean. The stars became still. My lungs stopped burning. I could breathe. Upon saying his vile name, I was standing, full of anger and purpose, on the gnarled wooden pier again, facing upward to the sky. In my rage, I can be anywhere, do anything. Vengeance is my path, and I must never once veer from it.

3

If I were to kill Edmond I would need to master my movement and most certainly I would need to be able to grab things. One of the men in Eleanor's room carried a knife on his belt. That would do just fine.

The stars disappeared. I was inside the hotel once again.

I stood over the sleeping body of the man with the knife. I did not like this man. His trousers and shirt were folded neatly atop a chair next to his too-small bed. His bulbous feet hung over the edge of the mattress.

I reached into the clothing to find the knife, which I did, but it was difficult to grab.

Eddddmmmmmooonnnnd, I thought, and the bitter name clenched my hand, and I made contact with the hilt. Before I lost my ability, I yanked it upward.

I was angry, and I was armed. I held the short dagger aloft. My instinct was to plunge it into the chest of this sleeping man, but I resisted. A mysterious murder the same night as a discharged pistol might prevent Edmond and his son from wanting to land here.

Before I could turn to leave I felt a sharp tickling at my feet.

I crouched low and noticed a white rat just under the bed. It had perched itself onto my toes, its nose turned upward searching for food or sensing potential predators. The rat was beautiful and rare with its dark red eyes sunken in pink. The fur was pure white but mangy or at least scarred from near misses with the hotel's cats.

I held my hand out to the rat and it climbed onto my palm, a trusting companion. I left the room to find the hotel's kitchen. I took a bottle of molasses from a cupboard and returned to the room.

I set the rat onto my shoulder and uncorked the bottle. I peeled back the sailor's bedsheets, poured molasses over his body and placed the rat on his chest. It began to lick furiously at the thick syrup. Its licks were wild, open-mouthed, revealing rusty, jagged teeth. In its hunger and enthusiasm, it had begun biting the man's belly, little bloody divots began to form on his skin. He twitched in his sleep, the pain surely would wake him soon, so I pulled the sheets back up over his body, up to his chin and pulled them tight around his neck.

He awoke in confusion. He began to twitch and squirm.

"What is that? What is that?" his excited voice lifting on each iteration. "Ow! Oh, God. No! No!" he fought and squirmed but I held the sheets tight.

I leaned in close to his ears and whispered, "It's an adorable albino rat who's very hungry. Let him eat in peace."

He didn't even look to the voice in his ear. He screamed and thrashed his head about.

I had achieved what I came to achieve. I had physically manipulated an object. Several objects, in fact. And I had acquired a knife. I let go of the sheet. Double-checking my work,

I reached for the open bottle of molasses and successfully grabbed it. I tossed it onto the man's bed and left.

Then I was back at the fishing pier listening for his screams in the cool night air. They were faint but satisfyingly audible.

The remainder of the week, leading up to Thursday, I practiced picking things up: rocks, fistfuls of grass, glasses of wine. I cut my initials into the side of several tree trunks. Often I dropped the knife and spent fifteen or more minutes attempting to pick it back up.

I would breathe steadily and hiss Eddddmmmooonnnd until I had a firm hold again.

Whatever life my body had, it was made manifest by my rage toward the man who had killed me.

On Thursday evening, from below the gnarled wood planks of the dock, I watched as a brig pulled into port, but well before that I felt Edmond's arrival. I planned to kill him on Friday night.

From the damp below the dock, I watched a cavalcade of the soles of men as they escorted the hunched Edmond, along with his much younger son, down the walkway into a carriage which carried them toward the hotel.

That night I entered his room and rifled through his belongings. I found a diary, detailing the mundanities of daily life on a merchant ship. There were no mentions of any thefts or bribes or even murders. I found the date only about two years earlier when Edmond left me for dead in Nulogorsk. All he had written was "Pietr caught a marlin today. He saved the bladed snout and plans to craft it into a decorative sword." I found fur hats and polished leather shoes. But inside a small wooden box, I found another knife. It was dull and bent slightly near the tip, a lesser blade than the one I had just procured, but I knew this knife. I bought it in Rome—how many years ago—and had thrown it at Edmond (and missed) the last night we faced each other.

I watched Edmond sleep. He was so peaceful, and I was enraged. The audacity to find solace in such an insidious life.

I crawled into his bed and curled my body next to his. I leaned my head against the side of his and whispered, "I'm alive, Edmond. I want you to see me when I end you. I want to cut you from chest to navel. I want to show you what you're made of. I want you to see your weak humanity spilling out of you. And the last thing I want you to see before mercy swaddles you in her arms is my face."

"Edddddmmmmooonnnnd," I hissed, and he stirred. I steeled myself as he began to turn his body toward me.

"Edddddmmmmooonnnnd," I hissed again as I grabbed the knife at my side. I would not wait until Friday night. I would end him now. I did not know if his death would return me to my own, but I did not care. My life ended when he killed my father and took me from my home. I could not miss what I never truly had.

Edmond gasped and rolled over. And as he did, he grabbed a bell by his bed. He tried to ring it, but his clumsy hand sent it jangling to the floor. There was a knock at the door. He did not respond. I could see his labored breathing, his eyes staring up toward the ceiling. Another knock and the door opened. A servant stepped inside. "Sir?" the servant said.

Upon seeing Edmond's still body and registering no response, the servant ran from the room, and I could hear him calling down the hallway.

"Edmond," I said, trying to grab him, but I could not get

hold of his body or nightgown. The small dagger that was a second ago clutched in my fist had fallen onto the plush duvet. "Edmond," I urged again, my tangible body failing me.

From the door emerged two people: Eleanor and Theodore. I recognized Edmond's face in Theodore's, but Theodore's complexion was more wan, and his eyes heavier somehow, in spite of being several decades his father's junior.

Eleanor leaned down to Edmond, cradling her unborn with one hand and touching Edmond's face with her other. Theodore stood uneasily back. Eleanor and Edmond had not registered my presence on the far side of the bed, but Theodore clearly sensed something that he did not like.

"He has no fever," Eleanor said.

"Father, can you hear us?" Theodore asked.

Edmond stirred, a flash of recognition, and he lifted both his hands toward his children. They each took one of his hands, and they both began to weep. Softly, not heaving sobs, but gentle tears that fell off the jaw like drops off a melting icicle on the first spring day.

"My son," Edmond rasped. "My exquisite daughter-in-law. I wanted to see you once more."

"You have no fever, father. You're going to be okay," Theodore protested, but his voice belied his knowledge that this was the end. "You'll see your new grandson very soon."

But Edmond would not. He had lived a long and happy life, a life of safety, of pleasure, of privilege, of wealth, of success, and finally, of family. He had seen his son live with the same joy and comfort.

"That my children are here with me as I leave this earth is all I ever wanted," Edmond said. "Know that my life has been happy, and my death even happier."

I lifted up my fists to strike him, and let out a rasping scream of anger and despair. A smile curved across his aged face. My fists came down and connected with nothing. I groped for the dagger, but in my frenzy, my body would not cooperate. I made contact with nothing. No one in the room could even see me. Edmond squeezed his son's hands and let out a soft exhale that rattled as gently as a breeze through a leafless tree. And with that, Edmond died.

The couple held each other, and wept quiet tears. I longed to sob too, but I could not. Once again, for the final time, my life had been taken from me, yet I was not dead. Crying, even wailing, could not truly express the desperate, perfect loss I felt in that moment.

I could not even open my mouth to begin such an expression. Where had my mouth gone? Where was my face?

As the younger couple comforted each other, I lay silently, curled next to Edmond's body, the shape of a mourning wife. All hope was lost, and I wished I were alive so that I might die. But that would not happen. It may never happen.

4

I believed the invisible path I followed had misled me, had betrayed me as Edmond had betrayed me, leading me with false promises and theatrical deception, only to drop this curtain upon my head just before the final scene.

Days later there was a funeral. Everyone wept but me. I stood behind a tree and watched, unnoticed by anyone except for Theodore. He looked even worse than the night his father died, his eyes dark and haunted. At one moment I felt him looking straight at me, but as I studied his eyes, I saw nothing. Like the eyes of a fish, they were upsettingly empty.

I spent the next several weeks in the coastal water of St. Augustine, as Eleanor and Theodore moved forward with their lives. Eleanor was exceptionally healthy, but Theodore continued his pallid decline. His condition could be attributed partly to a half-knowledge of my presence, but I was beginning to believe he was also ill in some way.

My curiosity pulled me, at least for a short time, out of my depressive state. I followed him, watched him eat, bathe, talk, attempt to conduct business meetings in town with Eleanor's father, but everyone, including Eleanor, had noticed his weakening health.

One night, I watched him in his room. He turned in early, as Eleanor was still preparing herself for bed. He had already fallen fast asleep atop the covers when Eleanor, in her silk night-gown, entered from the toilet and stood over the frail man, her skin and hair radiant, her posture like an Athenian sculpture. Theodore, in a too-large night frock and thick socks, looked like a troll too tired to ask his riddle.

"Sweet Theo," she whispered through freshly painted lips. "Sit up and let me look at you."

"My darling Eleanor," Theodore grumbled, in a liminal state. He sat up slowly on the edge of the bed, and she leaned forward to straddle him. He then glanced back toward the end of the bed a couple of times. I had disrupted his comfort. "I do love you so, but I do not feel well tonight," he said.

"You must have some energy left to love your wife," she said, glancing backward over her shoulder to where his anxious gaze had been. I was hiding behind the armoire, believing I was well out of sight, but her eyes locked right on me. She seemed to look at me steadily, then turned her head back to Theodore.

From behind her on the nightstand, she produced two glasses and a bottle of sherry. "Your legs are so cold, I think a drink will warm you up."

They clicked their glasses together, announcing "to our love," and drank.

"My dearest," she said placing her soft hand on his thick chest, "surely you remember what it is like to be young, to be impatient, to want something before you can have it."

She bit her lip and then his earlobe.

"Want and need are inseparable, love," she said, "when you are young." She lifted his frock over his head and gently pushed him down onto the bed.

It was doubtful that this young beauty should be so phys-ically desirous of such a dried fig of a man. I distrusted and respected her with equal intensity.

She disrobed and straddled his torso. She heaved her body up and down and moaned so convincingly, as The-odore barely moved a muscle. I watched her watch his ex-pression closely, and at the almost imperceptible moment of his climax she let out a satisfied cry, undulating her spine, decreasing tempo and intensity with each wave until they were both still.

She dismounted him gently, like a trained rider from an injured nag. She put her gown back on and ran her fingers through her hair, and I watched in confusion as she removed one earring, palming it carefully in her right hand.

"My dear, you should get some rest," she said gently kissing his forehead, "but share one last drink with me first?"

She picked up both glasses and handed him the one in her right hand. I knew suddenly what she was doing.

"I love you," she paused, and then, "husband."

"And I you," he said, clumsily repeating her childish smile back to her, "my wife."

"Down the hatch," she said, and drank the rest of her sherry like a whiskey shot in a lawless saloon.

He reflexively did the same.

I watched his face contort for a second, and his eyes flashed the same emptiness I had seen before. He coughed several times and finally laid down to sleep.

Dunce! I was such a fool to let my mind nap in the presence of this woman.

The earring in her right hand, a small cylinder easily mis-taken for a glistening gem, a vial of poison. His wan face and empty eyes worsening since he arrived from Europe. She had been slowly poisoning him each night since his return.

She laid next to him, but I could tell she was not asleep. Eleanor and I, from our separate corners of her room, watched over the next two hours as yellow foam gradually formed at the corners of Theodore's mouth, and Eleanor wiped it away, sweetly, with a handkerchief. His breathing stiffened and slowed, and by dawn it had stopped. When she was certain he was dead, she held his body tightly and cried, an honest cry, a cry of love, but also a cry of remorse. She would inherit Theodore's and Edmond's immense wealth. She would birth her child. She would be free for the first time in her life from the men controlling her, but her tears spoke of the cost of that freedom.

"Sweet Theodore, I couldn't let you die without the sweetest good-bye." She kissed his forehead. He was smiling in death. Like his father before him, he had lived a privileged life. And his final conscious moments were in a passionate embrace with his wife.

"No!" This time my shout was heard. Eleanor sat up. The tears had ended, but their salty trails left lines on her face.

My own face felt hot, not with anger, but with woe.

She arose, stepping toward me. She did not look bothered, just studied me for several moments with curiosity and a touch of compassion. "I hope my face shines with such vigor when I am your age," she said. "Let those words be the last exchange we ever have."

She caressed her belly and left.

Over the next several months, I moped about St. Augustine hoping to find solace in the police's investigation into Theodore's death, but all that came of it was a report that the sherry he drank before he died was a gift from a member of The Duke's

Own. Perhaps someone he or his father had betrayed years ago had finally gotten him back. Others were certain Eleanor had murdered her husband. She told the investigators she was with him his last night but did not drink any of the sherry, as pregnancy had made her feel unwell.

Meanwhile I made an effort to cheer myself up by haunting Edmond's crew members, some of whom I remembered from my final days.

Instead of knifing (or hungry-ratting) them in their sleep, I would spend several days replacing their clothing with similar but noticeably different clothing. Or I would put spiders I collected in the fields inside their boots. Sometimes I would write messages on their mirrors like "God does not like what he sees, Timothy. Repent." They would think themselves mad and behave so publicly. Eventually I would drive them near enough to suicide that if they didn't choose to end themselves, I would do it for them, and no one else knew the difference. Each man's slashing of a wrist, or drowning, or plunge from a high ledge, came on the heels of erratic public behavior. Soon the town was abuzz about Ocean Madness, the intensified awareness of which made my task even easier. And it began to explain Theodore's sudden death as well. The ship from Barcelona was cursed, the town believed.

It was fun, I could admit, but it could not bring back Edmond. I am not a ghost, I told myself, but I am certainly behaving like one.

Eleanor gave birth to Theodore's child: a boy. She named him Gregory. And seeing Edmond's eyes once again, knowing he could live a whole new life through his grandson, free from judgment for his crimes, destroyed what little was left me. I was empty of meaning, of hope, and of life. I did not understand why I still existed at all.

This is what failure feels like.

Hunched over a sleeping child, the oblivious offspring of a vile man who never paid for his transgressions, who died happy and unaware.

Failure feels of fever, of hot blood under cold skin, bumpy and painful to the touch.

Failure is the sound of a gentle snore of an infant, ignorant to its sinful heritage, its putrid ancestry. The baby cutely flexes its fists through empty dreams.

I could have waited at that sleeping child's side for decades, watching it grow older into adulthood, into understanding, until the moment I could tell him who his father was, what his father did, and then what?

The grown child would say, "Sorry about the actions of a man I never knew?" He would exhume his grandfather's corpse and allow me to stab it in the gut and say, "Revenge is mine, Edmond?"

What I wanted had been stolen from me. That's not true. Something stolen can be returned. What I wanted had been destroyed.

For hours each night, I lurked around Gregory's crib watching him sleep so sweetly. I grew to adore his fat fingers and bubbling lips. My heart had not changed, but revenge was no longer in reach, so I did the only thing I felt I could do. I helped raise a child.

Eleanor never remarried. She inherited the fortune of her murdered husband and lived with Gregory in a mansion in St. Augustine. She possessed him as her father had possessed her, doting lovingly on him and stashing him selfishly away.

The boy was polite and good natured, if prone to occasional spoiled fits. I kept a close watch on him, sometimes singing to him as he slept to calm his nerves. I visited Eleanor often, helping her keep her books balanced and to cook. I never knew if Eleanor was ever again aware of my presence, but there were occasions when she would pause while reading or sewing to look around the room, as if she sensed me there. She kept a loaded pistol by her nightstand, but she had always done that.

Gregory was schooled at home. Eleanor taught him piano, grammar, arithmetic, and Christian verses. They sang hymns together, recited poetry and Greek classics.

Sometimes when Gregory practiced his piano alone, I would sing quietly from behind him. At first, he would stop playing, frightened by the unseen voice. But over the years he grew used to it. He would sometimes tell his mother that their house was haunted, but she would tell him not to play devil's games.

Gregory grew into a handsome young man, and Eleanor, like her father before her, controlled his social life with an iron fist. By the time he was sixteen, he rarely was allowed in public without her at his hip. Many other prominent families paid visits to Eleanor and Gregory, and like Eleanor, I too became quite interested in weeding out the less desirable options.

Delilah Thomas, a pleasant enough fourteen-year-old, was brought by to meet Gregory. Eleanor took a liking to the young lady, but Eleanor had not seen inside Delilah's home. I had.

For every young woman who came to meet Gregory, I spent a week secretly living in her home to find out everything I could. Delilah had a weak immune system, nearly died at age two, and routinely fell ill. I doubted she could survive childbirth, let alone have the child make it out unscathed. I wrote an anonymous letter to Eleanor about this, and the courtship of Gregory and Delilah was off.

The Winchesters introduced their daughter, Bernice, but Bernice, behind closed doors, was a monster, shouting at no one and throwing objects. She screamed until she was red-faced and near collapse, and would conclude her tantrums by sobbing bodily into a pillow. I felt empathy for this troubled teenager, but I also could not have her marrying my Gregory, let alone carrying his child.

For months Eleanor introduced Gregory to young women hoping to find another wealthy family to join into her own.

On Gregory's seventeenth birthday, Eleanor surprised her son by announcing he was intended to wed Letitia Van Alston of the Pensacola Van Alstons. They would marry in two years' time. Gregory smiled, but it was a false smile, borne of matriarchal tyranny. Gregory wrote often in his diary that he did not wish to marry anyone, let alone someone he never chose. He wished to play the piano for a living and travel the world. He would never do either.

I liked Letitia fine. She would be a healthy and loving

mother, perhaps not as fearsome and strong as Eleanor, but a good mother nonetheless. Despite Gregory's inner complaints about the marriage, he was a dutiful son, husband, and eventual father.

I spent the next two years keeping an eye on Gregory, but I knew it would be time to leave soon. I did not know exactly where I would have to go next, but eventually I would start to move. Lovely young Gregory helped me find my path once again. It was not a path of brick or dirt or stone, but a feeling within me. An intuition that my existence had purpose and meaning. And I would follow this path where it led.

By this time, learning the lesson of the sea's dissipation of my body, I found I could be many places at once, and I began secretly living in several homes simultaneously. I was particularly drawn to slobs and sloths. Perhaps it is the captain in me to demand better of people, or rather to demand that they demand better of themselves. I would tidy up squalid bedrooms and barn lofts. I would attempt to strengthen tenuous relationships by writing letters to people.

In cases where someone appeared beyond help and where they seemed a danger to others, I would terrorize them like Edmond's sailors until they changed or rid themselves from the earth. I would lurk behind them in mirrors. I would whisper to them in dark rooms. I would put centipedes in their mouths while they slept until they thought themselves mad.

It passed the time.

And every day I thought about Edmond's happy face as he died, him seeing only the faces of Theodore and Eleanor while never seeing mine. He never smelled my rotten breath, heard my gravelly voice, tasted his own nervous bile, or felt my blade in his belly.

Those watery eyes of Edmond's, clear and content as he looked into his son's eyes, were the same deep, thoughtful eyes of Gregory as he looked into Letitia's eyes on their wedding. Gregory had taught himself to accept the path he did not choose for himself, and I knew I could do the same.

I stayed in St. Augustine, because remaining with Gregory was my path. Gregory and Letitia had four children together, three daughters, then finally a son. They named the boy Gabriel.

It had been a quarter century since Edmond's happy death and my greatest despair, and here I was now cooing over newborns, each with their father's eyes. In every baby, I saw Edmond looking right back at me, and yet each time I felt such joy at the miracle of birth.

In 1892, when Gabriel was four years old, Gregory died unexpectedly, when the horse he had just dismounted kicked him in the head outside his home. The town mourned. Letitia, Eleanor, and the three daughters mourned. Gabriel was too young to fully understand what had happened to his father.

Letitia, overwhelmed by the tragedy, moved away from St. Augustine along with her children. Eleanor tried to stop her, tried to keep her family like gold in a safe, but Letitia could not bear it in Florida any longer. Outraged by this theft of her granddaughters, Eleanor removed Letitia and her children entirely from the family will. Eleanor died wealthy and alone ten years later of heart failure, sitting by herself at a long dining table after her servants had cleared the prime rib but before they had served the cobbler.

Letitia had to rebuild her life as a working-class single mother. Gabriel grew into adulthood, and married a young woman named Hannah. They had children, and while those children would not grow up with the wealth of Gabriel's grandparents, the love they felt from their parents would be riches and wonders enough.

I paid my respects at Eleanor's grave, and then I too set out. It was time for me to move on. I did not know to where, but I was certain it would become clear. The path reveals itself to the faithful traveler.

I walked across Florida. I didn't have to walk to move from place to place, but I did. In the decades that followed my transformation in Nulogorsk, I had grown quite comfortable in my new body. No longer did I struggle with simple human functionality as I had those first few weeks in St. Augustine, but in all my previous travels I had never been to America, and I wanted to see it on foot.

It was a beautiful place, but not a good place. Slavery and genocide of natives had been vocally decried in the latter part of the 1800s but were tacitly allowed to continue under different names. Wealth inequality, political instability, ever-expanding industry coughing black smoke into pristine skies, all fueled by an ignorant and hateful philosophy of manifest destiny—a spoiled, rich child's justification that everything he can see belongs to him.

The land itself was stunning in its endlessness, its diversity, its loamy soils and prolific wildlife. I saw my first cottonmouth in a swamp near Tallahassee. I named the snake Lora because, like my giant friend once did, the serpent had eaten a turtle in a single unchewed bite.

I stayed in New Orleans for twelve years. It was economically depressed and politically corrupt, but it was where the path led me. Since the night I was taken from my burning home, my path had always been clear. The night Edmond died, I lost my direction, my hope. But I had found my path again, and I would follow it for as long as it would guide me. The path was my meaning and my comfort. From New Orleans, it led me to Memphis, which had been decimated at the end of the nineteenth century by yellow fever. The city had just begun to turn itself around, as trade along the Mississippi brought more jobs, new homes, and a burgeoning musical spirit. I spent many nights over the next decade falling in love with deep-throated hymns of love and loss.

I could have stayed in Memphis forever, but my path had taken the shape of the Mississippi River, and I secretly lived on a trawler for two years, following a fourteen-year-old fisherman named Thomas. I dripped latrine water in his ears as he slept to give him infections. I cut serrated lines in his boots which caused one to tear while he was on the port deck. He went overboard and delayed his crew by almost an hour. Plus the usual nighttime whispers and centipedes in the mouth that had become a staple for me.

Thomas was a handsome and charming boy. I had followed him growing up in Memphis. Like all babies, he was a cute one. But Thomas's father Matthew was an insecure and controlling man. Matthew expressed his insecurities through hitting his wife, Laura, Thomas, and the other children. Thomas was bright enough to escape his father's reach at an early age, and he found honest work, unlike his father who, in 1910, was gunned down in St. Louis by a French spy who, through mistaken information from his government contacts, mistook Thomas's dad for an influential Spanish dissident.

Thomas exasperated me because he put everything into his work and would not settle down with a family. I eventually finagled a meeting with a lovely woman in Minneapolis named Pauline, and he was so frustrated with his constant illnesses and madness on that fishing ship, that he left the river to raise a family. Minneapolis's winters forgave no sins. And shortly after the birth of his second child, Thomas fell into the frigid waters of Lake Minnetonka while ice fishing. He found himself trapped below a thicker layer of ice. He could not recover his position, because his muscles stiffened. No one saw him fall, so there was no one to pull him out. In minutes, his body seized up and hypothermia painfully ended his life. His body would not be found until spring.

Pauline and her children abandoned the brutal cold of Minnesota for a warmer climate, and my path led me away from the freezing north as well. I saw Sioux City, a fledgling river city, growing rapidly with the influx of Dust Bowl refugees. But I did not stay long. The path guided me deeper into America's economic pain, as I reached Enid, Oklahoma, a town with more oil derricks than jobs. The oil discoveries of the previous three decades had brought fortune to the city, but as the Great Depression sat its unbearable weight upon the young nation, the population was either crushed or dispersed or both. The epicenter was Enid with its metal derricks pumping up and down, great hammers cracking open the earth. The wealth of the oil boom brought fortune to Enid, but only to those who owned the quickly eroding land.

I watched with trepidation the rise of highways, the proliferation of vehicles, the dispersion of white society from urban centers like dandelion seeds planting homogenous weeds across the plains. Oklahoma, like much of South Dakota, Nebraska, and Kansas, was flat and dull, endless plains of corn and wheat, marred by oil towers and electrical wiring.

The wretched remnants of the Depression eventually died of starvation, died of war, or worst: died of old age preceded by decades of suffering under the centralized greed of industry. Dizzyingly tall skyscrapers housed securely the richest bankers and investors in America. Tycoons perfected the alchemy of turning blood into gold. Seeing the mud-smudged faces of children across western Oklahoma throughout the 1930s made me wish my path would serpentine itself to the financial centers of New York or Chicago. I wanted to find a new gang of thieves who could help me tear apart these institutions brick by brick, dollar by dollar, and place it back to the hands of the farmers and grandchildren of slaves and indigenous tribes.

But my path was so clear to me now, so vivid in its intentions, I could not abandon it. My path did not lead me to New York or Chicago. It led me instead to Texas.

6

In 1953, I arrived in Amarillo. My path took the shape of a gravel road, leading to a dusty trail, leading to wooden steps which rose up directly to the home of Moses.

Moses owned a ranch. He owned horses and cattle and chickens and dogs. He had a wife and a tractor and a barn. He had six children. He had a lot of whiskey. Moses yelled at his wife, Lola, when she failed to keep house to his liking. He yelled at her when she told him to get cleaned up for church. He yelled at her when he ran out of booze. He yelled at her when he had plenty of booze. He yelled at his children when they spoke out of turn. He yelled at them when they did not make their beds. He yelled at them when they ate too much or too little.

Moses's father had vowed never to lay a hand on his children, having learned from his own experience that beatings did not strengthen one's message. But Moses's father also was not around when Moses grew up, so Moses instead replicated the actions of his mother.

I also was not around when Moses was growing up. I was in Oklahoma trying to undermine oil barons who did not pay fair wages, nor provide safe work environments. I spent many years fighting an impossible battle against economic inequality, instead of being present for Moses's childhood. He was a healthy baby. At only two days old he smiled at me, and I knew he would be okay. But he was not, because I had not been there to help him, not there to help his widowed mother. Ignoring the call of my path was a mistake I vowed to never make again.

While Moses had failed at being a kind father and husband, he had succeeded at making a comfortable living for himself, buying a West Texas ranch and learning to raise livestock. But he was brutal and unstable, and I knew I needed to step back into his life.

I met the adult Moses while he was feeding his horses. Deciding immediate intervention was necessary, I hid in the corner of his barn and began to speak. I told him that I was the ghost of his dead mother.

"My momma ain't no ghost," he said, as if hearing voices were normal to him. Perhaps it was. "My momma would never be a ghost because ghosts can't hit folks."

"My child, you need to lay off the drink," I said to him. I wasn't great at these American accents, but I figured his mother had been dead for a while and he was perpetually drunk. "Your Lola needs you. Your church needs you. Your son. Your only boy, Jacob, needs you."

Moses thought about what I said, and for the evening he didn't touch a bottle, but newly sober Moses was more foul than drunk Moses. Lola eventually poured him two fingers just to calm him down.

I attempted many different voices, hoping to find anything that could reach him. I tried being Jesus. I tried being one of the horses. I tried telling him I was his subconscious, but he didn't know what that word meant. He never questioned the existence of the voices, but he certainly did not take them seriously.

I eventually cornered him in the barn one night. He was placing the last of his summer gardening tools away for an early winter, and as he turned around I was standing in the doorway. I held a lantern up to my face and he froze. His skin lost all color and he looked like he wanted to scream. I grabbed a pitchfork and pointed it at him.

"You'll stop your drinking this moment, Moses," I intoned. I stepped forward prodding the pitchfork until I backed him into a corner.

"Momma, no. Momma," he began to sob, reverting to a childhood he never really had. "Momma, your face. What happened to your face?"

I pushed him into the hay with ease and I tied his hands together. If, in his besotted state, he was going to mistake me for his mother, I would certainly go along with it.

"You'll stay here till you get clean, boy."

And I hid him there, mouth gagged, for an entire week. Lola and the children came to look for him, but I kept him quiet. I kept him fed. I kept him away from them.

Moses without alcohol, though, became more irrational, more unpredictable. I began to wonder if it was the alcohol that kept him stable. He would stare, silent and motionless, for hours on end at the ceiling, and then suddenly thrash his body about, throwing himself into walls, lifting himself to his feet and then diving like a dolphin into the air and face first into the floor.

He broke three teeth and dislocated his right shoulder doing this.

Within a few days, he began muttering to himself, and those utterances became full conversations with invisible people who were not me. I was the one voice he wouldn't listen to anymore.

I liked the feeling of ending the lives of people like Moses, but I did not like to do it myself. I'm not a serial murderer, and I would never want authorities to think there was a killer wandering the country. Most importantly, being mysteriously murdered makes one a victim, a man fondly remembered.

Here was Moses, fully mad, whether from the makeup of his brain or whether from the DTs. I only had to watch him destroy himself. There were no consequences for me, only for the wicked men of this wicked country, who were borne of other wicked men of other wicked countries.

But Moses proved me wrong. I had long believed he couldn't hear or see me anymore, but he saw me enough to drive a pitchfork straight into my neck from behind me. I had not been maintaining the ropes on his arms and legs, and he had worked them free.

I fell headlong and stiff into the frozen dung and dust of the barn floor. The middle tine had pierced my throat and stuck into the boards. I tried to gasp but could not. I could not lift my head, because my neck was staked to the ground. I struggled to my knees, kicking and gashing my bare skin against the cold, broken wood.

Moses walked up next to me. I could see his ragged boots and torn denim jeans. I could make out his crooked back from his broken shoulder. One of his eyes was swollen shut and a silver-dollar sized piece of his lower lip was missing, exposing the few teeth he had remaining.

I was not a ghost. I was bleeding, aching. Feeling the pain

down my spine and into my legs and toes. It went from fierce, to hot, to ticklish, to nothing.

I was not a ghost. I was an old woman, pinned down like the ragged centerpiece of a butterfly collection.

Moses stormed out of the barn shouting at whatever voices would listen.

"Eddddmmmmooooonnnd," I hissed.

And I was instantly inside the house. I had not moved like that in years, so used to walking, to feeling the grass and dust and rocks beneath my feet. Becoming so connected to my body that I nearly forgot I could move without moving.

But something was different. My head hung limp. The muscles in my neck torn loose by the pitchfork could not maintain the weight of my head. It must have also pierced something in my nerves, because I couldn't move my right arm either. I dragged myself to the bedroom of nine-year-old Jacob, Moses's son.

"Wake up, boy," I cried hoarsely. "He's coming to kill you. He's coming to kill you all."

Seeing me—a silhouette of an unknown old woman covered in blood and neck bent at an unnatural angle—must have been quite a sight, because Jacob leapt upward and ran screaming from his room.

I collapsed from the pain for a moment but managed to piece together enough strength to stand. As I got fully to my feet, I heard a crash from behind me. Moses had shattered the window to his son's room with a pipe wrench. He must have seen the light of Jacob's lamp. He did not even clear the broken edges before he climbed through. One particularly long shard sunk at least two inches deep into his inner thigh, and thick dark blood erupted immediately from the wound.

Moses poured his body into the room. I couldn't move. I thought of Edmond. I thought of my father. Moses was only feet from me. He raised his wrench over my tilted limp head. I heard a shotgun cock behind me.

In a split second, as the boom of the gunshot spread across the prairie, I had transported myself outside the home. Through the broken window I saw the boy, gun clenched in bloodless hands, a wisp of smoke from the barrel. On the floor, a silent father, his throat and lower jaw gone, a glistening parabola of red across the wallpaper.

Lola rushed in, immediately began screaming and hugging her boy. Jacob, of course, told his mother and the Texas Rangers that his father was a violent man and that he (Jacob) was only trying to protect his family when Moses broke through the window wielding a heavy wrench. He did not mention the crooked-necked old woman screaming at the foot of his bed. The truth he did not voice was that it was this woman he had been trying to shoot, not his father.

But one morning as the family prepared for church, I heard Jacob talking to his mother.

"I once saw a woman, mother. She stood at the foot of my bed. She had no face. What kind of person doesn't have a face, mother?"

Lola did not answer, although her own face said much.

"You don't believe me, do you?" Jacob asked.

"I suppose a woman who has no face is a woman who has no soul, Jacob." She put her hand on his and squeezed it.

"I'm scared I'll see her again someday, Mother." He leaned his head to her shoulder.

"You may," she said. "You may." And she kissed his forehead. Faceless.

I stood in front of the bathroom mirror. There they were, my eyes, my nose, my lips and teeth. Could no one see my face at all?

And what of my soul? Lola spoke from the Christian Bible. It was her genteel southern way of telling her son that I was not one of them. That I was forsaken by her God.

Or maybe the face *is* the soul. If you cannot see or understand the face of someone else, you cannot see them. This is why humans fear insects. Their faces make no sense to us. We cannot infer emotion like we can in dogs or horses or pigs or people. I thought of the eye of a fish I had once held in my hands, devoid of fear or intent, and how frightened I had been of its emptiness.

Over a century since Edmond left me for dead in that Nulogorsk harbor, many men had looked me in the face as they died. The terror in their eyes, in the corners of their quivering mouths, in their snotty, snuffling noses took on new dimension for me. Perhaps they feared mystery more than they feared death. Perhaps it was my faceless face that made them react so strongly.

But Eleanor saw my face. She acknowledged my eyes. She saw me for who I was. She saw my face. She saw my soul. Eleanor was different. I was no ghost. I was no demon. Even demons have Satan. All I had was murder.

I wanted murder to feel like a fever breaking. I wanted the satisfying plunge of a knife into a gut. I wanted the warm blood dampening my sleeves. I wanted the splattering wheeze of Edmond's final plea for mercy. I wanted his nose against mine. I wanted my name to freeze upon his tongue as his last cold breath pushed back against it. But murder has been a cloudless day. Murder has been a gently lapping wave. Murder has been the light rattle of leaves in a breeze.

My wounds from the pitchfork would heal, eventually, but a slight hitch in my neck and a limp would remain. Would I live forever? Beyond this version of America and all the versions after? Beyond humanity? Beyond the universe itself? A faceless judge, jury, and executioner of right and wrong? I hoped not. Lola could believe that I was sent by her god or her devil, but I was sent only by me.

7

Even with Edmond gone, the path had revealed itself, and I simply walked upon it, feeling its sharp pebbles crunch beneath my feet.

The path led me out of Amarillo into the desert. I had seen maps of the new world. I had heard stories about the American West, but nothing prepared me for its empty beauty. Pink mesas, deep canyons with striped façades like neat stacks of fabric, billowing shelves of clouds held at bay by mountain titans. The dust was dry and thin, easily swept upward in tall spirals by blasts of hot wind. I saw tarantulas and scorpions, red ants nearly the size of my toes. I touched cacti, never tiring of the sharp prick. I caught a jackrabbit and ate it raw.

I did not believe I needed to eat. I certainly did not feel any ill effects from days without food or water, but seeing the nightmarish length and erratic speed of such a creature made me ravenous.

I could feel the lawlessness of the West. There was certainly a lawlessness to the sea, but everything at sea must eventually return to land. The desert did not require a returning. The desert could be a person's eternity.

The hot air and sun surely could ruin a traveler, but at night, the purple sky brought frosted air and coyote howls. The American Southwest is nature's surrealist masterpiece. A place for getting away and for coming together. The desert upsets stale notions of sensibility, and invites newness in every form.

Lola's Bible spoke of forty days and nights in the desert, a temptation and a test. Before that, there was forty years in the desert, a punishment and another test. My trial was less strenuous, as it felt like a place I could live forever. It was so like the sea to me, a horizon of near limitless possibilities, most of which would never materialize.

I had grown to enjoy dreaming more than achieving, the anticipation more than the actuality.

Like many before me, in the desert I found a sign. Mine was literally a sign, by the side of a highway:

WELCOME TO NIGHT VALE
IF YOU LIVED HERE YOU'D BE DEAD BY NOW

A sense of humor is attractive.

The news when I left Sioux City was dominated by a financial crash, men in tall buildings flinging themselves to the pavement below after losing millions. Nebraska and Kansas had been covered in signs reading "NO JOBS / NO OKIES / NO BLACKS." When I left Amarillo, I heard of a war in Korea that was not to protect land or people, but to protect ideas about money. I was dubious of visiting another town. But such is the path. The path led me here, to Night Vale, and here I would stay for as long as the path directed me to stay. The path was fulfilling me, helping me find that which I thought had vanished.

I did not know the town of Night Vale—I did not even know what state I was in. I only knew that it was where I should be.

Near the edge of town, there was a young girl who waved to me from the front porch of her home. I said, "Hello, young lady."

The girl beckoned me with a wave of her hand. When I approached she leaned into my ear and said, "There are angels here."

I played along, asking, "Do you think I am an angel?"

"No," the girl frowned. "THEY are an angel."

She pointed to a being at least eight feet tall with half a dozen wings and hundreds of eyes who had been quietly standing behind her. The being let out a cacophonous honk like several broken French horns, and a cylinder of black enveloped the porch, the negative image of a sunbeam.

"My name is Erika," the angel boomed.

"Hello, I am a faceless old woman following an invisible path."

"I see your path," Erika said. "It is a good path, because you believe it to be. I also see your face."

Erika placed one of their many hands on my cheek and ran a finger along my eyelids, my lips, and eventually into my nose. I did not wince. I understood that touch was part of how the angel experienced the world.

"I believe you will be with us for a while," Erika said pulling their hand away. "I think you will like it here."

"Come visit me," the girl said. "My name is Josefina."

"I will," I said.

"Hey," the angel called after me as I walked away along the road into town, "can I borrow fifty cents?"

In the center of town, several people (some of whom were wearing what looked to me like hats made of internal organs) pointed and shouted "Interloper!" as I passed. Then those same people returned to walking or reading their newspapers on park benches, and ignored me. I felt remarkably at home.

Everything in Night Vale felt clandestine. Night Vale had a secret police force within the public police force. This secret police force spied relentlessly on its inhabitants, and every home bristled with poorly hidden surveillance microphones. There were helicopters that hovered above, representing numerous shadowy organizations, and the night sky was filled with mysterious moving lights. There were suspicious people in dark suits and sunglasses standing along most street corners who would quietly mumble into tiny antennaed devices. Along one of the streets a black cargo truck passed by. On its side was a white emblem of a labyrinth. The truck was travelling west toward the scrublands and sandwastes, beyond the edge of town. In its partially covered bed were stacks of crates. Following the truck was a black sedan. It pulled up next to me, and two men got out. They were not wearing hoods, but instead hats.

"Hello," said the man who was not short.

"We won't take up too much of your time," said the man who was not tall.

"Who are you people?" I asked, finally voicing the question.

"Good citizens, I suppose," said the man who was not short.

"We wanted to let you know we're awfully sorry for all the trouble you've gone through," said the man who was not tall. "We feel just terrible about it."

"But glad to see you made it here," said the man who was not short.

"Welcome to town," said the man who was not tall, and they got back into the car.

"Don't be a stranger," called the man who was not short from his open window, and they drove off. The only real communication I would ever have with the Order of the Labyrinth.

No one watched them drive by. The citizens showed no curiosity. The crates simply moved across the desert. They always had and always would, and it remained no one's business. Not everyone gets to know everything about everybody. Except me. I do. But I no longer have any interest in revealing all that I know.

There was a man named Leonard Burton who told the news of the town on the radio. At all hours of the night and day, I could hear him broadcasting his show. I wondered if he ever slept, so I snuck into his home late one night and found him sleeping. A curious impulse made me turn on the radio in his room, just to see. He was on air, broadcasting the current time and temperature.

While watching Leonard sound asleep in his bed, I called into the radio station and Leonard answered the phone, "Greetings, caller. You're on the air with Leonard Burton. What's your question?"

I hung up the phone.

"Oh, it appears we have lost them," said the Leonard on the radio. "Well, no matter. It's shaping up to be a beautiful night. I hope you are tucked in safe and sound somewhere." The Leonard on the bed smacked his lips and rolled to his other side.

Night Vale challenged my basic notions of what it even meant to be on earth, let alone a human being bound to basic laws of physics and philosophy. Yet here I was, a dead woman who was not dead, following a path only visible to myself and the angels. My vengeance, while seemingly lost at Edmond's death, was still achievable. In this impossible town, I felt natural. This town was where the paradox that was me belonged.

Night Vale was something more than a town, though. In the same way that I was a ghost and also much more than a ghost. I may never learn what I am. I know I will never learn what Night Vale is.

Each citizen in Night Vale is interesting. Each citizen is frightened by their government but more frightened of the sky. Each citizen had something to hide or something to hide from. Maybe each citizen had their own invisible path they were following, and maybe their paths had led them here too. The desert was the only place Night Vale could be, and it was the only place I could be.

8

I made a home in Night Vale. I made several homes. Secretly, I lived in everybody's home at once. I took an interest in each person's eating habits, book selections, fashion, and dating. More than anything I took an interest in their secrets.

A secret feels like falling from a high rock into cold water.

Enrique Herrera, who owned a newsstand near city hall, flirted daily with Winona Preston, who worked for the parks department cleaning trash off the lawns near Enrique's kiosk. Every day he would tell Winona a joke. They were bad jokes like "What did the scorpion say to the rattlesnake?" Answer: "Wickedness is an immutable yet subjective product of our evolution." (Night Valeans have always found great humor in the illusion of free will.) And Winona would give Enrique a flower from the public garden if the joke made her laugh, which was most days.

One day, Enrique's wife, Maria, came to see her husband to share the great news that she found several kittens floating in mid-air about six feet off their back porch, and she thought they should adopt them. Enrique, so fond of cats, blushed as he said yes. Winona, watching all of this, frowned and walked away. Enrique and Winona did not speak again.

Enrique never told Maria about his flirtation, just as he had never told Winona about his wife.

A secret feels like fingers tightening into a fist.

The City Council in Night Vale is a single-bodied being of many torsos, heads, and voices. In the early twentieth century, they developed an earthquake machine that they could turn off and on at will. They began to put out regular predictions of when earthquakes would take place and how intense they might be. Then they would cause their predictions to come true.

Night Vale citizens planned accordingly, saving themselves untold property and bodily damage. The people of Night Vale interpreted these predictions as divine wisdom from their central leadership, and this bolstered the City Council's power.

A secret can sometimes feel like cancer, in that we don't know we have it, and once we feel it, it may be too late.

I met Donald in Night Vale. Donald's father, Jake, died from a hunting accident, accidentally shooting off the side of his skull, when Donald was still an infant. Jake had remained in a coma for three years before the family removed him from life support.

Josefina and the angels she lived with helped little Donald and his mother, Linette, through the tragedy, bringing them food, keeping Linette company, and even looking after the baby while his mother worked.

I played with Donald too, and kept him calm at night so that his poor, overworked mother could get some rest. She had two jobs just to keep the two of them fed.

I wanted Donald to grow up to be a good man, but he had a secret. He did not know he had that secret, but it would eventually destroy him. In this way, he was not special. Many men before him had been destroyed by the same secret.

I did not want Donald to know the terrible secret he possessed until he was older. A secret such as this was a lot to bear for a child, and I felt only an adult could truly understand. So I protected Donald, the child, from his secret. I protected Donald from everything. I loved him.

Love feels like a well-paying job. Love is work. Love demands your time and requires experience and skill and attentiveness and diligence. But it is rewarded. Love, when treated respectfully, like a profession, keeps you alive.

Love of children kept me alive. Protection of Donald until adulthood kept me going. Donald, like all of the boys before him, had a secret. It was the same secret, generation after generation. But I loved all of those boys. I helped raise them. I helped them grow and mature and become good men, good husbands, and ultimately good fathers. I loved them right up until the day their first son was born.

The path had led me to flee my estate on the Mediterranean. It had led me to Vlad's blade in a Barcelona port. It had led me away from Albert's embrace to the empty mountains of Sardinia. It had led me back to my friends and to Venedict's bar in Nulogorsk, and then into the fire, into the air, and into the water. The path had led me to Florida, to the Mississippi River, to Texas, and then to the desert, to Night Vale, to Donald.

And on a golden afternoon in 1987, the path led me to a gentle child, a handsome child. That child was your father. His name was Craig. He, too, had a secret. It is the same secret you have, Darius.

DARIUS

2020

Look at those toes. One two three four five. Five toes on your little foot.

Look at that smile. Tiny teeth, but much larger than they seem.

You're holding my finger, Darius. Yes you are. Mommy's busy getting your big sister ready for mass. She doesn't need her big strong boy crying, so if grabbing my finger keeps you entertained, by all means, I'm happy to provide it for you. You're not the first person I've met with an affinity for fingers.

Such simple thrills you have. I tried to read to you, but you didn't want to hear it. You're tactile, physical, different from your father in that way. He liked listening to music and reading books. He was passive, but you are active, completely in your body.

The way you kick your legs, and jostle your waist. I think you might be quite the dancer. Most people don't like being in their bodies. They pose and posture and use sheer force to fight or protect or block passage. But most don't know what it means to discover each muscle, find their lines, sit with their pain.

I sit with my pain. There's little else to do most days. I know diet can affect mood. I don't think I can have oranges anymore. They make me upset. I can feel my head tighten, and I have less patience or concentration. I get grumpy when I eat oranges.

Such a shame for a girl who once lived near orange groves, but we get old, don't we, and our bodies change. The body changes more than the mind. The body says, you've had too much wine, but the mind says wine is delicious. And the body says: "Fine then I will make your sleep miserable, and you will become so sick when you drink wine you will no longer want it." And we no longer drink wine. We still desire it, sure, but want it? No.

You're right. This isn't interesting to a baby. I'm being a dullard. Let's play with fingers some more.

What a laugh you have. That is your father's laugh. There is no question of that. Although I will say there is something even more familiar in your laugh.

You know, when Craig was your age, he was unhealthy. It wasn't his fault, but he was born prematurely, and until he was five, he coughed a lot. Your grandmother worried constantly, taking him to the doctor, getting him medicine. Your grandfather held him each night, and rocked him to sleep. Even the slightest noise and Donald would rush in to ease him. And when Donald or Marina couldn't be there, I would be. I looked after your father every single day.

You're healthy as healthy goes, but I will look after you every single day too. It's helpful that your father left your mother so much money. He was so responsible with his finances, and after some arguing with the insurance company, his term life finally paid off. You will live a comfortable life, Darius. I'm glad of this. Your father's brief life led up to you. He lived so that you could live. And here you are.

Yes indeedy here you are. Ah boo boo boo.

Money aside, I want to do anything I can to help your mom. You must know that she loves you so much. I hope you learn everything about what made your father a good man, but never forget that it is your mother who will raise you. Take you to school, change your diaper, get you medical care, hug you, kiss you. She's a part of the narrative too. Your father didn't always remember that about his mother.

I used to talk to your father when he was your age, you little cutie pie. And his father before him. And his father before him. And his father before him. On and on and on.

The world is so incredibly old.

Oh, yes it is. OHYESITIS. bahbahbahbah.

Craig, when he was a baby, used to make little speeches to me. He would talk and talk, all kinds of gibberish, although I don't think it was gibberish to him. His thoughts, untethered from formal language, were the narrative of nature, like the babbling of a brook or the hiss of a snake, meaningful even for lack of codification.

Can you say codification?

You don't say much at all. You just smile and laugh. And cry. You do cry, but not as much as your sister. I can't tell if you feel less sad, or feel less desire to express sadness.

Sit with your pain. It's the best thing you can do for yourself. Take care of yourself, Darius, so that you can take care of others.

Oh! You touched my face. You're grabbing my nose. You are!

That's sweet. You don't even know yet that I don't have a face, let alone a nose. But you can see one. You can feel one. You feel my nostrils, don't you? Your mom doesn't like it when you put your hands on her face. Babies have lots of bacteria on their curious little fingers. Putting them in their mouths, their butts, on the dog, wherever.

I'm not worried about bacteria. You can grab my nose all you want.

Yes, those are my lips. I'm a bit surprised at what you think you can see and feel. You have no one yet to tell you that your reality is not real, so anything is possible, I suppose.

Your father never touched my face when he was your age, but he saw it. I know he did.

I'm so curious to see how like your father you'll become, and how different. As old as I am, watching the slow evolution of people across generations is fascinating. You come from a long line of men, little one, each of you so similar to the previous.

Your father was Craig, a high school English teacher, whose father was Donald, an industrial air conditioning salesman, whose father was a farmer named Jacob, as was his father, Moses, before him, and Moses's father was a fisherman named Thomas, whose father, Matthew, was a longshoreman. Matthew's father was named Gabriel (isn't that a pretty name? Gabriel.) His father was named Gregory. Gregory was poor, but he was born rich to a father named Theodore, whose father was a man named Edmond, a man I once loved and trusted completely.

Each one of you is so similar to the next, but you're all unmistakable to me.

I could line up every one of you, across hundreds of years, as ten-month-olds, and I'd know each of your names just by your faces, even as they're still in their chubby nearly toothless larval stage of facial development. I would know you by your eyes, your movements, your patters, your fingernails, your skin, your smells. I have known all of you better than you have known yourselves.

I have followed each of these men from the Mediterranean, through Central and Eastern Europe. As far east as Nulogorsk and as far west as Night Vale. I have lived secretly in each of their homes; on ships, in lean-tos, in servants' quarters, in mansions, and in middle class apartments. I can't order them to do what I want, but I can certainly manipulate the situation so that they will make the best choices for themselves, and ultimately their children, their baby boys, who will carry on their legacy. A very smart man once taught me how to do that. Oh, he was evil to the core, but he was so clever.

You must grow up big and strong, Darius, like all these men before you. You must marry a great spouse, like all of these men before you. The person you marry—like Amaranta, or Marina, or Linette, or Lola, or Pauline, or Laura, or Hannah, or Letitia, or Eleanor—will be strong and caring and will stabilize your home, will protect you through wisdom and medicine and love and grace. They will not be perfect, but they will never betray you. The two of you will have a child. You will keep having children until you produce a son.

And you will have me with you every day (Ohyesyouwill!) to make certain you will be healthy and loved and cared for, every day until the day you die.

Little Darius, with your brown eyes and fat fingers, this is hard to imagine now, but you will die. Everyone does. One day Amaranta will tell you about it and she will explain it in a way that will scare but also comfort you. Every child learns about death, and I trust your mother will know exactly how to tell you. "Why don't I have a dad?" might be a question that starts this conversation. Or "where is our dog, Bubbles?" or maybe just a straightforward "does everybody die?"

The hard truth is that almost all people die. I will not. I

keep on living so that I am afforded time to do what it is I am supposed to do. To follow my path. But we'll get to that. We have your whole life to get to that.

You just grabbed my finger again. I'll try to tell you all of this boring old lady stuff in a singsongy voice.

You like that?

Oh! You do! Good for you.

Every man in your lineage is now dead. YESTHEYARE.

Craig got distracted and lost control of his vehicle and crashed into a deep canyon.

Donald died of numerous cancers. He smoked some in his youth, and he drank a lot. But mostly it was the asbestos swatch that covered his mouth as he slept every night after his son was born.

Jacob shot himself in the head when he tripped on rock that was not there a moment before, and he fell into a tree trunk. He was holding his shotgun loosely against his shoulder and with the safety off.

Moses went mad, claiming he could hear disembodied voices. While fighting the ghost he thought he saw, he was shot dead by his son.

Thomas drowned in a frozen lake when a strange, long hand pulled open a fissure in the ice beneath him.

Matthew was assassinated by a French spy visiting the United States, when the spy mistook Matthew for an important Spanish dissident named Mateo. The spy had been given incorrect information, from an anonymous letter.

Gabriel was falsely imprisoned for murder, which he did not commit, but the evidence that was planted by an unknown person led to his public hanging.

Gregory was kicked in the head by a horse after the horse was startled by an old woman whispering in its ear.

Theodore was poisoned by his wife, Eleanor.

Edmond died peacefully in his sleep after a lifetime of wealth and ease. He got everything he wanted, despite destroying an entire family with his lies, murder, manipulation, and utmost cruelty. His elaborate plot on my father did not stop at killing my father. He wanted to make sure my father's only child suffered as well, so that my father's legacy and lineage was ruined completely.

I cannot go back. I cannot kill Edmond. I cannot cause him pain. I cannot tell him what joy his last, frightened breath would bring to me, because I missed my opportunity. But Eleanor showed me the first step in my path, when she fed Edmond's only son that poison. In Theodore, I saw Edmond's eyes, and I saw them struggle with comprehension. I saw Edmond's thin lips upon Theodore's face stretch into a jagged gash, like a knife wound, and fill with foam and bile. I saw Edmond's stout body and broad shoulders live again in his son's stout body and broad shoulders. And I saw them heave and gasp and finally sag in painful asphyxiation for minutes until he died. My path was clear as clear could be.

I would have to make sure Eleanor raised a healthy boy. And Letitia. And Hannah. And Laura. All the way to Amaranta. And I would make sure those boys grew into good men, who married good spouses who would give birth to good sons. And once I knew those baby boys would be healthy, I would take from Edmond what he sought to take from me: lineage. He destroyed my family's future. And I will return the favor forever.

Before each man died, I would remind them of the secret of

their cursed history, their secret they could never have known, could never have done anything about. And, dear sweet baby Darius, I swore to each man that I would raise their son. I would make sure those boys were happy, and healthy, and follow the best choices possible. I would talk to and play with each of those baby boys, like I'm talking to you now, little one. (Ooh, you love kicking those chubby little legs about, don't you? Yes. Who's got a gorgeous smile? It's Darius! Yes it is!)

I swore that no man in Edmond's line would ever have a comfortable death. Edmond's debt will continue as long as I exist. The curse will never end. Each man will be forced to sit with their pain, to sit with my pain, to sit with the pain their ancestor never had to sit with.

I would make sure as he died, that each would see my face again just as he did as an infant. And each man would know. They would recognize me, and they would remember what I told them.

I didn't get a life, Darius. I didn't get a family. What I get instead, again and again, is the dawning epiphany of horror on those men's faces, faces that look exactly like Edmond's. And each time it delights me. It fills me with purpose.

One day, just like your father, and Donald, and Jacob, all the way back to Gregory, you too will die, and it will be my doing. I will be with you on that day, and I will remind you. You will suddenly, for the first time, remember this conversation we're having now.

I don't know when your death will be. I don't know how it will be. But, Darius, it will be.

Maybe you'll again be lying on your back, naked and alone, kicking and gurgling and grabbing at me, just like you are now. I think that would be a poetic symmetry. Don't you?

I can't die, young Darius. I have long wanted to, but I cannot. Perhaps this is because I don't truly want to. One day, many years from now, I may give up my vengeance. Give up my pain. But for now, I'm still quite happy sitting with it. Understanding what makes my body hurt. And through the centuries, I have found peace with my pain, and relief in my wisdom. Revenge is in my bones, my brittle old bones, and I cannot do anything with that but act upon it.

Okay, my baby boy. Now I want you to grow up big and strong and handsome and kind. We need to get you a good job, and a lovely spouse. And, of course, a baby boy to call your own.

Remember me, my nosey-wosey, baby boy. Remember my story. One day you'll have a son, and that will be the happiest day of your life. And of mine.

Oh! Looks like someone made a messy mess. Don't cry. Shhh. Let me get you all cleaned up.

There. Out with the bad pants. Let's just wipe your behind up all clean. Yes. And get you some new pants. You like your new pants, do you?

Remember what I said, little Darry. Many many years from now I will watch the horror and confusion and betrayal spread across your precious little face, and in that brief moment before the end, you will understand.

Ohyesyouwill!

Now, get some rest, little one.

I hear your mother coming.

WANT MORE NIGHT VALE?

Well you've done it now. You've read all of this book, and now there's none of it left. (Except the secret pages we hid. Let us know if you find them.) In any case, while this is the end of the book, it doesn't have to be the end of your journey into Night Vale.

If you enjoyed this novel, we recommend you join us in our ongoing *Welcome to Night Vale* podcast, which has been telling stories about this strange desert town since 2012.

Our podcast comes out twice monthly online and is completely free. You can download it to your computer or listening device through Apple, Spotify, SoundCloud, YouTube, any of the hundreds of free podcasting apps (Joseph recommends Podcast Addict), or by visiting welcometonightvale.com.

All of the episodes going back to the very start are available to download right now. Or if that sounds like too much of a time investment, just hop right in with our most current episode. Or dabble around with ones that have titles you like. We're not here to tell you how to live your life.

Welcome to Night Vale also does live shows all over the world (more than four hundred shows in seventeen different countries at the time of this writing). These live shows are full evenings of Night Vale storytelling, with live music and guest stars, designed so that you do not need to know anything about the podcast or novels to enjoy.

Keep an eye on welcometonightvale.com to join us next time we pass through wherever you live. (Wherever you live is our favorite place to perform.)

Oh, and did we mention that we have a podcast network called Night Vale Presents with fourteen original shows made by us and artists we love? Visit nightvalepresents.com to see them all. We recommend *Start with This*, in which the authors of this book provide an easy and thought-provoking guide to writing—one short and simple assignment at a time.

See you out there.

ACKNOWLEDGMENTS

Thank you to the *Welcome to Night Vale* cast and contributing writers for nearly a decade of podcast episodes and touring live shows: Meg Bashwiner, Jon Bernstein/Disparition, Desiree Burch, Hunter Canning, Aliee Chan, Dessa Darling, Felicia Day, Emma Frankland, Kevin R. Free, Mark Gagliardi, Glen David Gold, Marc Evan Jackson, Maureen Johnson, Kate Jones, Ashley Lierman, Erica Livingston, Christopher Loar, Hal Lublin, Dylan Marron, Jasika Nicole, Tina Parker, Zack Parsons, Flor De Liz Perez, Jackson Publick, Molly Quinn, Retta, Symphony Sanders, Annie Savage, Lauren Sharpe, Lusia Strus, TL Thompson, James Urbaniak, Wil Wheaton, Brie Williams, Mara Wilson, and, of course, the voice of Night Vale himself, Cecil Baldwin.

Also and always: Jillian Sweeney; Kathy and Ron Fink; Ellen Flood; Leann Sweeney; Lola Cranor; Jack and Lydia Bashwiner; the Pows; the Zambaranos; Rob Wilson; Kate Leth; Jessica Hayworth; Dave Watt; Iain Burke; Christy Gressman; Adam Cecil; Julia Melfi; Grant Stewart; Vincent Cacchione; Nathalie Candel; Sarah Conboy; Lucy Goldberg; Angelique Grandone; Lauren O'Niell; Teresa Piscioneri; Emily Pojman; Em Reaves; Bettina Warshaw; Holly and Jeffrey Rowland; Kassie Evashevski;

Andrew Morgan; Eleanor McGuinness; Megan Larson and Christine Ragasa; Hank Green; John Green; Griffin, Travis, and Justin McElroy; Cory Doctorow; Janina Matthewson; Sarah Maria Griffin; John Darnielle; Aby Wolf; Jason Webley; Danny Schmidt; Carrie Elkin; Eliza Rickman; Mary Epworth; Will Twynham; Erin McKeown; Mal Blum; Dane Terry; the New York Neo-Futurists; and, of course, the delightful Night Vale fans.

Our agent, Jodi Reamer; our editor, Amy Baker; and all the good people at Harper Perennial.

ABOUT THE AUTHORS

Joseph Fink created the *Welcome to Night Vale* and *Alice Isn't Dead* podcasts. He lives in the Hudson River Valley and Los Angeles.

Jeffrey Cranor cowrites the *Welcome to Night Vale* and *Within the Wires* podcasts. He also cocreates theater and dance pieces with choreographer/wife Jillian Sweeney. They live in New York.

Find out more about Joseph Fink and Jeffrey Cranor by registering for the free monthly newsletter at www.orbitbooks.net.

LOOK OUT FOR

OUT NOW

Enter the monthly

Orbit sweepstakes at

www.orbitloot.com

With a different prize every month,
from advance copies of books by
your favourite authors to exclusive
merchandise packs,
**we think you'll find something
you love.**